The Lady of ɩ

~~ The Glen Highland Romance ~~
Book Two

Michelle Deerwester-Dalrymple

Copyright 2019 Michelle Deerwester-Dalrymple All rights reserved
ISBN: 9781792978043
Imprint: Independently published
Interior cover art by K.J. Dalrymple Copyright 2019

Cover art by German Creative

The Lady of the Glen

Contents

Prologue: On Learning a Lesson

E layne exited the MacLeod keep in a swirl of plaid and fury. Her cousin, Young James, followed right behind her and fell back as she visited her rage on him.

"What did ye do, just standing there like a fool?" she hurled at him, her gray eyes flashing. "Ye were here to support me in my claim to Ewan! What ails ye?"

James cowed back farther from Elayne's tall frame, stammering an incoherent response as the priest stepped into the muggy air. He lifted his chest in Elayne's direction, preparing for her insults.

"And ye!" Indignation shot through her with an uncontrollable, rabid fever. "What did ye do? Ye stood there in front of that witch and did nothing? Could ye no' see the woman is a witch? I showed ye the herbs! Ye saw with your own eyes the way she witched Laird MacLeod. Ye even started to condemn her, why did ye halt?"

Elayne's voice rose to a crescendo that grated on Father MacNally's every nerve. Father MacNally summoned all his patience and training as a priest to calm himself before he spoke to his Laird's daughter. Caught in the web of loyalty to his Lord Christ and loyalty to his Laird James MacNally, clan loyalty would, of course, lose. Plus, someone needed to finally put the spoiled harpy in her place, and he was truly the only untouchable man in the clan to do so. While he would incur the legendary wrath of the MacNally, the Laird could do nothing about Father MacNally's treatment of Elayne. This most recent escapade was the final straw.

"*Haud your wheesht*, lass! How dare ye speak to your priest and elder in such a manner? What has your father no' taught ye?"

Elayne's braying fell quiet as the priest clutched her arm and dragged her towards their horses. Anger and exasperation radiated off Father MacNally, rivaled only by the embarrassment that Elayne visited upon him. Jealously he could understand, as well as taking action if one was wronged, but falsely accusing a woman of witchcraft because she married the man Elayne wanted to wed? That bordered on hysterics. She put both Ewan MacLeod and his wife, Meg, danger; in addition, she risked the reputation of himself and the MacNally clan. Her thoughtless actions led Elayne down a perilous path. Now Father MacNally needed to set her straight 'afore it led to her own destruction.

"Aye, your father has spoiled ye for far too long," he growled at her. "He has let ye have run of the keep and of himself, surely out of guilt for his motherless daughter. Ye are supposed to be a lady, lass, one who brings respect to your clan, but this?" He waved a heavily clothed arm towards castle MacLeod, "This was unacceptable. Ye have reached the apex of repugnant behavior."

Her wide, gray eyes held notes of fear and bewilderment. "What?! Ye agreed to come with me! Ye said the situation had merit! Ye said —"

"I ken what I said!" Father MacNally hollered back. "And I said it based on your misleading rantings! Ye neglected to tell me ye planted your handkerchief? That she was invited to the keep and expected to leave when the old Laird passed? That ye called her a witch with no real cause, other than she had what ye wanted? That is covetousness and envy, Elayne! Two mortal sins and ye participated in them without accountability!"

Father MacNally threw her toward her mare as the insipid James scrambled toward his own gelding, wanting nothing more than to hide under a rock.

"What, I did no' such a thing! How dare ye —"

She did not expect the sharp smack that landed across her face, the priest's small hand leaving a stinging red reminder on her cheek. She gasped and placed her hand over the mark, her delicate features a mask of pain, surprise, and horror.

"Ye need a stronger hand, Elayne. We will ride home, and I shall expect ye at the kirk forthwith for your confession and penance. Ye will need to think on your selfish, willful behavior as ye scrub the floors of the sanctuary, cleaning both it and your dark, sinful soul. Only then will ye be clean enough to enter your father's house, apologize for embarrassing him, and mayhap, *mayhap*, ye will see the error of your spoiled ways and begin your life anew. Ye can nay have what ye want, Elayne. Ye can only have that which the Good Lord Jesus Christ gives ye. Get your arse to the kirk now, and I will meet ye in the confessional."

Finishing his cutting speech, the small man leapt nimbly onto his horse, gave a harsh glare to Elayne and her erstwhile cousin, and kicked dust into her face as he rode off back to MacNally lands.

***

Elayne MacNally departed *Broch Lochnora*, her head low, her spirits defeated. Her father had forbidden her to come. But she defied him, grabbed her cousin, the priest, and the horses, and explained her concerns about Meg and how the lass charmed Ewan with her witchy magic. Her cousin remained dubious, but the priest seemed almost over-eager at the prospect of witch hunting. When Ewan kicked her out, she was shocked not only at Ewan but that her priest departed so willingly, then reprimanded *her* instead! She believed she was right, so right, that Meg was using witchy powers on Ewan. It was obvious! But she must have charmed more than just Ewan — that MacLeod clan, too.

In this moment, though, she considered that she had made a mistake, perchance a grave mistake. Now she must return home, alone, with no prospects, the reputation as a harpy, and face the wrath of both the priest *and* her father. She was uncertain which she dreaded more.

Reaching the crossroads between her home and the kirk, she reined her horse to a stop. James had ridden ahead, most likely to throw himself on the mercy of her father and beg his forgiveness, the cretin. Everything inside her roiled at the prospect of facing the priest but facing her father frightened her to the depth of her core. Perhaps Father MacNally could offer some penance that would speak to her father's sensibilities and temper his ire. She sighed in defeat and nudged her golden mare towards the church.

Inside, colored light from the overcast sun dappled through the stained-glass window over the altar. Normally bright and cheery on sunnier days, the light of the church reflected her current emotional state. Rejected by her would be fiancé, reprimanded by her priest, and awaiting punishment by her father, Elayne felt a sense of lowliness unbeknown to her. She always attained what she wanted, either by commanding others or bending others to her will through her position as lady of the manor. Now that was all ripped from her, and her mind ached from the prospect of it.

Had she been engaged to Ewan? Elayne assumed so since they were bordering clans and both the oldest children of Lairds. Was she wrong to think such notions? And what of her commanding the priest to evaluate Ewan's new wife as a witch? Everything pointed that way, at least to Elayne. But maybe his wife was just a meek girl who captured his heart? Maybe Ewan MacLeod didn't want a brash woman. Elayne sighed deeply, acknowledging her lot. She knew her reputation — it was difficult to miss in the Highlands. Few men wanted a willful woman. Elayne stared at the crucifix hanging above the altar, a sense of hopelessness and loneliness falling over her. Mayhap she would not wed at all. Especially after rumors of this latest escapade made its way through the villages, who would want her then?

The door to the confessional was closed, letting her know that Father MacNally was seated behind it, waiting for her confession over this day.

And Father MacNally's animosity showed with her penance. *Scrub all the pews?* She thought the penalty did not fit her sin; unfortunately, she was not in a position to argue with the priest. As it was, once she exited the confessional, Father MacNally all but sprinted from his side and out the door of the sanctuary which slammed accusingly behind him. She cringed at the sound, and the stained-glass windows shuttered in his wake. She did not need to ask his destination — he was reporting on her to her father.

Pushing up her sleeves and twisting her dark hair up on her head with her handkerchief, she took this time scrubbing to evaluate herself. Elayne caused her father much strife in her twenty years on this earth. For so long he had put up with her willfulness, her brash, demanding ways, that she feared this may be his breaking point. Surely never before did her behavior merit a lecture and a penance such as she received today. As her dread for meeting her father increased, the more attention she gave her work. The longer this cleaning took, the better, thus her movements were sluggish, taking as much time for each task as she could. In the closet behind the sanctuary, she paused after finding the bucket, sat after tossing the rags in, then sauntered to the well for water.

Scrubbing itself was not difficult, but her back ached from bending over each bench, and taking frequent breaks elongated the process which did not bother her in the least. Late in the afternoon, the last of the pews shone under the colored light filtering past the intricate glass, and she dropped onto one of the benches, the damp of the pew seeping through her skirt to chill her skin. She brooded over the last fortnight, trying to understand what she had done. *Why had I gone so far with my accusations? Why was I convinced Ewan was supposed to wed me? Was this my comportment all the time, forceful and unpleasant? Violent even?* she wondered to herself.

As a leader in her clan, Elayne was granted much leeway — by both the clansmen and her father. She ran her father's keep, helped with accounting, wrote his letters, and she had grown to behave in a manner reflecting those responsibilities, but perchance she deceived herself. Perchance she needed to re-evaluate her life, her behaviors, her expectations, and that inner reflection weighed heavily in her chest. Elayne felt not only saddened by the events of the recent days but muddled. *What is my place in life now?*

With the sanctuary clean, only one task remained for her today — to return home and face the wrath of her father. She wrung out the scrubbing cloths, noting the worn, twisted fabric reflected her inner turmoil, and left them hanging to dry on the bucket in the sunlight outside the church doors. For the first time in her life, dread filled her completely as she began her short journey back home.

Chapter 1: It's Not Good to be the King

Methven, West of Perth, 1306

R ide, my King! Ride!" Declan MacCollough shouted at Robert the Bruce, slapping the Bruce's horse with the flat of his hand. Startled, the horse sprang into action. The Bruce and a few of his soldiers rode west, away from their foes, into the blinding sunset. Declan shielded his eyes to watch them leave, and once they were out of sight, he turned to rejoin the fray. A sudden, sharp pain burst on his shoulder, and he fell heavily to the ground, blacking out as he went.

His crusty eyes peeled open as he awoke in the barber surgeon's tent, lucky to be alive, he knew, and he wanted to keep it that way. Declan's days passed as he healed, and he learned the conflict between supporters of the Bruce and Comyn's allies had ended badly. Many of Comyn's followers were displeased that King Robert the Bruce lived and was in hiding from his enemies. Many eastern and lowland clans announced their displeasure as they retreated toward their homelands, raising concerns with the Highland clans that remained loyal to the Bruce. The battle, for certain, may have ended, but the ire between the clans and with England had not. MacCollough dreaded to think of what Comyn's clans and allies may try next.

The message for him came as he rested on the barber's pallet, waiting for another hot water treatment on his shoulder to prevent us from setting in. Thus far, the treatment was successful, as Declan poked the wound gently with one long finger. His head snapped up when he heard someone approach the tent, and a young lad from the northeast raced in, nearly tripping over Declan with the pressing missive. Declan managed to focus his less-sore eye to peer at the letter, written by one of his father's clansmen, informing Declan that his father had passed into God's good graces (which Declan sincerely doubted) earlier in the month. Declan, if he could be found alive, was needed at the keep to take his place as Laird of the clan.

Declan shuddered at the words. That task was one Declan did not anticipate or desire. If he put aside the disturbing memories of his father, the sense of loss he felt since his mother left, and the disaster of a clan he knew awaited him, that still left him with the fact he was now laird to one of the most uncivilized group of men in the Highlands. He must somehow put the situation of his clan to rights. He waved the young messenger away with one hand as he rubbed a burgeoning headache with the other. The idea of going home, however, did have some appeal. Many years at the side of a war-torn King wore on a man, and Declan was ready to go home, no matter its condition.

His journey back to MacCollough land was long and cool and gave him time to assess his current circumstances. The heat of Scottish politics and early summer pounded on Declan, making him wish for the Highlands all the more. The failed diplomacy under King Robert the Bruce regarding Comyn, followed by his horrible loss at Methven, left a hefty weight upon Declan's shoulder, which still ached where the surgeon atempted to repair it after the solid hit from a broadsword. He should be dead; most of the clans thought he died on the battlefield, and for now, he was content for it to remain that way. Indeed, his mortality and aching shoulder were the least of his concerns.

***

In his ruminations, Declan failed to consider that, of those Highlanders who thought him dead, the numbers may also include his own clan. He had not seen his homeland in nearly a decade. His physical appearance no longer resembled that of a young man. Once these realizations occurred to him, Declan sighed heavily. He would have an uphill battle with his clan just bringing it back under control, but to accomplish that feat as an unknown stranger? His stomach roiled at the prospect. As if returning home after his occupation under the King was not daunting enough.

His service under Robert the Bruce began when his father sent him to the king to learn warfare, "to make him more a man," his father claimed. Declan's whole body was bruised and damaged in becoming "more of a man." Instead of taking the time he needed to rest and heal completely, here he was riding his broken body, and if he were honest with himself, his broken spirit too, back to a place that had truly been hell on earth when he was a lad.

At least his work with Robert the Bruce netted him some sense of pride and imbued sympathy with the king, who promised to help locate his mother. More years than he cared to count had passed since she left, "abandoning him" his father oft-argued, and Declan retained no real memories of her. The Bruce claimed he had resources to help find her, even if it meant waiting until the Highlands settled after the battle at Methven. The Highlands always seemed to be embroiled in some sort of war, civil or not, and Declan did not anticipate the Highlands settling anytime soon.

And while the King's promise intrigued him at his basest level, the actual prospect of finding the woman tore at the hole in his heart. He had settled his grievances with his mother in his mind long ago — locked thoughts of her away so they no longer hurt to touch. To unlock that part of him was like abusing a bruise that would never heal. He prefer to never meet his mother again.

And as for memories of his father, well, those he locked away as well, lest he allow the past to repeat and form his own future. Declan's greatest hope for his life was to become a man entirely unlike his own father. Pushing these painful memories to the back of his mind, he lifted his face to the heavens, hoping the cool Highland air would provide respite for his fevered head.

The smell of the village reached him long before the village itself came into view — rotting animal flesh, garbage, and general debris hung heavy in the air of the dank moor that led to *BlackBraes* from the west, so unlike the sunlit glens from east and south. As he considered his current position and that of the clan, he promised himself he would physically clean up the clan as his first cause of action.

Villagers stared at him as he passed through the main gate of Castle MacCollough. Declan tried nodding at his people as he rode, but their empty faces did not respond in kind. He noted filth and disrepair as he entered the inner bailey and could not stop the groan that rose from deep in his throat. The men of the clan were accustomed to the coarse life of the last several decades, he knew. Pausing his horse at the inner bailey of the manse, sweating and sore, he decided he needed significant help if he were to make his clan refined again.

***

Clan Dunbar near Dornach Firth

The meeting had gone much longer than Laird Baldie Dunbar of Sutherland anticipated. Firelight flickered low in the hearth; in an hour, the fire would burn out unless someone added more wood or peat, and that was the last thing Dunbar wanted. He ran his hands through his graying hair in aggravation and fatigue. All he wanted at this late hour was his bed.

Ross stood at the side of the table, veins popping out of his forehead. His hatred for Robert the Bruce only grew with the recent message he received about those who helped him escape the English after the disaster at Methvyn, using simple trickery *again*. Ross repeatedly questioned Bruce's mental capabilities to anyone who would listen, and since he commanded the floor now, they had to listen. Baldie Dunbar did not like what he was hearing, however. Ross' complaints bordered on treason.

Baldie finally reached his breaking point. "Donald!" he yelled at Ross. He may have been tired and achy, but he was still a large man in his own right. Everyone at the table quieted.

"Ye canna mean what ye are saying. What ye speak of is treason, at least while the Bruce is still king."

"Ye dinna see, Baldie! He should no' be King! Once we have him — either disposed or dead — we won't have committed treason. The man doesna even have an actual claim to the throne. He canna defend us from the English. He is the worst Scotland has to offer! And this MacCollough, he helped the Bruce escape capture. We wouldna' be in this position if it wasn't for that lad! Do ye no' see how that makes him a de facto traitor himself? I have it on good authority that if MacCollough doesna send the Bruce to his castle, the decrepit pile of excrement that it is, then he knows where to find the pretender, if the MacCollough yet lives."

Baldie rubbed his hair again. He understood Ross' opinion, and on some level, dealing with MacCollough might help find the Bruce. But at this point, the Bruce was king, and they needed to do what they could for the cause of Scotland under his rule. And throwing accusations at a low-level Laird who probably knew little about the Bruce's whereabouts served no purpose. Baldie was so tired of these battles between clans which did nothing but further weaken the Scottish cause. He told Ross as much.

"Donald, I respect ye as a friend and peer, but what you speak of does nothing for Scotland. I willna be a part of this. 'Tis madness! Now, 'tis late, and I am weary. I will take my leave. Ye can do what ye feel is necessary, but for my clan, we are shifting our alliances to focus on the Scottish cause and that alone. I can tolerate these fractious escapades nae longer. If ye are wise, Donald, ye will follow suit."

With that, Baldie Dunbar rose and retreated to his chamber for much-needed sleep. A restful evening eluded him as he ruminated on this conversation with Donald. Baldie's thoughts kept returning to Donald's eyes — the more the old Laird spoke, the more disturbed his visage became, his eyes growing dark and hooded throughout their conference. Baldie had known the man for years, but Ross' reaction the recent events with the Bruce, and Laird MacCollough specifically, gave Baldie cause for concern. Donald always appeared to be strung differently than most men, and Baldie feared that the old man final lost all his senses.

Donald Ross and his compatriots were gone when he entered the hall the next morning, and a chill coursed through Baldie's wame at what Ross would do, and who would help him do it.

Chapter 2: A Matter Unsettled

Clan MacNally, Akedene, Western Highlands

L aird MacNally exploded when he learned where his daughter had been, and then his anger enflamed all the more after learning his attention-seeking priest and lily-livered nephew had the gall to with her. Earlier in the day his voice thundered throughout the hall, demanding to know where his daughter had absconded. Once the stable lad shared that he helped Elayne, her young cousin, and the priest saddle up, MacNally's face screwed up in frustration as he realized his daughter's intentions. Taking several deep breaths, he calmed and set himself in the solar to wait and attend to them once they returned. The lengths to which Elayne would go to secure herself a husband, Ewan specifically, spoke volumes to MacNally. Ewan would never set his wife aside for Elayne — in truth, MacNally was uncertain how she set her mind to wed the Laird of Clan MacLeod in the first place.

The priest managed to save himself, Christ notwithstanding, by coming to the hall as soon as the entourage returned. Throwing himself on Laird MacNally's mercy and speaking as rapidly as possible, the priest poured out the details to MacNally — that Elayne considered Ewan her intended, claimed his new wife was a witch to himself and Young James. Once the priest learned that Elayne misled him with her intentions, he left with her. Father MacNally also informed James that his daughter already submitted to confession and her penance while he came to the castle for his own forgiveness. MacNally's face betrayed no emotion during the priest's confession. Instead, the priest's words further befuddled him.

"Father, what prompted Elayne in this lunacy?"

The priest pressed the tips of his fingers against his lips. "Of that, Laird, I am uncertain. But she seems to be in a quest for a husband. Perchance she feels she needs more than what is offered to her here, as the daughter of the Laird?"

Laird MacNally scratched at his graying beard, a grumbling noise arising from the back of his throat. "She has all she needs here. Full run of the manse, full control, and whoever she weds will become Laird as she is a Lady. She has never said she needed anything more."

The priest did not respond but scanned his eyes around the hall in a telling manner. "She has lived here her whole life, and Elayne is nay one who prefers consistency. She has been nothing but a handful, always searching for something more, getting her way, doing what she wants. Mayhap she has reached an age where the confines of clan MacNally are nae enough for her."

James MacNally nodded in agreement. Mayhap his daughter needed something more in her life than to run his keep as the spoiled daughter of the Laird. MacNally dismissed the priest with appreciation instead of chastisement, him mind focused on his situation with his daughter. Father MacNally fairly ran from the keep, grateful to still have the skin on his back after the day he spent with Elayne MacNally.

For too long James MacNally had allowed his daughter to run the house with no accountability or direction from him. He should have raised her with a heavy-hand, set some rules, but she ruled the house and clan with an iron fist — her way was the only way as far as the care of the castle was concerned. His tall, dark-haired daughter commanded respect, and for a long time, MacNally was content to have her deal with the womanly duties and then some. He appreciated having such a strong daughter. Now, however, he realized that she needed more; she needed a place, a husband who could accept her headstrong ways and let her be herself, a husband who actually needed, nay, *welcome*, an iron-willed woman to take over the care of himself and his house. That blossoming idea convinced him that responding to the letter he received several weeks earlier was the best option for his daughter.

Sitting at the rough-hewn desk, he flexed his fingers several times before he dipped his quill in the ink and continued his message. Writing helped him tame his anger, which would surely resurface once Elayne found her way home. As for his wayward nephew, he would deal with *that* young man later.

Elayne entered the keep like a ghost, so unlike the insolent lass who left. Earlier, the house servants recoiled from the brashness of her voice that reverberated off the rafters, dictating everyone within hearing to their duties. Now she returned with nary a word to anyone, reticent, avoiding her father, humiliation casting a pall on her face. She did not want anyone, least of all her father, to see her. Shuffling upstairs, she made it to her chamber, where a small fire waited for her after her long ride home. Closing the door, she hid herself from the household. A confrontation with her father would soon follow, and she needed to collect herself before that encounter.

The heat of the day still hung in the room. A pail of water hung over the fire, ready to use for a wash. Elayne poured some into the metal basin and used a cloth to wipe her pale face and neck, scouring off dirt from the road and the church. She would need help removing her dress for a full wash but did not want to risk looking for Senga to help her. Loosening the ties on her bodice, she rinsed the damp cloth in the basin and wiped more of the road weariness from her chest and breasts. She carried the cloth to the chair and began to remove her shoes when her father stormed through the door, fury oozing from his pores like the heat from the sun.

"What in the name of *Christ* did ye think ye were doing?!"

Elayne didn't pause as she freed her feet from her leather shoes, stretching her toes in relief. She was more than accustomed to her father's rages and tirades. She remained silent to let his bluster blow itself out before speaking, especially since this time the bluster was well deserved.

"Ye *cannot* go around the Hi'lands, accusing people of crimes of witchcraft because ye want to marry a man! What were ye thinking?"

Too much bluster, Elayne thought and finished removing her stockings. She wiped the damp cloth over her feet, the sensation of clean, bare skin overriding her previous emotional upheaval.

24

Elayne's silence prickled James' fears more than her willful ways ever had. "Lanie, I love ye, daughter, more than ye can know, but these behaviors, I do not ken what to do with ye."

At this, Elayne stopped in her ministrations. *Do with me?* That phrase did not ring well in Elayne's ears, and she screwed up her face, finally addressing her father.

"Do with me? What is wrong with me that ye have to do something?" Her voice was strangely calm. She wiggled her toes, drying them, as she regarded her father, her slanting eyebrows straight with curiosity.

MacNally sighed heavily and stepped into the room, sitting on the large bed across from his daughter. He reached for her hand and looked on her as lovingly as a father could.

"Lanie, I think ye are bored here."

"Bored? Father, what can you mean? I have this whole keep to care for, plus assisting with the care-taking of the land and the clans people. Much needs my attention daily! How can I be bored?"

"Well, perchance that is the wrong word. But I see ye here, with only Senga for company. Ye do not have any close companions, ye don't have a beau —"

"Not anymore!" Elayne broke in. Her father held up his hand, his eyes hard. Most of his anger had expired, and his present focus was on the best future he could offer his daughter.

"Nay, my lass, ye never had Ewan, no matter how much ye wanted him. But that is the point I am trying to make. Ye are nigh on twenty years, and most young women are wed or hand fast. Most young women have a company of women to entertain, a mother to spend their time with. Ye have none of these, and mayhap much of that is my fault. I never wed after your mam passed. I never had more children. Ye need companionship, if for no other reason than one day ye and your husband will lead clan MacNally. So, I have an idea, if ye are up for hearing it."

The mystery of her father's idea both intrigued and frightened her. She enjoyed her life here at *Akedene*, itself surrounded by the mighty oaks for which it was named. However, she could not dispute that her father was correct. Over the last several years, she had perfected her home and land management skills, and her house ran better than the king's; she was sure of it. This perfection in running the clan meant she did not have her hands deep in the daily upkeep, and she found herself with too much time. *Idle hands are the devil's handiwork,* she heard said. There are only so many tapestries, so many books, to fill the extra time.

Elayne tossed the drying cloth back into the water basin and turned her pale gray gaze directly to her father, intrigued.

"Ye have my attention, father."

***

Clan MacCollough, BlackBraes, Southeast of Ullapool

As far as his revenant as a stranger to his own clan, good Torin and Duncan solved that problem in one auspicious moment. Declan came upon the giant Torin as the man was dumping muck outside the stables. When Torin turned at the sound of the approaching horse, Declan found himself knocked off his tired beast, the solid mass of man that was Torin enfolding Declan so that his toes barely touched the ground.

"We thought ye dead!" Torin exclaimed.

He laughed and cheered so loudly that Duncan, upon hearing the clamor, rushed over the investigate. Instead of helping Declan out of the suffocating grasp of his closest childhood friend, Duncan joined the fray. At least Declan knew that his return home was well received. While this alleviated some of his worries about becoming Laird, Declan was sure he would be crushed to death before he could see the interior of the keep. The two stayed with him for the rest of the day, informing Declan of clan news as they drank and celebrated the return of the prodigal Laird.

The next morning, Declan awoke from a hard, drunken sleep to an ungodly smell rising in a corner of the dingy castle hall. He managed to peer one eye at the corner where a pile of debris — leftover dog scraps, dirty rags, and what looked like ashes from the hearth — projected the odor of dying Highland cattle. Letting out a dismayed sigh, he closed his eye and tried to breathe shallowly as he considered his predicament.

At least the castle itself was in good shape, no disturbed or broken stone that Declan could see from his bedding in the hall. Not that the castle could even be called a castle. More like a large stone house, it was given the title of MacCollough Castle years ago to his grandfather (or was it his great-grandfather?). His father inherited the keep from his grandfather, both strong, hardy men, and the lands secure and animals well cared for. That, however, was where the accolades of Clan MacCollough ended.

Declan's grandmother died shortly after his father's birth and he was raised roughly as a result. Declan's own mother left soon after he was old enough to walk, and Declan was thusly raised by his father's rough hand. Declan and the men of his clan were all boorish men from uncouth backgrounds. Few women now lived in the village, most not wanting to live or raise children near such a large assemblage of wild men.

And the reputation of the wild MacColloughs traveled far across Scotland. When Declan was a tow-headed youngster, he enjoyed the title, roaring around like a bear cub himself. Now that he was a man, too soon approaching his 28th year and having served the king of Scotland, he realized those wild ways must be set aside. He heard whispers about who would be chieftain when Declan died, and many wondered what future the wild clan would have at all.

In his heart, Declan struggled with the idea of taking a wife and having children, bringing them to this harsh land, risking the legacy of his abusive father. He recalled his own pain at not having a mother to turn to when in need, and what, if any, woman who would wed him should leave as his mother did? Or perchance worse, die in childbed like his grandmother? These fears continued to rest heavily on his shoulders. But again, he pushed them to the side as he squinted his eyes open to scan the hall.

Several other clansmen sprawled in the squalor, snoring heavily, sure to awaken with headaches, dry mouths, and odorous bodies once the sun was high. Finding a meal in the unkempt kitchens was a challenge — half burnt, half raw meats were the usual fare, eaten off a spit or a dirty plate. Something as simple as butter (oh, did he miss butter!) was absent in the kitchens. For all the robust Highland cattle good Ian kept, a pat of butter was rarer than gold in MacCollough land. The whole clan was in a dire place, and Declan desperately needed a solution.

Declan stepped outside to relieve himself, kicking an odd, frosty bucket out of his way, scanning the yard as he pissed. Even after being home for several months, the lands looked little better than when he had left. While the buildings appeared well-maintained on the outside, for defense of course, the remainder of the lands and the interior of the buildings required significant attention. Coarse, ramshackle gardens grew haphazardly, lacking in care and finesse. Most of his men donned awkwardly stitched garments; while most men could sew if necessary, not a one could sew well, and the clothing exhibited that.

Then the sheer number of men in the clan could not be missed. Few women meant few mothers, fewer children. *A clan that does not breed, dies,* the Bruce cautioned him, a lesson Declan MacCollough would not forget his sage advice. After years in the king's employ and traveling across different clan lands, he could not help but compare those lands, those clans, to his. He did not like what he saw.

He shook off his cock and tucked it under his plaid, trekking distractedly back into the keep. Recalling the lass he spied in a village months ago, he hoped his solution for his clan was a sound one.

***

The scent of a fresh fire kindling at the hearth overrode the less pleasant smells of the hall as he returned. Declan watched his oldest friend, probably one of the largest, hairiest men in the Highlands, awake and poking at the fire, encouraging it to flame. Torin Dunnuck may be hairy, but like Declan, he found the Highlands cold and took every opportunity to complain about it. He was also the only man in the house who would deign to light a fire. On this morning, Declan was grateful.

"Are ye cold already? 'Tis only October, ye chilly fiend," Declan taunted.

Torin stood, his frizzy brown hair almost touching the beams of the room and smirked at Declan.

"At least I have mine arse out o'bed before daybreak, ye lazy lout." He tossed the fire poker to the side where it clanged against the hearth and reclined on a bench near Declan, shoving some dirty rags to the side. "And ye are the one always complainin' about the cold!"

Torin flicked his eyes to Declan, not bothering to hide his present opinion of his Laird.

"Have ye put more thought to your half-crazed idea?" Torin continued. "Ye know that most o'the clansmen will not take kindly to changes. Unlike us reasonable men," Torin raised his bushy eyebrows to Declan, "most men enjoy drinking binges and free reign."

Raising an eyebrow at Torin, Declan guffawed at the taunt. No one more than Torin wished for the rough ways of the clan to remain; he was the Laird's most staunch opponent to the idea of civilizing the clan.

The hall slowly warmed, brightening with the fire and daylight, which did little to improve the appearance of the room. Disgust filled Declan, and again he pondered how his home, his land, his clan had fallen into such an abject state, which only reinforced his conviction that the step he was about to take was the correct one. The solution, however, would cause more strife than the dirt and decay of the hall.

"I received a letter," he told Torin. "I dinna ken if 'twill amount to anything, but I have heard the woman is a force to be reckoned with, and I think, I *know*, that is what we need."

"But," Torin hesitated, "ye do not even know the lass. Don't ye want to find a woman ye love? What if ye aren't even attracted to her? What if — " he paused a moment, choosing his words wisely. "What if she leaves like your own mam did? Are ye no' concerned with history?"

Declan reclined on a cot near the hearth. The fire and daybreak chased away the morning chill, and Declan collected his thoughts, scratching absently at his golden beard. His oldest friend might understand his motives but still vehemently disagreed with the idea. Declan knew without a doubt that the rest of the clan would likewise not be convinced. Declan turned his pale hazel eyes to Torin's dark ones, trying to explain his motives.

"I ken that women are often used as pawns in power struggles between clans, and men of power usually have the upper hand when it comes to a choice of brides. It should be that way for me, but when I see my clan in such condition, I know I must choose a wife who can help me get my life, my home, my clan in order. If she can do that, then I will love her no matter her reputation, or her appearance."

Chapter 3: The Benefit of Literacy

I wrote a letter, Lanie," Laird James MacNally admitted to his daughter.

"A letter?" Her dark eyebrows rose.

"Aye, a letter. Do ye know of the clan MacCollough, east of us?"

"MacCollough? Ye mean the dark and dirties?" A look of revulsion crossed her face as she noticeably recoiled.

Her reaction was not what MacNally hoped for. As a neighboring clan, MacNally was familiar with the reputation the MacCollough clan garnered over many years. Nevertheless, James MacNally was familiar with the new Laird, having heard accolades of the young man from other chieftains; some praise passed straight from the King himself. MacNally found several avenues of opportunity with Clan MacCollough. In strengthening that clan, he would assist a neighboring clan and ally, and perchance find a more significant opportunity for his headstrong daughter as well.

"Well, I would not quite call the clan *that*," he rolled his eyes. "But it is a clan in need of some, um, female involvement. I know Declan. He is a good man in a rough place. He has spent the last several years at the side of the Bruce. *BlackBraes* could be a great clan but has lacked a woman's hand for generations, and the rough men are a testament to that."

He paused to scratch his beard. "The MacCollough has heard of ye. And ye, my lovey, ye are the strongest woman I ken, stronger than many men. I think, the MacCollough is astute in his request — ye can help bring his keep and his clan into a more reputable state. Ye will have a maid or two, and Senga can go with ye." Laird MacNally would never design to send his daughter to a man's house without a chaperone.

Elayne pressed her lips together in a tight, shrewd line. "Why father, are ye playing matchmaker? Are ye hoping that the Laird MacCollough will so appreciate my overbearing ways that he will fall madly in love with me and attempt to wed the harpy, as you have so callously painted me?" She threw her head back and barked out a short laugh. "Why father, ye have more gumption than I gave ye credit for."

MacNally laughed as well, in spite of his daughter's foul humor.

"Ye see, Lanie? It is that behavior, gumption as ye say, that is needed. I think it will be good for ye. It will allow ye to explore the world, use your skills in a way much needed, and if ye wed a man, a laird, well, the more's the better, aye?"

Elayne tipped her head to the side, measuring out her father's words.

"What did ye write in the letter?"

"Do ye want to read it 'afore I send it?"

Elayne shook her head, her dark hair falling about her shoulders. "Nay, father, a summary of the letter will suffice."

MacNally cleared his throat. "'Tis a short letter, truthfully. I merely responded that I was aware his clan lacked a woman's care, that cleanliness and medical care may be needed, and confirmed my daughter was exceptionally skilled at both. I wrote that ye were looking for life experience and adventure, and mayhap he would find your companionship useful for a time."

Elayne cut her eyes toward her father, sharing the same smirk he presented her earlier.

"Useful, eh? I sound like cattle."

"Nay, my Lanie, ye sound like a prize."

***

Actually sitting down to write the return letter, however, was another matter for Declan. Now that Laird MacNally agreed to Declan's proposal, he was at a loss as to what to write. How does a man respond to another man offering up his daughter? What details would he need to consider for receipt of the lass? James MacNally's letter did not entirely serve up Elayne on a platter, but given the reputation of the lass in question, Declan understood the letter's true intent. Elayne MacNally was known in much of the Highlands as a willful, spoiled woman, tall as a man and as outspoken as one. Having seen the woman in action, her reputation was well deserved. Declan, though, was a man who understood perspectives. He knew that just as Elayne earned a reputation as an aggressive woman, there was more to her than that, and a good reason why she acquired such a reputation. After all, her reputation as a harpy was the reason he wanted to meet the lass in the first place. Regardless, such rumors did not bode well for a woman. Whisperings and gossip made it difficult for any woman to live down a rumor, true or not. Having a reputation precede her made marriage for any woman difficult.

The one characteristic of Elayne he had learned, however, was that in spite of these supposedly horrible traits, she was actually a beautiful woman. Tales of her chestnut hair, gray eyes, and well-formed body reached him before he first saw her in the village. He noted her height, another rumored trait. She was tall for a woman, but as most men in the Highlands were taller than average, he wondered why this was so disconcerting for many. In truth, he didn't care about height — perchance he was more confident than most men? Or at this point, he just didn't care? Declan shook his head to collect his thoughts, dipped his quill in the stained inkpot, and began his letter.

Laird James MacNally,

I appreciate your Response to my letter, and the opportunity to improve our Clan with a strong woman's hand. While some might not consider such an idea, I truthfully believe BlackBraes would benefit Greatly with the assistance of someone as qualified as your daughter. An arrangement for a visit from her is welcome.

I do have to ask again if ye are seeking a Husband for your daughter as well, since ye indicated she is not currently betrothed. I must ask if I may try to woo her; BlackBraes does not have a Mistress as I lack a Wife. To allay any concerns, I am familiar with the chatter in regard to your daughter, and

you can be Assured I give them no credence. I would be
honored to take this time to get to Know your daughter
herself, and if she decides I am worthy of her, I would also be
honored to take her hand in Marriage.

We are nigh at the start of autumn, and I understand
that travel arrangements may take some time. Please extend to
Elayne the offer to write me as she would like, so she may be
at least somewhat familiar with myself and BlackBraes prior
to her arrival.

Again, thank you for considering BlackBraes and
myself worthy of your daughter.
Laird Declan Anders MacCollough

***

Young James took the post from the MacCollough
messenger and delivered it to his uncle and namesake.
Displeasure for Young James' excursion to the MacLeod's
clan with Elayne still simmered under Laird MacNally's
visage, but he was mostly forgiven (much of his actions
ascribed to being impetuous, which helped his case
immensely), but he did not miss any opportunity to get on his
Laird-uncle's better side. Young James hoped the letter from
the MacCollough was good news, and mayhap that would
completely remove Young James from his uncle's ire.

Laird MacNally took the letter without lifting his eyes
from the papers on this desk, much to Young James's chagrin,
and waved his nephew off. Usually a brave man, MacNally
hesitated to break the seal. He knew marriage options for
Elayne were limited — hell, *she* had to know they were

limited — and he blamed himself. She was, if nothing else, a result of his upbringing. While he was proud to have such a strong daughter, one who could run the entire clan single-handedly, that opinion was not one shared by most. He inhaled deeply and split the wax. After reading the first line, he broke into a run up to Elayne's chambers.

Elayne sat sewing by the window, letting the fresh cool air flow over her, using the last of the bright sunlight to help her make close, tight stitches. Always perfect — nothing less was good enough for her. Everything she put her mind to, she endeavored for perfection, commanded it. MacNally only hoped that the MacColloughs would understand her desire to have her life lived in a specific manner. He knew this trait could often be read wrongly — but she too would need to learn to temper her desire for perfection with acceptance that humans, most definitely the MacColloughs, are not perfect.

He knocked at the chamber wall as he entered. Elayne glanced up from her sewing and gave him a slight smile, one of the few ways she took after her mother.

"Lanie, I have heard back from Laird MacCollough."

At his pause, Elayne braced herself. "What is the news, father?" She returned her gaze to her sewing, feigning disinterest.

"He writes that he would be honored with your presence and your company in helping set his house in order. He writes that he hopes ye find both himself and his home worthy of such a visit."

Elayne's hands didn't pause as her gray gaze regarded her father. "Do ye think he is honest? Is he reputable? I dinna ken the man, so I must defer to ye if ye think this is a sound decision."

Her voice shook, but her strength still shone through her words. If Declan MacCollough was the man James believed him to be, then Elayne should have naught to fret over. If nothing else, certainly the Bruce's faith in the young Laird should be evidence enough. James nodded pensively.

"Aye, daughter, I ken him to be an honest, reputable man. I am certain your dignity, and your virtue, will be in safe hands. But," and here he hesitated a moment, his gray eyes searching hers.

"Remember, they are only human. They have lived without a civilized touch and may be resistant to ye and your ways. There will be many rough men who see ye as an interloper, and ye may need to have more of a soft hand at times to help him get his house into order. Ye must be accepting of them as they will have to be accepting of ye. Do ye ken what I am saying?"

Elayne nodded. "Yes, father. I understand."

"Fine," MacNally smiled. "I will write MacCollough this eve and let him know your answer."

Chapter 4: Preparations

Upon receipt of James MacNally's letter announcing his daughter's arrival within a few days, Declan surveyed his main hall with a discerning eye. Advancing through the kitchens, he returned to the hall and made his way up the dark, stone stairs to the upper chambers. He peered into each chamber, regarding the blue room the longest. The bright, cavernous chamber had been his mother's. Before she left for good, she first left his father's room. Though it sat empty for years, it could be considered the cleanest room in the keep. Other than a heavy layer of dust, the chamber itself was neat — bedding made, chamber pot discretely under the bedstead, pitcher and basin centered neatly on the table near the window. Even the candle was devoid of dripping wax, waiting to be lit for an evening.

Declan's own chamber left much to be desired in terms of cleanliness. While he did put items back in his trunk, the room itself appeared well-lived in. Food remnants, stacks of furs, dirt from his shoes tracking across the floor, and the less than fragrant odor that resulted made him grimace. Once again, he questioned how his house could sink to such squalor. And what example was he setting for his men? The truth was, he wasn't. The hall below testified to that. He was impelled to put his castle in some order, so the poor lass didn't run screaming from the disaster that was the keep. This challenge needed more than he was capable of handling, being from the lands for the last several years. Racing back down the steps, he called for Torin. Perhaps his seneschal might have a solution.

Declan found Torin in the stables, his typical hiding place, brushing dust and sweat off his large walnut steed. While the chill in the air testified to the strong hold of autumn, the beast still sweat profusely, as did the horse. Seeing the sweat and dirt on the man, Declan's hopes sank. Torin was not one who ascribed to the "cleanliness is next to godliness" philosophy, but Declan needed to see if Torin had an idea.

"My good man!" Declan called out and Torin turned to him. Torin held up a filthy hand, clasped Declan's hand in his, and clapped him on the back, sending dust and sweat flying.

"What brings ye to the stable? Do we need to ride?"

"Ooch, nay, Torin," Declan told him, trying to shake off the pounding he just received from his friend. "I need to pick your mind a bit."

"My mind? Well, I daresay I'm flattered. What do ye need?" Torin tossed the brush to the side, his full attention dedicated to his Laird.

"I have received confirmation from MacNally that his daughter will arrive in a few days. While she will help put the house and whole domain into rights, the keep as it stands leaves much to be desired." Declan pressed his thumb to his lips. "I dinna want to scare the lass away 'afore she even enters the hall."

Torin cleared his throat, suppressing a laugh at Declan's description. "Well, Laird, we could try to rouse up some young ladies or married women without children who can come to the hall and help clean a bit."

Declan pondered the idea. It was sound, to be sure, obvious even, but the problem lay in the fact that women were few and far between in the clan, which is why he was in his current predicament. This would be a good start if they could find a lass and her father willing. Perchance then more fathers might permit their daughters to partake in the MacCollough castle if the whole of the clan, the keep, and the lands were mended.

"Can ye think of any women who may want to work at the manse?" Declan asked, *or any fathers who may permit them?* Declan thought. "It is too much for one woman, and I don't expect a clean keep, just one that looks less like a . . ." Declan struggled to find the right word.

"Disaster?" Torin offered. Declan furrowed his eyebrows at his man-at-arms but did not deny the man spoke the truth. Declan shook his head in resignation.

"Aye, well, at least clean a room for the lass 'afore she arrives. Do ye ken anyone?"

Torin rubbed his fingers in his russet beard, thoughtful.

"Aye, Old Ian trusts ye, the man that ye are. He has an older daughter, named Bonnie, and she may welcome coming to the keep as house help. She may even be able to stay once your MacNally woman arrives and serve as company for her. Do ye want me to inquire?"

"If ye would, Torin. Try to complete the task today, and if she and her da are amenable, have the lass come to the keep tomorrow."

***

Once her father sent the letter, approving her visit to MacCollough, Elayne began packing her belongings. Her father indicated she would leave soon, if she desired, and Elayne was nothing if not prepared. She considered what items she may need, not only to put the strange man's house in order but to bring the whole clan and village into a civilized age. Her trunk sat next to her bed as she filled it with her necessaries. In addition to her bodices, kirtles, and skirts, she packed papers, ink, and quill, plus some books and herbs. She was evaluating if she needed to raid the kitchens for more and bring her own pitcher and basin — *who knows if he even owns one*, she thought — when her father approached.

"Ye are packing already? Ye do not leave for a few more days?" he inquired.

"Ooch, nay, father. It is more preparing for packing," she told him. "Ye ken I prefer to be ready."

"Aye, that is for sure," he agreed.

"And father, I am glad that ye are here. I want to settle your mind about something."

MacNally stood up a bit straighter, wondering what could be on his daughter's mind *now*.

"I ken ye are worrit for me and not just the traveling," she began, folding kerchiefs into a stack on her bedding. "I ken that I am strong willed, and my more brash behavior and opinions have caused ye grief in the past," she admitted, pausing to look her father nearly eye to eye.

"I want to apologize for my behavior with Ewan MacLeod," she continued earnestly. "For some reason, perhaps since we had done much with his clan over the years, I believed we were going to be betrothed. That a betrothal to him would not happen, I never considered. My miscued expectations dictated my actions, and for that I am sorry. Ye can rest assured, father, that I can temper myself, now that I no longer have those expectations."

Her explanations pleased her father, as the concerns for her loud, willful ways was never far from his mind. Though he did not believe her fully, James MacNally gave her a lopsided smile and nodded.

"I ken that, Lanie," he said. "Sometimes we get an idea in our head, and it just willna leave."

"Aye, that is for certain, father. And I also apologize for bringing poor Young James and the priest with me. It reflected badly on them, and it could have led to grave repercussions for the MacLeods. Once settled, I plan on writing a letter in apology."

Of course, she would — she would have all things done her way. The fact she acknowledged her error, however, moved him. Perchance she learned more than he realized. Perchance she was not as spoiled or willful as her reputation led everyone to believe. "I think that is a fine idea, Lanie."

"And I would like if ye did not punish Young James or Father MacNally further. They were just following my wishes."

MacNally paused, then nodded again. "I think ye have become wise beyond your years, Lanie. I will take your words under consideration."

When MacNally spoke again, his voice was low, almost sad. " Ye ken ye do not have to leave, Lanie. *Akedene* is your home, and if ye wish, we can find a strong man here for ye."

Elayne sensed her father was becoming overemotional, and it touched her heart, even if he was lying to appease her.

"Aye, father. That I ken. But I have lived at *Akedene* my whole life. Perchance travel will grant me stronger perspectives." Again, she must have her way, his pride in his daughter choking him.

"Aye, Lanie," James MacNally said, hugging her close, "but it does not make ye leaving any easier."

Chapter 5: When Introductions Run Amok

T he wagon was full of trunks and travel bags on the day of Elayne's voyage. Senga had informed Elayne and her father that over her dead body would Elayne travel to a strange man's vulgar clan alone. For all her wrinkles and gray hair, Senga could be a force of will to match Elayne, and James was not one to argue with her.

Even though she exhibited a tough exterior, Elayne was relieved to know she would not travel on this journey alone, even if her only chaperone was an old woman. Senga helped raise her, the only mother figure she had really known, and Elayne did not relish leaving Senga behind. And if the state of the MacCollough keep was as appalling as her father intimated, the extra set of hands would be well received.

Cool, overcast skies welcomed her as she stepped out from her father's castle hall to the inner courtyard. She managed to hide the shaking in her hands but feared her father might recognize her nervousness and cancel the trip. Senga was already in the back of the wagon, reserving the wagon seat next to Ramsay, the stable hand, for Elayne. James MacNally helped her step up into the seat, and his hand lingered on hers.

"Keep ye safe, Lanie. If ye need anything, or ye just want to come home, send for me immediately."

Elayne adopted her mask of iron will — eyes narrow and mouth grim, the one most Highlanders recognized from the Harpy — and responded in her most authoritative tone. "Of course, I will, father. And now that I will not be here as the woman of the castle, ye must find yourself someone, a new wife. Otherwise, this keep will fall apart without my strong hand!"

She smiled at her father as he winked back. He hoped perhaps this adventure would be good for her — she had seemed less terse, less shrewish (as much as he hated that word) than she had earlier in the summer. Though she previously apologized for her actions, MacNally's concerns for his daughters had not yet abated. She would always be headstrong and formidable, which would be just what MacCollough needed to bring civilization back to his clan. James slapped the horse's haunch.

Elayne's head jerked as the wagon leapt forward with the horse. The village road met the main road through the thin woods and low brush, the horses settling into a steady gait, pulling the wagon at a strong clip. If they kept up this pace, Elayne believed they could be at MacCollough's before sunset. Senga hummed quietly to herself in the back of the wagon while Elayne admired the view. The few trees burst full of autumn leaves, casting a cheerful landscape over the road, while still allowing the snow-capped mountains in the distance to present their commanding stance in the background. She noted a few Scots pines, still full and deep green contrasting against the mountains. Birds called out in high, clipped songs, flitting above them. The high, sweet smell of thistle, heather, and white lace relaxed the travelers, and Elayne rested against the back of the wagon bench, feeling calm for the first time in months.

The brush cleared to the south, opening to a wide glen that expanded as they approached Clan MacCollough. Shortly after entering the glen, they ate a midday meal of cheese and bannocks, downed with cups of cider. Elayne took the reins so Ramsay could eat as well. The sun had long since crested its zenith, nearing late afternoon, when Ramsay suddenly sat up high on the bench, his head turning toward the trees.

"Mr. Ramsay?" Elayne began.

Ramsay held up a hand to silence her when she heard the sound as well. Hoof-beats, loud and fast, meant riders. The wood and hillside could mislead them, but to Elayne, the sound came from the east.

Large riders in green and black plaid burst through the brush on Ramsay's side of the wagon and Elayne heard Senga gasp. She hoped the woman would think to crouch in the back of the wagon to hide. Elayne sat up taller, narrowing her eyes as the man nearest to Ramsay addressed them.

"Who are ye? And what are ye doing trespassin' on our land?"

"Trespassing?!" Elayne screeched. She put on her haughtiest look and glared at the man who spoke. *Reivers?* she wondered. " I dinna ken who ye think t'be, but this road is a royal road, one for public use, and we are in our full rights to travel on it."

The man fair giggled at that. "Ye rights? Ye
pretentious bitch! We will show ye what we think o' your
rights to the road!"

At that, two men jumped onto the wagon. Elayne
strained to push away the man closest to her, but he grabbed
her wrist and yanked her off the wagon bench. Another man
threw Ramsay to the ground, where he landed roughly in the
dirt, and the men in plaid gathered the reins and rode off with
their wagon, hooting and heckling over their prize. Elayne
watched in horror as Senga's frightened face peeked over the
back edge of the wagon. Standing in the middle of the road,
hands clenched at her side, Elayne began yelling for all she
was worth. Pretension be damned.

"Ye bastards! Ye vile thieves! I shall have your heads
for this!"

The men on the wagon were too far down the road, and
if they heard her, they did not react. Elayne dusted off her
skirts, then reached over to Ramsay and offered him a hand,
assisting him to his feet. He also brushed the dust off himself,
then looked sheepishly at Elayne, wringing his hands.

"Milady! Please forgive me!" He started to cry, actual
tears leaving tracks in the dirt on his cheeks. Frustrated,
Elayne waved his apologies off.

"What were ye to do, Ramsay? Fight off all of them?"
She sighed heavily and peered down the path. She would
definitely call this an adventure. "Well, it appears that we will
be walking the rest of the way to Castle MacCollough. 'Tis
fortunate I wore comfortable shoes."

With that, she threw her shoulders back and began to
march over the dusty road, Ramsay scrambling to follow her.

***

The late afternoon sun was losing its glow as Declan returned from his discussion with Ian regarding Bonnie, Ian's eldest daughter. Conversations with old Ian took longer than anticipated. The lass was more than eager to leave the monotonous work of her father's house and start monotonous work at the keep, much to her father's chagrin. Declan repeatedly guaranteed her safety, and Ian finally acquiesced. The opportunity sent Bonnie into a small packing flurry as Declan left the chaos of the croft.

Crossing the yard to the road leading back to his castle, Declan attention focused on dirt kicked up by riders from the west, highlighted by the setting sun. Anticipating Elayne's entourage, he rode toward them and was perplexed to see his own clansmen in dirty plaid arrive with a lone wagon. He raised his hand to signal the riders over, and Bran galloped up, a childish smile plastered on his face.

"What is this?" Declan asked, a sinking sensation spreading across his belly.

"My Laird! Trespassers on our land, so we relieved them of their bounty!" Bran's belly shook horribly as he laughed, and Declan's befuddled state worsened when he saw an older woman's frightened face appear over the wagon seat. He pressed his hand against his forehead, panic rising as he pieced together what transpired.

"My Christ in Heaven, Bran, what have ye done?" Declan called back as he dismounted and sprinted to the wagon. The men grew unnaturally quiet as they watched Declan reach over the side to help the small woman down.

"And ye are?" Declan asked, his anxiety rising.

The woman's eyes, wide under her kerchief, spoke more than she did. "I'm Senga," she replied.

"And ye were escorting who?"

"Lady Elayne —" was all Senga could say before Declan spun on his heel, racing for Bran's horse.

"Ye fools. Did ye not hear that I had guests from MacNally's land arriving today from the west? Christ's blood! Ye have assaulted and robbed our guests! The lady of that clan!"

Declan mounted his steed and raced off in a cloud of dirt and plaid, and two of his men still on horseback had the wherewithal to follow.

Gloaming cast the sky in a gray haze when they found two figures walking down the road toward *BlackBraes.* Declan wanted to hang his head in shame — how could this have happened? What a horrendous first impression, and to leave a lady, the daughter of a laird, to walk an unknown road to a stranger's land? He wasn't sure which emotion he felt more — impressed that she had kept walking or contempt at his men's behavior, which reflected back on him.

"Milady," he called out as they approached.

The woman turned her startling gray eyes up at him, and Declan filled his gaze with the infamous shrew. She was long-limbed, but taller than expected, as tall as a man if he had to guess. Her vibrant, dark hair was wound into a braid around her head, creating a halo, and even though the road was dirty and she had just walked the last hour, she looked refreshed and alert, as if this were nothing more than a walk in a garden. Her gray eyes, however, flashed her indignation, and Declan braced for a tongue lashing. He was not disappointed. Her reputation, evidently, was accurate.

"Really?" she began, making the connection as to his identity — the illustrious Declan MacCollough, attempting to rectify the behavior of his clansmen. "*Milady?* Given the conduct of your men, which I presume they were since ye wear the same plaid, one would question your language. Is this how ye welcome guests into your lands? Is this how ye welcome a lady of another clan? With thievery and besiegement? It lends credence to the rumors that your clan is naught but a collection of uncivilized lack-wits!" The longer she raved, the louder she became.

Declan sat upon his horse and endured the well-deserved verbal assault. After all, she was not mistaken, and he and his men earned the tongue-lashing. He lay his hand on his chest and bowed deeply over the reins.

"Milady, ye have my sincerest apologies," his voice calm and earnest. "I hadna ken that my men were patrolling, and though I told my men to expect guests, my message obviously was missed, and I accept the blame for such shortcomings. Can ye forgive me?"

Elayne was momentarily taken aback by the fair man's response. Many men would have not cared that she and her servants were put out in such a manner, but this man took responsibility and wanted to rectify it. She raised one slim eyebrow to him.

"Declan MacCollough, I presume?"

"Aye, and ye must be Lady Elayne MacNally?" She nodded in response.

Declan dismounted in one swift move and enclosed Elayne's hand in his.

"Again, my apologies. My men and I rode here as soon as we learned what had transpired. Your servant is presently resting at my hall, and we shall escort ye and your man back to *BlackBraes*."

Elayne regarded the road. With no wagon or extra horses, how did he mean to escort them? Before she could ask,

Declan grasped her around the waist with one arm and put out his hand. She stared at it.

"My Laird, what —?"

"Boost up," he replied. She stepped on his palm and pulled herself up on the saddle. Once she settled atop the horse, Declan swung himself up behind her. Elayne cut her eyes sidelong to him.

"Laird MacCollough, I daresay this is quite inappropriate."

"Aye, it may appear so, but this is the only escort we have at the moment, so shall we make the best of it?"

He prepared for another shrieking outburst, but to his surprise, she further cocked her eyes at him and replied coolly, "Indeed."

That comment intrigued him more than her outburst. Perhaps the rumors about Elayne were exaggerated, but since this was their first meeting, he elected to err on the side of reserving judgment.

Elayne watched as Ramsay saddled behind one of the other clansmen, and Declan reared his horse around, making a nickering sound with his tongue, and the horse took off full gallop through the wood.

Chapter 6: Paradise Unclean

They arrived at the castle, coated in dust and sweat, and the first thing Elayne wanted was a bath. Her traveling kirtle was caked in grime and stains while the bodice of her chemise clung to her wetly. Though this was not the first impression she wanted to make on the laird, his first impression left much to be desired as well, so she did not overly concern herself. A bath, a clean gown, perchance some food, and she would feel her normal self again.

However, upon entry into the hall, her hopes for the bath and food dissipated. The overall presentation of the hall made her gorge rise. Ages-old dirt and filth climbed the walls, creeping from a completely blackened fireplace. Debris piled in the corners of the room and the residual stench forced Elayne to breathe shallow through her mouth. She dreaded seeing the kitchens, let alone eating anything from it, and she absolutely feared entering her own chamber. Sudden, stark concerns about her decision to come inflamed her brain, and another light sweat broke out over her body.

The look on Elayne's face cast Declan into an absolute
state of fear, certain she would depart his land 'afore even
entering the hall. He took her hands in his again, catching her
wide gray eyes with his pleading gaze.

"Milady, as you can see, there was good reason for me
to write your father in regard to your attributes. I dinna ken
how to run a house. I have been a soldier, camping in the
outdoors for the past several years, and my father, the previous
laird, took even less interest with the house and village than I
have. There has no' been a woman's strong hand in the land
for decades. I would ask that you take this all in, evaluate what
needs be done, then help me accomplish it." *Please dinna run
away in fear,* he begged to himself.

Unblinking, she narrowed her eyes. In typical Elayne
fashion, she felt the harpy inside rise up and prepared to give
this young laird the dressing-down of his lifetime. His earnest
hazel eyes, however, caused her to bite her tongue. She did not
know him, his history, or his conditions of the last years, but
his tone, while not pleading, suggested an imploring need.
She also promised her father and herself before she left
Akedene to temper her outbursts.

"Normally I would loudly protest such a treatment of a
guest," she replied honestly. *No need to be coy,* she thought.
"Thus far the hospitality has been sorely lacking and this place
—" She cast her eyes around the sorry state of the hall. "Well,
I will not let loose my tongue on ye. 'Twould appear that ye
dinna need that right now. My father informed me of the
conditions of your household, and I will temper myself
because it is obvious ye ken what is lacking. However, I
canna begin to help ye in the present state I am in. Please tell
me that my chambers are in a somewhat better condition than
this?"

She pulled herself up to her full height. With her head high and shoulders thrown back, her eyes nearly reached his. Those eyes, while hard as flint, engaged him, and he desired to do all he could to keep those eyes on him. From her speech, he discerned she was intelligent and spoke her mind, often loudly. Declan could easily see where the rumors came from. She had strong expectations, and Declan wanted for his whole clan to rise and meet them.

"I assure you," he told her, "that your room is in much better condition. Perchance a layer of dust from lack of use, but otherwise in excellent shape."

One of his men leaned toward him, speaking in his ear. Declan glanced back to Elayne, a bright smile lighting and softening the handsome structure of his face. A flame of yearning lit within her, a smoldering need she had not before experienced. Elayne deduced he was not a man who smiled often, and she wanted to see him smile at her like that again.

"Your maid, Senga? Ye will find her in your chamber as well."

Relief flooded Elayne, and she allowed Laird MacCollough to guide her up the stairs to her room.

***

The blue room, as Declan called it, was larger and cleaner than she expected. Though he was correct about the thick layer of dust, the remainder of the room was well-kept, and dust was simple to eliminate. Someone tied the tapestry over the window to the side, allowing the last rays of the setting sun to pierce the room, casting a fine glow on dust motes dancing in the air.

The large bed was in the corner near the window, a dark plaid coverlet folded over a layer of furs. A table with a washbasin (*no pitcher,* Elayne noted) stood to one side of the ashy fireplace with a chair at the opposite side. Her trunks were not yet in her room, and neither was Senga. Declan guessed at the reason for her concerned appearance.

"Your servant is apparently attending the kitchens, searching for vittles for ye. Shall I send for her?"

While Elayne truly wanted a bath more than anything, Senga was already retrieving food, and she would ensure it was edible. Elayne nodded her head.

"And my trunks?"

"Aye, those are still out in the wagon. I shall have them retrieved for you straightaway. Shall I light the fire for ye?" Declan asked.

"Nay, that I can accomplish myself. Thank ye."

Declan stepped toward the door when Elayne addressed him again.

"This room, my Laird MacCollough, whose is it? I have the notion 'tis no' yours. It nary looks lived in a'tall. The dust means it has been unoccupied for a while. . ." she trailed off.

His hazel eyes darkened at her question. "My mother's chambers," he told her curtly and left the room.

As he exited, Senga appeared in the door. She waited until Declan had passed through the length of the hallway before entering Elayne's new chambers with a wooden tray of food. Elayne, contemplating Declan's abrupt shift and hasty departure, lifted the cloth covering to see what miracle Senga managed to perform in what was surely a catastrophic kitchen.

"Kipers, cheese, and potatoes, milady. Not the meal I was hopin' for ye, but the most edible of the lot. The bread looked a wee bit moldy. Ach," she paused, pulling another cloth off the tray, exposing a small pitcher of ale. "The ale looked good enough, no surprise there."

"No' need for commentary, Senga. I am just glad there is food. I am starved, as ye must be." Elayne reached for the tray to set it on the basin table, smirking at Senga as she did so.

"I hope your trip to the castle was a pleasant one?" Elayne teased.

"Ooch, Lady Elayne! Those MacCollough, I have ne'er seen a rougher bunch of beasts! They rode the wagon over every ditch and rock on the road! I'll be certain to have bruises all along my backside!" Senga, not one to miss an opportunity, cut her frosty eyes back to Elayne. "And ye, miss, how was your ride back?"

Elayne knew that Senga must have seen her atop Declan's horse, his arm around her waist, and she did something that rarely happened — she blushed — and threw the cloth from the tray at Senga.

"Well, he is a handsome sot," Senga said. "Even if he has his work cut out for him with these beastly men."

"The good news is our job is no' with the men. We are to help get this house and village in order, encourage other lassies to come. It shall be Declan's job to see that his men treat the lasses in the fair way they deserve."

"Ooch," Senga said again. "The Laird may have'ta die trying on that one."

***

Elayne picked at the kippers and hard cheese as Senga resumed her servant duties, first kindling the fire then directing pail after pail of water heated and poured into a bath. She and Senga managed to wrangle a sheet draped over a large metal basin from some clansmen below. The water was warm enough when Elayne stepped in, and she would have enjoyed putting her whole self in at once, but much like every other bath basin she encountered in her adult life, her legs hung askew over the tub. Not a one was ever long enough to accommodate her height.

Senga sorted through Elayne's trunk, pulling out necessaries and lining them on the mantle. Thankfully, she had also shaken out the coverlet and furs so Elayne would not have to sleep in a dusty bed this eve. Her less-than-vocal evening at this new place did not go unnoticed by Senga, who commented on the unusual behavior. Elayne waved her off with a wet shake of her hand.

"Dinna get your hopes up that I am now quiet and ladylike. I am just evaluating my situation. But more than that, I am truly tired. I ache all the way to my bones and the bed looks so —"

She did not finish as a loud crash and yelling from below interrupted her. She looked askance at Senga and reached for her robe. Senga, knowing that look well, tried to stop her.

"Milady — this is a strange house! Milady, ye are only in a robe!" Senga's words fell on deaf ears as Elayne stormed out of the blue room, ready to give these discourteous sots a piece of her mind. *Who behaves like that in their laird's castle hall?* She wondered to herself as she descended the stairs in her bare feet.

Elayne reached the bottom of the stair and absorbed the scene before her. When she arrived at the hall, she could see that someone may have started to clean the years-worth of clutter and grime that plagued the place. But after so long unattended, the effort was nay more a drop in the ocean, and now Elayne could understand why. She first saw a horse somehow managed to enter the main hall, with a man atop it no less. Once she was able to close her gaping mouth from that sight, she watched as large Highlanders wrestled behind the horse, making it skittish, and it kicked into several tables, sending pitchers and mugs crashing into the sparse rushes on the stone floor. Men and the horse trampled food, peat, dirt, and clothing, and a couple of dogs ran wild, eating what fell to the ground. Any attempt that someone had put into cleaning this hall before she arrived was lost in this cacophony of men, beasts, and chaos. Declan was nowhere to be seen.

"What do ye THINK ye are doing in this hall?" Her shrieking voice carried over the noise, reverberating into the corners.

The man on the horse reigned the beast in and the raucous clansmen stopped to stare at her. Feeling suddenly vulnerable in just her robe, she pulled herself up to her full height, buttressed by the extra height of the stair, and glared at the strange gathering.

"First, this is your laird's hall, which should be treated with respect as an extension of your laird! Second, animals belong in the barn, NOT in the hall!" She cut her eyes to the man on the horse. "Third, someone attempted to clean this hall, and your gross conduct has rendered that a complete waste! Ye must take your atrocious behavior out of doors. If ye are going to behave like beasts, then ye should be outside, like beasts!"

For a moment, the hall was silent, then the dark-haired man on the horse burst out laughing, followed by the rest of the men in the hall.

"And who do ye think ye are, ye lass, to tell us, the men of clan MacCollough, what to do?"

"She's my future wife," a voice carried over the din, and Elayne leaned off the step, peering around the horse, to see Declan at the doorway. He stood with his arms crossed, his blond hair unbound and full around his head. His face betrayed no emotion, but his words surprised Elayne, and she found herself standing a bit taller, a wide smirk plastered on her face.

"Declan! What do ye mean? We grapple here all the time!" one of the wrestlers protested.

"Well, no more, Duncan. The lady is right, we have lived as uncivilized beasts for too long. If we are to survive as a clan and make our mark, we must act differently. The lady is here to help us with that."

The men paused, letting Declan's words settle into their ears. Many of them, sending angry glares toward Elayne, exited past Declan. As the horse clomped out last, Elayne surveyed the hall that now resembled a battlefield, and then caught Declan's eyes. His intense, golden gaze moved from her face, then down to her gown. Her body burned under that gaze, and she blinked to regain her composure, clasping the robe more tightly around her curves. She decided to ignore his "future wife" comment, certain he had said it more for impact than truth and continued to smirk as he walked over to her.

"Well, Lady Elayne, I can say for certain that ye made an impact this evening."

"That may be true, but I certainly didna make any friends," she responded as she walked back up the steps to her now-chilled bath.

Chapter 7: Lies Do Not Become Us

Clan MacNally, Akedene

J ames MacNally rode into the courtyard near dusk and noted a figure standing in the shadows near the gate. Dismounting, James handed the reins to the horse-master and cautiously approached the figure. The man stepped out of the shadows, and James was pleasantly surprised to see his older nephew, Alistair, waiting for him. The lad fidgeted, anxious, his dark reddish-brown hair nearly standing on end. They embraced warmly, and James escorted his nephew inside, calling out for some bread and mead.

Stretching out on a chair near the hearth, Alistair graciously accepted the rations and gulped the mead, foamy drops sticking to his light beard. James sipped at his own goblet, patiently waiting until the Alistair finished drinking to learn the reason for his visit.

Alistair belched loudly and wiped his sleeve across his mouth. He sighed deeply.

"Thank ye, Uncle, for the hospitality. I rode hard after talking with Young James."

"Really?" James MacNally raised his eyebrows. "What did the lad say to ye to cause ye to ride like the devil?"

"The news from wee James was alarming, Uncle, and I could not believe it until I spoke to ye directly. 'Tis not true, is it, that ye sent Elayne away to find a husband?"

James scratched at his beard, trying to understand Alistair's concerns. What did it matter to the lad if Elayne was entertaining a husband?

"I did no' 'send her away,' as ye put it. Aye, the MacCollough did indicate an interest in wedding Elayne if she could help him bring forth civility to his clan. I am of a mind, knowing Elayne, that she will be wildly successful."

"And what of our clan?" Alistair asked.

"What? What do ye mean?"

Alistair's brow furrowed toward his uncle. "Our clan!" he exclaimed. "Ye are not a young man, Uncle. Now that Elayne is to be gone, who is to lead the clan when ye expire?"

James inflated his chest. He felt at the peak of health, and his body exuded strength. Other than some graying on his head, he looked as youthful as when he first wed. He opened his mouth to say as much, but the impetuous youth cut him off.

"Surely not the MacCollough? Wee James said he heard ye claim that if Elayne does her job, then *she* and her husband would lead both clans?"

"Why does that surprise ye, Alistair? It is not unheard of. Many clan lands in this area are groups of two or more clans with one laird. My marriage to Elayne's mother brought the Blars clan as part of the MacNally clan. Why are ye surprised at this?"

Alistair's tawny eyebrows shot upward this time, and he leapt up from his chair at his uncle.

"Ye would have an outsider as laird of the clan?" He slammed his hand on the table.

"Nay," James shook his head, keeping his temper controlled. "I would have my *daughter* and her husband lead the clan. Elayne would not wed someone too weak to lead. I trust her discretion in choosing a husband. MacCollough could well be that man."

"Are ye a fool, Uncle?" Now Alistair came close to James, setting James on edge. He sought to rein in his irritation, knowing Alistair was just a hot-headed youth, but his hands curled into fists, regardless.

"A fool?" James asked in a low voice.

"Yes! How can ye rely on a woman to make a choice such as this? And to a strange man ye dinna ken? She should wed someone in the clan proper! If not that, ye should have the leadership of the clan descend from your line, and since ye don't have a son, it should —"

"Should what?" James interrupted, his face hot. "Descend to ye? Ye are the eldest of all my nephews. Are ye using this moment as a play for power?" The reason for his nephew's visit was now readily apparent. Making questionable assumptions was evidently a MacNally trait.

"Uncle," Alistair curbed some of the wind from his words, "I dinna mean it that way."

"Nay, but ye did. Ye want to suggest that ye are the best candidate for my position, as though I am an old man on my deathbed, not a strong man in the prime of life. And ye are also suggesting that mine own daughter is somehow more daft than ye are and that her decisions canna be trusted. Further, your claim suggests that if Elayne were to wed, she would not have a son, who then could be a direct line from me."

Now James stepped toward Alistair, who shrunk at his uncle's voice. He feared mayhap he poked a sleeping bear, and presently that bear was angered.

"Nay, Uncle, I never would imply —" he tried to explain.

"But ye did!" James roared. "How dare ye imply my daughter is a fool, barren, and that ye would be a better choice? What put such crazed ideas in your head?"

He stepped back from Alistair, afraid he might inflict physical violence on his own nephew. He cast a hard look at the lad.

"Ye are a fool for even coming to me with this. If MacCollough had done something to call his ability to lead into question, ye would have had a stronger claim. If my daughter's safety were in danger, or if there were a legitimate concern, I would hear ye. But this pathetic play for power before Elayne is even wed speaks more to me than anything else. Your actions today tell me even if I had to select a successor, I should not select ye. Now get ye gone from my sight."

***

From his chamber window, he watched his nephew ride off. Both Alistair and wee James were his sister's sons, and she could be almost as willful as Elayne. In fact, it seemed to be a pervasive character trait in his family, so MacNally should not be surprised by his nephew's words. What angered most him was Alistair's accusations regarding Elayne and the certainty the lad espoused about his own claim to laird-ship.

Above than all that, Alistair's insane words made Elayne's absence more real. James MacNally had to admit he worried about his daughter. Ramsay relayed the encounter they had with MacCollough men, and MacNally wondered if he made the right decision. He felt a throb begin behind his eyes and rubbed his forehead, hoping to stave off the oncoming headache his nephew wrought.

James MacNally missed his brash, willful daughter. She only left the day before and his heart ached for her terribly. Her loud mouth drove him to a frenzied state sometimes, but he realized now how she filled the keep, and a huge emptiness settled in. He started to wallow in parental self-pity when a pair of warm, slim arms wrapped tightly around his midsection. James placed a large hand over the small ones cradling him.

"Are ye weary, my Laird?" a serene voice asked from behind him.

"Yeah, Mari, 'twould appear so."

Mari leaned her head against James' back, pressing her body into his.

"No' too weary for me, my Laird?"

He turned to face her and pulled her in close.

"Never too tired for ye, my love."

He kissed her deeply, and for the first time enjoyed his lover in his chamber, out of the sight of his daughter. Not having to hide Mari from Elayne excited him to his core, and he took Mari to his bed.

***

Alistair did not ride for home when he left. Instead, he sped past MacNally's tenants and the darkening crofts, the cooling air easing his tensions. Autumn was fiercely upon them, chill and dank, but the air this eve was just what Alistair needed to clear his head. Not only was he dejected from his uncle's harsh reprimand, James' unflattering characterization of him fueled fierce anger at his core, burning deep. He grasped the reins as his mind whirled, wondering what his next step should be.

The drone of the horse's hooves lulled him into a contemplative state. He knew MacNally would live a long while, so perhaps he was premature in his confrontation with James. The fact that Elayne, a mere woman, would be set up in a higher position than he unnerved him. *He* was the first-born male of the family. *He* was the one who trained with his uncle's men. *He* should be the one to lead the clan! The more he mulled over the conversation, the more incensed he grew, until he had an epiphany. *"MacCollough could well be that man."* MacCollough could only be *that man* if he were present to wed Elayne, and an idea formed in Alistair's mind that could alter that arrangement.

At the fork in the road, instead of heading further north toward home, he veered east, nickering the horse into a gallop, eager to see if the idea blossoming in his head could work. The lands of clan Ross lay far to the east, and he rehearsed his ideas as the night drew long. He knew that it would be a full day before he arrived and riding to the point of exhaustion benefited neither him nor his horse. Alistair rode into the brush, tied his horse off near a low bush, and wrapping himself in his plaid, fell asleep.

When he arrived at *Balnagown*, seat of Castle Ross, doubt reared within. He had only partial information, and the design that cultivated in his mind smacked of treason. It would take much for one clan to turn against another. But rumors abounded that Ross and several other clans did not support the claim of Robert the Bruce, that Ross personally was enraged that Bruce escaped, yet remained king. And then Alistair had one bit of repute few were privy to. Alistair recently learned from a drunkard in a tavern that the MacCollough was the very man who assisted the Bruce's escape from the English and the collaborative Scots. Mayhap Donald Ross and the full power of his clans could eliminate MacCollough as retribution.

A sentry stopped Alistair at the portcullis. Alistair looked in awe at *Balnagown* — a much larger stack of stone than Alistair's home, even larger than his uncle's. While Alistair gazed skyward with his mouth agape, the sentry took his reins and asked him a question. Alistair shook his head to refocus and looked back at the sentry, who repeated his question.

"State your name and business at *Balnagown.*"

"Oh, aye. I am Alistair MacNally, and I have some interesting information for Laird Ross, if he be available."

The sentry grunted in response and led Alistair and his horse toward the stables. Dismounting, Alistair left the horse in the hands of the stable lad, and the sentry escorted him into the expansive main hall. The sentry pointed to a bench, and Alistair sat, waiting as the sentry delivered his message.

Donald Ross entered the hall shortly, and Alistair was taken aback at the man's person. Expecting a brawny Scottish warrior in full plaid, instead his eyes rested on a short, balding man who seemed to find growing facial hair difficult. Alistair rose and bowed to the man. Ross gave a brusque bow in return.

"What business do ye have here, mon? Gillivry speaks of your supposed "interesting" information?"

Alistair scratched his chin and struggled to suppress a smile. Now that he was here, and Ross was present, his scheme to dispose of MacCollough and help promote himself as the eventual leader of Clan MacNally solidified — surely Elayne's discretion would be seriously called into question if she aligned herself with someone who was executed as a traitor. Mayhap he could wed the unpleasant lass, thus securing his position.

"Laird Ross. I thank ye for your time. The news I have is in regards to Declan MacCollough — does that name mean anything to ye?"

Donald Ross drew himself up to his full height, as short as it was, his nostrils flaring.

"Aye," he responded. "And what does that name mean to ye?"

"Ooch, correct me if I am misinformed, but I have heard it said that ye consider MacCollough a traitor, and ye want his head on a pike for his aiding the Bruce to escape. Am I wrong on that account?"

"What ye speak of is treason," Ross said.

"What if I ken where ye could find MacCollough?" Alistair pressed.

Donald Ross blinked at Alistair a few times, cautiously selecting his next words.

"I had heard the man may be dead."

Alistair scoffed. "Oh, nay, Ross. The sword did not end his life, only cleaved his shoulder a bit. The man lived, returned in secret to clan MacCollough after his father died, and is back at his keep, trying to wed and regain control of both his lands and the MacNally's."

"So, the rumors are false? The man yet lives?" Delirious light shone in his eyes.

"Aye, and he is back on his own land."

"What, with the wild beasts of the north? That clan is little more than a pack of animals!"

"Well, not anymore," Alistair informed him. "He has returned, is wooing Elayne MacNally herself in hopes she can help him tame his wild clan, and once wed, will eventually reign over two Highland clans — the very man who removed the Bruce from your grasp."

Ross was silent for a long while, then extended a hand toward Alistair, an alliance of two unstable minds forming.

"Come, young MacNally, to my chambers. We have much to discuss."

Chapter 8: Paradise Reclaimed

Clan MacCollough, BlackBraes

Sunlight barely touched the dewy earth when Elayne rose and donned her most worn dress and kirtle. Declining Senga's assistance, she coiffed her hair back in a dark kerchief, then marched downstairs to the kitchens where Bonnie was already at work at the hearth. Elayne had learned of Bonnie's employ the evening before, so she decided to let Senga catch some much-needed rest.

"Good morn," Elayne called out, and Bonnie jumped back, raising her fire poker like a sword. "Ooch, my apologies! I dinna mean to give ye a fright."

"Aye, 'tis nothing. I wasna prepared for anyone to be awake at this hour. I have been here the last day and from what I have seen, did nay expect anyone to rise 'afore noon."

Elayne gave Bonnie one of her classic smirks and tipped her head toward the hall.

"Someone needs to start cleaning up after these beastly men, but 'tis too large a job for one woman." Elayne turned back at Bonnie. "Truth, 'tis too large a job for two women, but 'tis all we have. If ye are finished here, can ye help me find buckets and we can get to work?"

Bonnie nodded and reached over the hearth for two wooden buckets. Filling them from the cisterns, they entered the main hall together. Remnants of the previous night's escapades littered the surprisingly empty room and Bonnie gasped. Elayne surmised Bonnie had entered the manse from the kitchens and had not yet seen that damage.

"Aye, they made a bad mess even worse. And then some." Elayne rolled her eyes. "I fear 'tis too much work for us, but I dinna ken anyone else who can assist. I hope ye are up for a long day of scrubbing."

Elayne moved toward the hearth near on the far side of the hall, deciding to start at one end and work toward the other. Bonnie skipped to keep up with her long strides.

"Milady, pardon my asking, but who are ye? Are ye the woman the men discussed, come from another clan to try and tame this one?"

"Well, aye, I'm Elayne MacNally. But 'twill not happen unless the laird is on board with the idea. He appears to be, which bodes well. When I reprimanded the men for their chaotic behavior in the hall yestereve, MacCollough supported my declarations. That will go long in turning this clan around."

"Is this horse shit?" Bonnie exclaimed.

Elayne smirked again. "Let me tell ye what I stumbled onto last night."

She then regaled Bonnie with what she saw while on the stair in her robe. Bonnie laughed uncontrollably while the morning and the debris of the night before waned. All too soon the sun was high in the sky and, unlike most of the scrubbed hall, both Bonnie and Elayne wore coats of grime. As Elayne emptied yet another bucket of thick, brackish water outside the keep, she heard Bonnie giggle behind her.

"Ye are no' what I expected, milady."

"And what did ye expect? A tiny, witless woman, unable to do for herself?"

"AYE! 'Tis exactly what I expected."

Elayne allowed herself a rare giggle and turned back toward Bonnie.

"Well, then I am fortunate my reputation did no' reach ye. So, we are here, but we have no other help? Have there been no women in the keep 'afore this?"

Bonnie nodded. "Aye, and few women in the clan as a whole. Ye have to travel past the village toward Clan MacKenzie to encounter more."

"I heard rumors, but we canna always believe what we hear," she flicked her eyes toward Bonnie to show what she thought of gossips. "I would like to ken why no house help or kitchen maids live here, or why the men have no wives? And then where did ye come from?"

"Ye are right about rumors. Truth be told, some women are tenants for Clan MacCollough. But for years, Laird MacCollough's da and grandda both lost wives, so nary a woman's hand has helped in the running of the castle, tenants, or village. Generations of rough men chased most women away. My mother and da are tenants, but we live far off, closer to the village." Here she paused for a moment. "I can see why the Laird wants for a woman's touch. Too long the men have run wild. The clan is shrinking, few children fill crofts or even this very hall. I heard the MacCollough tell my da the future of the clan is uncertain."

Elayne nodded. A chill coursed over her at the mention of "children." She knew she came here to help the MacCollough gain control of his house, to bring a woman's touch in a rough place, but she also recalled the Laird's letter to her father offering marriage. Her mind had so long anticipated joining with Ewan and the MacLeod clan, she never entertained wedding anyone else.

Now that she had regained her senses and her pride, she had an offer to consider which prompted another thought: *How could she decide to marry a man she barely knew?* She rode on a horse with the man and heard him speak a few sentences the eve before — those two events encompassed all her encounters with Laird MacCollough to date. How could one want to wed sight unseen, person unknown? Surely love, consideration, and desire had to play a part in whether two people should wed?

***

The sun struggled to push past the clouds until noon, giving up its battle to the chilly day. Pushing sweaty hair off her face, Elayne stood at the outer door to the kitchens, dumping another bucket of sludge water, grateful for autumn with its golden flora and cooler weather. Bonnie finished her share of the kitchen cleaning, with Senga cleaning and arranging Elayne's new chambers. Elayne told them they rest and partake in a meal before they continued. While the kitchen needed more scrubbing, the domain was reasonably clean enough to prepare a repast without worry of making them ill. Bonnie offered to assemble a quick meal after they cleaned the layer of grime off themselves. Elayne took advantage of the offer to pilfer a clean cloth and bucket and fill it with crystal water from the cistern outside.

One side of the kitchens was partly sheltered, providing a clear space near the garden wall to wash. She untied the kerchief from her hair, letting the long walnut locks trail down her back. She washed her hair and face with the cool water, relief from the work of the morning washing over her with the water. As she worked the wet cloth under her kirtle, along her chest and shoulders, clean water displaced the sweat and grime. Once cleared of the initial layer of grit, she leaned against the cool stone wall, closing her eyes, relaxing with deep damp breaths. At the sound of scattering stones, her eyes popped open, and she glimpsed the Laird himself.

"Pardon, milady," Declan bowed toward her, "Bonnie told me ye where to find ye."

"And what do ye want?" She heard how clipped her voice sounded, but sweaty and tired, she really didn't care.

"Have ye spent the whole morn cleaning?" he asked with incredulity.

"Aye."

"Why?"

"Why?" She sprang up off the wall. "Ye only have poor wee Bonnie to help ye with the whole of the castle, and she has only been here a day! Ye need more, nay, an army, to begin to have this stone disaster in order — who else would ye expect? 'Tis a part of how we get a house in order. A clean palette if ye will."

Declan considered this statement, his gold eyes searching hers. Elayne felt a bit exposed under his intense gaze, her kirtle wet and clinging to her breasts, her damp hair loose and clinging as well. She could only imagine the impression her dirt-streaked face made, and she used her hand to wipe her hair back from her forehead.

Her impression on Declan, however, created the opposite effect. To see her work so hard for his house squeezed his heart — she had been in his house but a day. He had never known another person to take such pride in the castle and land, certainly not his father, and here this lovely iron-eyed woman stormed in, took charge, and worked herself into a sweaty mess — *a gorgeous sweaty mess,* he thought to himself — just for him. And she a lady no less! She enraptured him both physically and mentally, and the damp kirtle that exposed the rounds of her breasts did not help his situation. He surprised himself, desiring her in all her dripping, grimy beauty.

"Milady, ye need an army to clean?" he asked.

Elayne was nothing if not decisive. "Well, it would help. The kitchens are getting clean, and we have a start in the hall, but we have only just begun in those rooms. Then there are still the solar, the stairwells, and the whole upper castle that needs attention. The gardens, the courtyard . . . " Her voice trailed off as she appraised the gardens behind Declan. "Truth, it will take more than a fortnight to get the entirety of the manse in order, even with assistance."

Declan did not miss her use of the word "we" and a small smile broke across his face. Elayne saw the play on his lips and gave him her smirk in return.

"So, have ye an army, my Laird?"

"Perchance I do, Lady 'Layne. Enjoy your repast, and I shall return in the hour with your army."

Her smirk grew. "Aye, my Laird," she told him, disbelieving, and went to eat.

***

Elayne and Bonnie busied themselves cleaning up from their midday meal, an easy moment of cheese and bread (with the mold cut off), and found in a corner cubby, wine that had fortunately not turned. Elayne was beginning to despair at her limited diet — this was her third meal of bread and cheese, and as she peered around the kitchen, she noted the considerable lack of food stuffs that typically fill the kitchens of a keep. Senga pointed out the same earlier in the morning. Elayne dreaded at the prospect of bread and cheese again for her supper.

Bonnie noted Elayne's gaze. "Yes, limited food here, aye?"

"Aye. What do the servants or clansmen who abide inside the walls eat?"

"I dinna ken," Bonnie stated. She shrugged. "I ate at home until I came here. Perchance those who do live near eat at home?"

Elayne inspected the kitchens again. The whole of the kitchen area was smaller than what she knew at *Akedene,* cramped even, most of the storage areas completely empty. At least the kitchen boasted a few cooking pots. She sighed. These men, this clan, were true barbarians. Her mind thought back to the golden-haired man she encountered in the garden. The Laird seemed so different from these wild men he lorded over. *Why such a difference?* She considered what task she took on with the MacCollough, if this were a life she could live. The offer of marriage hung heavy in the air, like thick smoke from a hot fire. She wondered if she would ignite or smother here.

Elayne heard a chaotic sound from the great hall, loud voices, clomping, and she raced from the kitchens, dread filling her. *Please, not another horse!* she thought. What she found brought her to an abrupt stop, mouth agape. Several men, dozens it appeared, collected in the hall, full of dusky shirts and muted plaid. Declan stood at the helm of coterie, near the door beam. He caught sight of Elayne as she stopped short and gave her an exaggerated bow, gesturing towards his collection of men.

"Your army, Madame." That slight smile pulled at his lips again, and instead of smirking, Elayne snapped her mouth closed and felt herself with an actual, face-alighting smile.

"My army?" She tilted her head toward the crowd of men. "For what, my Laird?"

"For cleaning, upkeep, heavy lifting, cooking," he told her. Elayne burst out in a loud laugh at the prospect of men cooking in the kitchens. "And anything else you may need them for," Declan continued.

"Dinna piss on my leg and state 'tis rain," she shot back. "Are ye joking? They are men!"

"Nay, no pissing," Declan said, his smile expanding, crinkling the corners of his eyes. "And aye, for cleaning. Perchance if they have to clean for themselves, not only will they take better care of their clan, but they will see the need to civilize themselves for women and the clan as a whole."

"Ahh, ye have a vested interest in this ploy. Well, then, let's put your beasts to work!"

She climbed up on a bench and clapped her hands loudly over her head.

"My good gentlemen!" she called out. "I hear ye have been recruited to help clean up the keep, the grounds, and mayhap your clan! I will put each of ye to work and together we will have this complete before nightfall!"

The grumbling of the men grew as she spoke, and a large russet-bearded highlander in the front spoke out in protest.

"Who are ye to tell us to clean? 'Tis women's work! Ye should clean, ye Highland banshee!" Raucous agreement followed his speech. Declan stepped forward to put the man in his place, but Elayne stayed him with a light hand on his shoulder. *Banshee? 'Tis a new title,* she thought. She drew herself up to her full height and brought forth hell from her voice. She was the harpy of legend, and Declan was pleased to see it. This was the Elayne of legend he wanted for his wife.

"Who do ye think *ye are?* Ye have been told I am to be the lady of this keep, wife to your Laird, and disrespect to me is disrespect to your Laird! This clan has run rampant without a civilized hand. Your venerable Laird had the good conscience to take action, and now ye spit at his efforts? Ye should be ashamed! If ye dinna listen to me, then ye are no' welcome in the hall!"

She flicked her eyes briefly toward Declan at that threat, and he slightly inclined his head in agreement. Elayne then turned full force back to the crowd.

"Aye, now step forward and I will assign each of ye a chore!" Her voice carried through the hall.

The crowd continued to grumble, each man glancing at another for guidance of what they should do, when one lanky young man waded through the men to stand before Elayne. He appeared worse for wear in his dull, rumpled plaid but looked up at Elayne with a sense of pride and respect.

"Milady," he bowed to her, "Hamish Morgan of Clan MacCollough, at your service." He awaited her command.

"Aye, Hamish, I thank ye. What skills do ye have, if any?"

"I am naught but a tenant crofter, but I have a fair hand in my garden."

"The kitchens are no' well stocked, Hamish. We should starve this winter without sustenance. I would have ye work with Bonnie to evaluate the kitchen stocks, then work the garden, gathering anything that is ripe and help us determine what we need to plant for next year. If we hae' a well-stocked kitchen, we can have full evening meals in the main hall, and more to sell in the village. Are ye amenable to that?"

"Aye, milady!" He all but jumped toward the doorway, obviously ecstatic to avoid cleaning the privies. That job, she considered, she was saving for the large russet man who first contradicted her. *Petty but just,* she thought. She hoped her short speech to Hamish made an impact on the remainder of the men, both in regard to contributing to the keep, and the desperate need for the work. *How did the clan survive this long?* she wondered. *Did they eat raw squirrel?*

With Declan's help, she worked her way through the crowd of men, assigning duties they considered well below their stations but much needed. Once the crowd mobilized and the castle filled with the sounds of cleaning, moving, and scrubbing, Declan lifted his hand to assist her as she stepped down from the bench.

"Well, Lady 'Layne, your reputation was not undeserved. Ye handled that crowd of men well, and I am impressed."

Elayne found herself blushing and scolded herself on the inside. She looked him in the eye.

"'Tis ye I need to thank, Laird MacCollough. Ye were true to your word of bringing an army. Not the one I had anticipated, mind ye," Declan chuckled at that, "but this will save Bonnie and I much work. I am used to hard work, ye ken, but this task seemed insurmountable. Perchance I can focus on forward management as we unearth these stones."

"Your presence here, just in the last day, has made quite an impact on the keep, on the clan, and on me. Milady, may I —?" Here he stopped, then used his free arm to pull her close, her nose nearly touching his.

"May I thank you properly?" he breathed at her. She barely had time to nod as he pressed his lips gently against hers. Her heart pounded in her chest at the gesture, her lips responding to his. He lightly worked her lips, pressing deeper as the kiss grew longer, and she let her arms move around his shoulders. She had been kissed before, but only light pecks, childhood kisses, and now she was in the arms of a full-blooded Highland man who kissed her deeply and with wanton exuberance. Her mind spun, and she trembled as he devoured her mouth.

Declan had to pull himself away and step back. He had not lain with a woman in several long months, and Elayne enticed him in a way he had not thought possible. She may be rumored to be a harpy, but Declan was willing to risk that a woman with the title must be passionate in order to obtain it, and he was not wrong. He took many risks when he broached the idea of bringing her here, and the reward, to him, was worth the gamble.

He inhaled shakily, gaining control of himself. Taking her hand in his, he kissed it gallantly, nodded to Elayne with that small smile still on his lips, then left to find a chore and make himself useful.

Chapter 9: When A Door Opens

T he hot bath that night was, if possible, more welcome than the one from the previous evening. Declan ensured the large metal tub was filled and steaming when she retired at the end of the night. Not only was much of the castle clean and the grounds clear, specific labor had been assigned — Hamish in the gardens, a few other men as hunters, and a list to Declan of what else was required for a functional kitchen and keep. She also elicited a promise from Declan to write more letters, encouraging fathers to allow their unwed daughters and sisters to come to MacCollough lands and mayhap find a husband. They would find employment in the castle grounds in the meantime.

Elayne sunk herself into the water, up to her chin, letting her knees stick out, her grimy hair floating around her. Though the bath soothed her body, her mind remained active, listing what was needed from the clan to civilize the men, what they must acquire on the next market day, and what were they going to eat the next few days until the cupboards were filled. The clan accomplished so much in one day, but the incomplete list, adding to how most of the men of the clan did not hide their animosity toward her, caused a headache to flare behind her eyes. She rested her eyes and reclined her head, trying to emancipate these thoughts. Water splashed over the edge of the tub, and she heard the door to her room creak.

"Bonnie?" she called out behind her, opening her eyes, "can ye bring me some soap for my hair? It feels thick with dirt, to be certain."

A hand placed the soap on a small stool near the tub, but the flash of plaid was not Bonnie's dress. Elayne squeaked and tried to pull as much of herself under the water as possible.

"My Laird! What are ye doing here? I'm indecent!"

Declan's eyes roved over what he could see above the water and wanted to see below. That small smile tugged at his lips, and Elayne found herself once again smirking back in spite of her state of undress. His behavior was improper, but as he gazed at her, the intensity in his eyes bore into her. She found herself not caring about impropriety. His desire for her showed plainly on his face, and tremors of excitement coursed through her.

"I dinna think ye are indecent," he said softly. He stepped around directly in front of her and pulled the stool closer to the bath. "I think ye are beautiful. More beautiful than I anticipated."

He tugged his own grimy shirt over his head, exposing his firm, lightly furred chest, and tossing it to the side. He lifted the soap and sat on the stool at the foot of the bath. She watched him like a hawk, waiting to see his intentions, when he reached beneath the water and grasped her foot. Pulling it from the water, he began to rub the sole with his thumb, soap frothing between her toes. Elayne gasped sharply, then groaned in pleasure and relief.

"We are unwed, yet here ye are, in my bath, touching me. One would question your intentions, Declan."

"Aye, I'll nay lie, what I am thinking is nay honorable at all. Ye can rest assured, this is the most we will expose to each other for now."

Elayne allowed herself to settle into the bath, enjoying the foot rub and the silence for a brief moment.

"Then why are ye, here, if not to ravish me?"

"Ye certain do have a tongue on ye," Declan told her.

"'Tis something ye already ken, Laird, so answer my question."

Declan shifted to give attention to her other foot. "I want to talk to ye. This keep has no' been in such a refined state since before my grandfather was Laird. I have seen ye in action, and if ye are a harpy, ye are by God an unbelievably effective one. But I dinna think this so. I would see ye more as a *Cailleach*."

His shoulders relaxed as he spoke, seeming more comfortable with her than she had seen in the last few days. This type of intimacy was unfamiliar to her, and she felt edgy, adjusting to Declan and his apparent ease around her. "Ye are no' afraid to get your hands dirty, unlike what I ken about most ladies."

At that Elayne rolled her eyes. She had heard much in her life on how "most ladies" should behave; however, she kept her lips closed, relishing the words Declan spoke. Other than words from her father, she was not attuned to encouragement. *Harpy* was hardly an endearment. *Cailleach*, though?

"Ye think me a winter hag?" Her damp forehead furrowed.

Declan shook his blond head. "Nay, a powerful woman, taller and larger than life itself," he explained. "In just two days, ye have made it your mission to create a better clan for my people." Here he paused, considering. "*Our* people, now, I think. And ye should ken I told Torin — "

"Who's Torin?" Elayne interrupted.

"Ooch, aye, he is my oldest friend, my man at arms, and very well the largest man ye will meet in the entirety of your life."

Elayne lifted her hand above the water, gesturing at Declan to proceed.

"I told Torin, if ye did that, regardless of how ye looked, I would wed ye."

Elayne turned her head, averting her eyes in discomfiture. She never fit the preferred, diminutive, pale standard of loveliness, and she knew it. With that in mind, she did try her best to present herself as womanly as possible, her height notwithstanding. While she did receive some compliments, Ewan ended up marrying a tiny, pale woman, and Elayne's sharp tongue drove off other potential suitors. But to hear comments about her beauty, or lack of it, from a brawny, handsome man who kissed her so passionately earlier pained her. Even if her situation were nothing more than an arranged marriage, she had hoped he would find her somewhat attractive.

"To my surprise," Declan continued, his voice husky, "ye appeared on my lands, statuesque, controlled, with dark hair and flashing eyes, and your sharp tongue, and I find want it all. And last night!" He leaned back on the stool, tugging her leg out of the water as he laughed. The softening of his face touched a chord in Elayne.

"The robe clung to ye, and I ken. At that moment, not only was I gifted a powerful woman, one worthy of the status as wife to the Laird of the Beasts, she was a beautiful woman to boot."

He dropped her massaged feet back into the water and moved closer to the head of the bath. Reaching into the water, he clasped her hand, and Elayne flinched back cautiously. The ferocity in his eyes unnerved her. She knew the danger in permitting him to draw too close, but she again felt her heart race and did not pull away.

"I ken this is naught more than an arrangement," he explained, "and we need some time to grow familiar with each other. And I ken if we do wed, we will surely fight and disagree." He moved in to kiss her hand, and she found herself pulling closer to him, the round top of her breasts rising above the water like alabaster moons.

"But ye bring passion, 'Layne, so if ye are agreed, I would like to raise the banns and wed ye 'afore the snow flies."

Elayne was not sure if it was the cool evening breeze or the earnest proposal from this fair blond giant, but she felt in her heart that she could possibly love this man — the respect he had displayed over the last few days alone were worthy of marriage. She captured his face in both her hands and raised up to kiss him. She stroked her lips against his. Her lips parted, and his tongue pressed forward. Her head was spinning, and she was exposed to her waist as he gathered her in closer, his tongue exploring deeper, breaking past her icy exterior.

His breaths came hot and fast to match hers. Declan caressed her wet back, following the droplets down to the curve above her buttock. His naked chest pressed against her damp breasts, and Elayne suddenly understood how fierce and commanding this intimacy was. As his lips moved from her lips to the curve of her jaw, she placed her hands on his chest and gently, unwillingly, pushed him away. Sinking back into the relative safety of the tub, the water growing chilled, she kept her eyes downcast.

"My apolog —" she started. Declan held up his hand.

"Nay, lass, I apologize. That was too much, I think. I should no' have pressed my advantage."

"Ooch, nay, I daresay it was just right," Elayne disagreed, and Declan's eyes lit up in response. "But we need to wait until we are wed for more, methinks."

"Oh, aye, forsooth!" Declan agreed, almost too quickly, his eyes shining like an eager lad's. Elayne laughed at how he resembled a schoolboy. After her cool interactions with him previously, this warm and desirable side of him captivated her.

"And I think we should do this again, soon." She flicked her eyes at him, coy, and he reached toward her again, teasingly pressing kisses on her face and hair until she laughed and splashed him.

He sat back on his heels, his hair damp from her bath.

"Too soon?" he asked, and she splashed him again as he removed himself so she could finish her now cold ministrations.

***

The next Sunday, Elayne found herself kneeling next to Declan in the small kirk, scarcely attended by any of his clansmen. While this did not bother Elayne, as she preferred the smaller audience, having more men in attendance would have lent credibility to her position in the overly masculine clan. And truly she was disappointed at the lack of support the men showed their Laird. *Perchance they did not know any better?* A few of the clansmen accepted Elayne's presence, Hamish in particular. She wanted to believe it was affability, but it was probably the food — most likely a result of the warm vittles from clean kitchens.

Late morning rays filtered through the window slits and the few stained-glass windows in the cold stone church, casting tinted sunlight across the aptly placed altar. Elayne's thoughts drifted to the past several days as the priest's Latin droned on. Declan's offer to have unwed daughters come visit and work in the MacCollough castle was accepted by neighboring clans, and travelers were set to arrive as early as tomorrow. Market day would follow, and Elayne fidgeted as she listed necessary items in her head.

A light touch on her hand brought her back to the kneeler in the church, and she looked to see Declan's hand covering hers. She brushed his hand with her thumb and watched his eyes move imperceptibly toward her, a bronze gaze that she caught with her gray one. Her heart fluttered at the gesture, again surprised at her body's response to him.

The more she pondered her impending marriage to the Laird of the most unrefined clan in the Highlands, the better she felt about her life. After her misadventures and abhorrent behavior in regards the MacLeods, she needed a stronger focus in her life, as her father claimed. She had thought the visit to Clan MacCollough would be a minor diversion, not a real prospect of marriage, yet here she was, kneeling in a church, pledging her troth to a virile Highlander who made her insides quiver, and enjoying a chaotic life she had not believed possible.

Sipping wine from a communal cup and eating a small piece of bread, they waited until the priest commanded "*Vade ad Deum*" and they exited the church into the bright daylight. The reception left much to be desired; no one cheered as they exited. Declan's attentions toward her, however, made up for it.

"Twenty-one days, my Laird," Elayne spoke to Declan as they strolled back to the keep, her arm laced through his. "Can ye wait that long? Or is that enough time for ye to change your mind?" She gave him a wry grin, and he eagerly took her teasing bait.

"I may have to see how far I can get with ye in those days. No matter how loudly ye yell at me whilst I try." He mockingly flinched as she reached out to smack his arm.

"Ye get too far and ye shall find yourself wed regardless," she laughed at him.

Declan flexed his arm, tightening his hold on her, and escorted Elayne into the hall. Bonnie and Senga (whose cheers would wake the dead, Elayne was certain) knew about the kirk visit, but most clansmen, at least those who could read, may not learn of the Banns until they saw the notice on the church doors. Declan wanted to prepare himself for the potential onslaught of clansmen questioning his sanity. He barely had Torin's support, and the gruff man made himself scarce as of late, spending more time in the stables.

To appease some concerns of the clan, Elayne ventured an idea to Declan, suggesting a large feast in the hall that evening. His reticence was noticeable — he knew few would not care about his decision to wed, so long as he did so, but many in the clan were not happy with Elayne, her changes, or with his unadulterated support of her commands. Those men may not be swayed by a fine meal. Elayne thought otherwise.

In need of advice, Declan sought out Torin in the stables and found the giant half covered in hay, wiping down his stallion. Torin looked up as Declan entered, putting his pig-bristle brush to the side.

"So, ye did it?" he asked flatly, his face stoic. Declan pursed his lips in response.

"I tole ye I would. I said if she —" but Torin cut him off.

"Aye, I ken what ye said. But ye dinna ken the woman. She is bossy as hell. And no' well-liked by any in the Highlands. And taller than a man!"

Declan's brows twisted at that last, petty critique. "What? Ye are taller than a mountain — her height should only be a problem for short men! And what is her height to ye?"

Torin shook his head, "'Tis unnatural."

Declan could not control his mirth. "Well, 'tis fortunate ye dinna have to wed her."

Torin puffed his chest up and directed his sullen gaze to Declan. "Please, my old friend, tell me ye have thought this all through. Are ye certain this is the path ye want to take? Your father —"

"I ken what ye think," Declan interrupted, trying to control his frustration, "but I am no' my father, and she is no' my mother." He paused, kicking at the loose hay on the ground, his faith that his oldest friend and seneschal would side with him on this matter fleeting. "'Tis my hope we have a chance for something better. To make this whole clan something more than the wild clan, something worthy of respect of the King. Is that too much to ask?"

Torin sighed deeply, hanging his head. He clapped his bear-claw of a hand against Declan's back, rocking him nearly off his feet.

"Nay, my friend. Your happiness is nay too much at all."

Declan was not certain Torin meant the words he spoke.

***

The oppressive heat from the fires throughout the hall bore down on Elayne, sweat dripping over her back and between her breasts clad in her slivery-blue gown. The gown and her comfortable blue slippers were a pathetic attempt to impress the crowd below, she knew that; however, old habits died hard, and she was raised to dress for an occasion. Her betrothal was no less one of those occasions.

She had written to her father to inform him of the upcoming nuptials, so he would be present to see his daughter wed. Thinking on her father, she realized just how much she missed him, how long the last several days in this strange castle had been. Most of her life was spent in or near *Akedene*, the past fortnight the longest she had ever been from home. Tears formed in the corner of her eyes. She pushed those thoughts to the side and gathered her wits for the announcement feast.

Bonnie managed to employ several brawny men to arrange the tables at Elayne's request, since the men seemed more receptive to Bonnie than they did Elayne. As a result of their efforts, the hall rivaled those of the larger, established clans of the Highlands. A proud smile spread across Elayne's face as she wound her way toward the Laird's table. Declan reserved the seat next to him and stood as she neared, pulling out the chair like a courtly gentleman. Though attired in a shining gown and seated at the head of the room, she was, for the most part, ignored by everyone else in the hall. She had hoped perhaps the men would stand in respect like their Laird, but they were all too involved in the food spread on the tables, not that she blamed them.

Compared to the diet of cheese and bread of her first few days, assigning hunting and gardening to the younger men proved to be a fine decision. Platters of spit-cooked rabbit, quail, and even some savory, plump venison graced the tables. Her mouth watered at the heavy aroma of roast meat. The gardens produced bright kale apples, pears, and late-season berries, which Hamish collected, saving the plumpest fruit for this evening. Large pottery bowls contained steaming porridge while the smaller ones held honey. Large crockeries of cider made the rounds among those feasting, froth spilling onto the tables. Elayne knifed a piece of rabbit from a platter and closed her eyes as she relished the hot meat.

As the eating wound down and the drunken laughter increased, Declan banged his hand on the table. The noise of the hall diminished, everyone's attention focused on the Laird. He grasped Elayne's hand, helping her rise with him.

"Gentlemen and ladies," he nodded around the room, "this feast tonight is in celebration!" He raised his hands, pulling Elayne's long, slender arms up with his, his smile and the cider lighting up his face.

"Tonight, we celebrate the betrothal of Clan MacCollough to Clan MacNally. Lady Elayne has agreed to pledge her troth to me, and we are to be wed in less than a month!"

Most of the Highlanders were inebriated, which contributed to the jovial cheers that rose up at the announcement. The reactions of two men in particular, however, did not go unnoticed by Elayne. Her smile faltered as she noted neither Torin nor the large russet man who questioned her cleaning chore days ago (*Duncan, his name is Duncan,* she repeated the name to herself) showed any excitement, spiking her concern. Turning her focus from them, she instead admired Declan, letting his joy in the moment wash over her. He caught her gaze and gathered her in his arms, pressing his lips on hers fiercely, eliciting rousing catcalls and more cheering from the benches.

On the surface, it seemed that most of the clan approved of the forthcoming union, at least while drunk.

Chapter 10: Action Speaks Louder than Words

Market day excited Elayne for many reasons, not the least of which was meeting several women who elected to work at the keep. Declan explained he thought more families would have welcomed such an opportunity for their daughters. Elayne knew better — the notoriety of the Wild Clan or Beast Clan, though not completely accurate, was no misnomer. Few fathers wanted to send their young women into a beast's den. Four lasses, however, fancied employment at the keep, much to the joy of both Bonnie and Elayne, as it would lighten their workload.

Elayne worked hard her entire life, but after weeks of keeping up with Clan MacCollough, she was bone tired. For Bonnie, these young women represented something greater. Becoming the official chatelaine of the keep pleased Bonnie, happiness tugging at the corners of her lips and eyes. At first, she put on an air of seriousness when Elayne discussed the title with her that morning. Bonnie was concerned that Senga may be offended, but Elayne reassured her that, given Senga's advanced age, she did not want to take on such heavy duties.

Frigid air welcomed Elayne, Declan, and their entourage as they approached the village which bustled with activity, full of colors and sounds. Declan gave her an almost chaste kiss as they went their separate ways. He needed to collect late rents with Torin and other clansmen, a job that would busy him for most of the morning. He offered to send Torin to find her when he could. Elayne scoffed and promised him she would be fine shopping on her own. Spending the morning meeting other tenants, inspecting wares, and purchasing much-needed victuals for the kitchens delighted Elayne. She felt a bit stir-crazy after so much time putting the castle in order that this time outside in the crisp morning air was a welcome change.

Elayne and Declan intended to meet the new house servants near noontide, which gave her several hours to herself. Pulling a wooden cart behind her — *I am nothing if no' prepared,* she thought — necessities for the kitchens topped her list. At the moment, she was none too particular about the offerings for those items. With new people and better functionality of the hall, quantity over quality was her moral of the day. Elayne was continually shocked at what the MacCollough keep lacked. In her life at *Akedene*, any desired item, whether a spoon or trim for her gowns, was immediately on hand. Certain this contributed to her horrible reputation as spoiled, she took it upon herself to rectify the gaping lack of supplies at *BlackBraes,* spoiled reputation be damned. Her velvet money pouch, heavy with coin, banged against her leg under a small slit in her skirt as she approached the first few stalls.

Once again, she was struck by the noticeable shortage of women in the village. Back at *Akedene*, buyers found women in most of the stalls, selling everything from foodstuffs to sewing. The few women she did encounter were direct kinsmen of the MacKenzie clan just north of the village, not MacCollough women. The dearth of women also showed in the absence of household items she would typically find in a marketplace — lace, embroidery, baked goods. Perchance not *necessary* items, but valued ones, nonetheless. Instead, the stalls outside *BlackBraes* showcased millwork, metalwork, and dried meats.

Elayne began with the dried meats and purchased raw meat as well, placing the wrapped vittles in her wagon, then selected grains and vegetables from respective stalls to supplement their present supplies. Milk was plentiful, as Torin ensured someone milked most of the Highland dairy cows housed in his stables, but the butter churn in the corner of the kitchen collected nothing but dust.

She also purchased wares for the kitchen to replace rusted or broken items, a small sturdy knife for necessity, and in one of the last stalls, she was surprised to find delicately carved wares, in particular a wonderfully carved wooden box. Filigree etched the edges while a falcon graced the lid. The box was the type of gift fitting for a wedding present, and she wanted it for Declan. Elayne smiled at the wrinkled man behind the stall, inquiring at the cost. He looked up at her and, like many of the men she had traded with this morning, raised his eyebrows at her towering presence. Shrugging it off was second nature to her, so she widened her grin and inquired to the price again.

"'Tis dear, milady," he began in a cautious tone. She softened her gaze to put the man at ease.

"Tell me your price, my good man," she told him.

"A shilling, milady," the old man croak, looking down at the wares.

"Aye, a fair price for a fine piece of workmanship," she responded nonplussed, pressing the coin into his wrinkled palm. She tucked the box in with the kitchen wares to keep it hidden until she could surprise Declan with it on their wedding day.

She pulled the cart to the open area at the end of the stalls near a worn cistern and bucket. Using a small cup, she scooped up some icy water and drank greedily. The overcast sun seemed brighter and told her it must be nearing noon. She glanced around the stalls to see if Torin was anywhere to be found when someone grabbed her arm. Expecting Torin, she was shocked to see her cousin, Alistair.

"Cousin!" she exclaimed. "What brings ye here? Do ye have word from father?"

"Nay, Elayne, I wish the news were as good as that." Alistair's face displayed no joy. Elayne hardened in response.

"No' something has happened to father?" Her voice rose in panic. Alistair cringed, hoping the harpy would not surface and draw unwanted attention.

"Nay, nothing with your father. It concerns the Laird MacCollough and the danger ye face here."

"Danger? Surely ye jest." Elayne was confident in her own judgment, but after her misconstrued escapade with the MacLeods, doubt about her discernment crept in. She knew Declan for so short a time — more of an arranged marriage courtesy of her father, but she trusted her father's judgment more than her own. Her father would not send her some place where he would fear for her safety. Alistair tugged her arm again.

"Ye have to leave with me. There is a question as to the validity of the Bruce's kingship. Many powerful clans are calling him to task, searching for him, and your Laird MacCollough helped the Bruce escape capture. MacCollough is seen as a traitor by many. He canna be trusted, Elayne. He is a violent man who leads violent men. Ye must come with me, and I will return ye to the safety of your father's home."

Elayne raised one sleek eyebrow at her cousin. She was educated about Scottish politics; she had heard from her father that the Bruce killed Comyn, his competition for the throne, but her father sided with the Bruce, as did most clans aligned with her father. News of clans who did not follow the Bruce had lessened, and the idea of Declan as a traitor was so comical, Elayne nearly laughed at Alistair. The stark intensity in his eyes, however, killed her laughter in her throat. The apparent rage bubbling under his skin sent a shiver down her spine, and she cast her eyes about to see if anyone from the keep, particularly the giant Torin, were nearby. Of course, they weren't. The old man at the end stall would be of no use if Alistair forced her to go with him, and her small knife was buried in her cart by the cistern. Elayne cursed her luck, drew herself up to her full height so she could stare Alistair in the eye, and braced herself. Perchance her height and her reputation as the harpy would send him on his way.

"Alistair, what ye speak of makes no sense. My father is an ally of MacCollough, a friend of the Bruce —"

"I have only just learned of these developments, Elayne," he interrupted, tightening his grip. "Your father does not know of these conflicts. I rode straight here to you upon learning of them! He can no' want ye here with a man who may be tried for treason."

"In that case, Alistair, I will contact my father. We will deal with this accordingly."

"Nay, Elayne. Your father would no' want to associate with this man or for ye to remain here with him! Ye must come with me now."

He yanked forcefully on her arm, dragging her toward his courser reigned to a nearby tree. Tripping on her own feet, she reached out and smacked him in the face.

"Unhand me, cousin! What do ye think —" Her tirade was cut off by a large hairy arm crossing over her shoulder, clasping Alistair by the neck.

"Is this man disturbing ye, Lady Elayne?" Torin asked, wagging his bushy eyebrows. Elayne had never been so grateful to see the man.

"Nay, Torin, my cousin was just leaving." Elayne looked pointedly at Alistair.

Torin released his grip on Alistair's neck and stepped back beside Elayne. Hate and fury contorted Alistair's face.

"Ye are making a mistake, Elayne. I promise ye that," he spat out. Torin moved toward him, and Alistair stumbled back toward his horse.

"Are ye certain ye want the man to leave?" Torin inquired. "We can keep him here, let MacCollough deal with him."

"Whilst the idea does hold interest, let the poor lad go. He is all bluster, by no' much brains."

She and Torin watched as Alistair rode east, deeper into the wood. Elayne rubbed her temples which throbbed from the unpleasant encounter. Her cousin had not acted in such an aggressive way 'afore. *What prompted him to behave so now?* she wondered. Torin grabbed her cart handle, and they walked back toward the center of the village.

"I do wonder what he was trying to achieve, here," Elayne thought aloud. "He was determined that I no' reside here any longer."

"Could he be trying to prevent your marriage to the MacCollough?" Torin said it without inflection, but Elayne glanced towards him, fairly certain the giant shared Alistair's goal. Her cousin's intent, however, escaped her.

"Could verra well be. Though why, I dinna ken," she admitted.

***

They found Declan near the village center, not far from the blacksmith. Five young lasses and their fathers trekked to the village, entrusting their women into Elayne's responsibility. Her willful reputation netted one benefit, apparently, and the virtue of these lasses was not one she would take lightly. Unlike her pre-arranged marriage to the Laird, these women had no marriage prospects (*Not yet! she* thought with her wry grin), so she must ensure their safety and honor while in her care. Declan clasped each father's arm, introducing Lady Elayne — with noted emphasis on the word Lady — and made personal guarantees to each nervous man.

Further complicating the exchange was the "wild man" reputation of the clan. Few women and men compared to beasts did little to allay a father's concern, especially these fathers from other clans. No father wanted his daughter in the hands of a fiendish-sounding group of men, Elayne knew. In light the rumors about his men, Declan's letters focused on the changes he had already made within his clan, the presence of a Lady of strength, renown, and piety (Elayne barked a laugh at his word choice), his own upcoming nuptials, and his hopes for other young men of the clan to find wives and have children.

The latter part of the letter smacked of bribery, that the women may wed to a higher station, to be more than a tenant or cottar's wife. The subtle bribe brought back thoughts of Meg and Ewan, causing a moue of discontent flash across Elayne's face as they wrote the letters. The discontent passed as quickly, though, as she put the thoughts of her failed plan to wed Ewan from her mind. She was now aligned with someone much different than she ever anticipated, one she responded to in the most passionate way. *God's plan, not mine*, she told herself, and she hoped for the same for these lasses coming to the keep.

Making her own promises to each father with Declan, she faced the group of anxious-looking young women. Most wore muted homespun skirts and leather work shoes, but one blonde girl, in particular, wore her MacKenzie plaid wrap proudly. Elayne nodded in acknowledgment and smiled broadly at the girls in what she hoped was a maternal way. A few of the lasses smiled back, and that was a good start.

"Hello, my lassies! I ken ye may be worried over this change, and believe me, a new living situation can be frightening." She showed more teeth to convey her understanding. "However, instead of fretting, think of this as an amazing adventure. 'Tis what I did when I first came here. This place is a bit different from your home to be certain, but with your help, we can rally and make this clan your new home."

The lasses smiled at that part. Elayne noted their appearances and posture, playing matchmaker in her mind. The shorter blonde lass seemed especially engaging; perhaps Hamish would have an affection for tiny blondes?

After allowing a moment for the lasses to bid their families goodbye, Declan, Torin, Elayne, and the clansmen escorted them back to the keep. The men kept to the rear of the group while Elayne, not one for idle small talk, did her best to chat with each lass heading back to *BlackBraes*. Learning their habits, preferences, and skills, she could best place them for work in the keep, and perchance encourage the most appropriate men to find interest. Leaving home was frightening prospect for even the most stalwart of women, and if Elayne could reward these women for taking such a risk, she would do so.

***

Bonnie and Senga welcomed them to the keep and assumed their care-taking from Elayne, showing the lasses to their sleeping areas and proving a tour of rest of the keep. Declan ushered Elayne up to his chamber, bypassing the more public study off the hall, not hiding the urgency on his face.

Once he escorted her into his chamber, much improved since her first visit she noted, he closed the door and secured it with the metal bar that clanked into place. Elayne did not miss the impropriety of his actions. She pulled herself up to her full height and braced herself for Declan's next words.

"What in the name of Christ happened in the village today?" The intensity in his eyes burned like fire.

"The village, ye mean with Alistair?" she asked in a reticent tone.

"Aye, Alistair, your cousin, Torin says?"

Elayne patted her hair, collecting her thoughts. She would be lying if she did not admit Alistair's words placed doubt in her mind regarding the man in front of her. To this day, Declan had been naught but a gentleman, one loyal to her oft intractable ways. He gave her no reason to question him or his intentions and was completely open about his desire to wed her. Alistair's insistence, regardless, tore at her mind.

"Do ye want to marry me for what I can do for ye clan? Is that the only reason?"

"Wait, what?" Declan's brows furrowed in confusion. "Lady 'Layne, I have told ye that I want ye. Yes, for the prestige ye can bring to the clan, your strong hand in helping me tame it, aye. But do ye doubt that I find ye attractive as well? That I burn —" Here he stopped. "My apologies, 'twas inappropriate to say that to ye."

"Nay, my Laird, please continue the thought," she waved with her hand.

"I ken we were both distressed at the prospect of an arranged marriage, and when I met ye, I was more than pleased with your figure, your visage, that accompanied the strength of ye," he paused. "Is it me? Do ye no' find me attractive?"

Declan was fairly confident in his strong looks — women had told him this often — perchance Elayne preferred dark men more like Torin? He heard the rumors of her intention to wed Laird MacLeod but was too familiar with the man's appearance. Elayne nearly choked in laughter at his suggestion. Her wry grin returned, and Declan blew a sigh of relief that she did not view him as a troll.

"Nay, 'tis not your looks, my Laird. I do, in fact, find ye verra attractive." A blush flared on her cheeks. "Nay, 'tis not that. Did ye want to wed me to claim both my clan and yours? For any selfish or treasonous reason?"

"Treason?" Incredulity painted his whole being. He clasped his hand to the plaid at his chest. "'Layne, I was the

one who helped the Bruce escape the English! I pride myself
on being one of the men who helped him retain his crown, the
most loyal of Bruce supporters! How has your cousin accused
me of treason?"

"I dinna ken for certain, Declan," she told him. "He
said that the Bruce was no' the true king, that this kingship is
to be questioned. Clans are rallying against him. They plan to
unseat him, and ye shall be charged with treason. He claimed
my father would no' want me to wed ye if he knew the desires
of the clans. He wanted me to leave with him today."

"Aye, Torin conveyed that to me well. He said your
cousin put his hands on ye."

Elayne giggled at the implication. "That may well be,
but only after I had smacked his face the first time. I was
readying for a second when Torin interfered." She flipped her
hair with pride at the memory, then refocused on Declan.

"That is no' my largest concern," she continued. "Why
would my cousin express such concern over my wedding?
And suggesting my father, who arranged all this with ye,
would no' approve? He supports the Bruce. I dinna ken his
meaning with ye."

Declan ran his hands over his head, his hair standing
on end like a Scottish wildcat. *Fitting,* she thought errantly, *for
the Laird of the Beast clan.*

"Your cousin did no' want ye to wed me? So, treason
could be why, though it seems far-fetched."

"My father would no' agree to joining to a traitor, but I
dinna think Alistair kens the true mind of my father. That
reason is dubious as well," Elayne added.

Declan nodded in agreement, her meaning clear.
"What does that leave? He did no' want ye to wed me. Is there
a reason he may have, himself?"

Elayne rolled her eyes heaven-ward in understanding.

"Of course!" She paced the room in anger, her skirts whisking against her legs, punctuating her anger. "The wily weasel! He fancies himself a Laird! He does no' want ye to be Laird of both my clan and yours!"

"But your father lives," Declan started, "why would he think —"

"He's an impetuous youth, my Laird. Do ye no' ken what ye were like at that age? He sees my father as an old man. Ugh, the craven leech!"

Declan rested against the door. "Aye, I do recall myself at that time, and ye make strong sense. Your cousin can no' become laird as ye live, are to be wed to a Laird, and could have sons. He fears ye will displace him." His eyes widened in shock. "Ooch! I wager he plans on trying to wed ye! That would explain the elaborate story-telling!"

Elayne fell back onto the bed in resounding laughter. "I would never wed that boy. My father would no' permit it even if I did! He is naught but a weak lad."

Declan did not share her humor. He stepped away from the door to stand before her.

"But his actions are no' to be laughed at, 'Layne," he rationalized as he gazed down at her. "Treason and rallying the clans are large threats. I fear he may be serious and try to derail our betrothal."

The chamber fell silent, heavy with consideration, as they pondered Declan's words.

"I have an idea, my Laird," Elayne said suddenly. She raised her face to Declan, her eyes almost twinkling with mischief.

Chapter 11: Without Consent of the King

E layne rubbed her hand over the thick furs covering Declan's bed, patting the space next to her. Declan took the hint and sat close, pressing his leg against hers. This close, he was so much more male; his muscled body and masculine scent overwhelmed Elayne. Though she was a tall woman, he was so much larger, overall — broad shoulders and chest, and sitting, he seemed to dwarf her. All of this registered with her as he seated himself. He reached over and clasped her daintier hand in his large, calloused one. They sat together for a quiet moment in the dying light of the day.

"He will try to have my father intervene," she said.

"Aye, most likely," he agreed.

"And the wedding, I ken for certain he will interrupt it. He will try to prevent it," Elayne continued.

"Aye, for certain."

She inhaled deeply, gathering a bit of courage. An idea sprung to mind as they discussed her cousin, one that would circumvent Alistair, his protests, and any attempt he would make to halt their wedding. The idea, though, was brash and completely immoral. Now that Elayne had come to know Declan a bit more, she feared he would not go along with it. Taking another breath, she boldly placed her other hand on his leg as she spoke.

"There is something we can do. 'Twould ensure Alistair, nay anyone else, could stop our marriage."

"What are ye saying —" Declan stopped when she tilted her head behind them, eying the bed. "Wait, are ye suggesting—?"

She gestured toward the bed again and didn't stop the evocative curl of her lip. Her idea of lying together, using ancient hand-fast laws and the church's position on intimate relations to secure a marriage, would guarantee a wedding. Declan, on the other hand, look scandalized.

"Lady 'Layne!" He nearly jumped off the bed, only to be pulled back by her hand he still held. "'Tis inappropriate! To lie with ye before the sacrament of marriage —"

"Secures our union. That I ken," she replied, unflappable.

"Outside of your virtue, milady, what of my clan? I have spent the better part of the last year trying to reclaim my clan, rid it of its offensive reputation. How would taking your virtue look? I would be nothing more than the head of the beast clan —"

"Not if ye wed me afterward. My virtue would be in question for what? A fortnight? And that is only if anyone learns of it. And what happens to your beast clan if I can no' stay? How will ye rebuild the reputation if I am no' here?" *What other Lady would have your clan?* she did not say aloud, the insinuation clear.

106

Her words gave him pause. Next to him on the bed, she regarded him with half-slanted gray eyes, her chestnut hair still elegantly coiffed and curling into the deep bodice of her dress. He had not failed to appreciate her wonderfully presented cleavage, sneaking glances at her bust throughout the day. Her voice and indomitable attitude, though decried by many, were reasons he agreed to this arrangement. Perhaps he if found her unattractive or respected her less, this offer would not offend him so.

She could see plain on his face that he was weighing the options in his mind. Elayne decided to make the decision easier for him and started to tug at the strings holding her bodice together. She pulled off one side of her kirtle as she sat, dropping it to her waist so one breast was fully exposed. She placed her hand on her chest, enticing Declan to action. With her hand still enclosed in his, she tugged him toward her.

"Ye are to be my husband. We are to be wed soon. Take me to bed, husband."

***

Declan could not argue further. The sight of her half-dressed on his bed was his undoing. He reached for her, not sure if he was intending to shake her back to her senses or remove her from his bed. What he did was kiss her, full and hard, grasping her arms with his hands, holding her to him. Elayne did not hesitate. She kissed him back with full fervor, parting her lips as his tongue caressed hers. His grip on her was strong, bearing her back to the bed as his mouth worked her lips, then skimmed her jawline to her neck. Chills ran along the path his lips made, imprinting him onto her skin. When he brushed his mouth past her neck to explore the top of her breasts, she gasped and arched into him, the novel sensation of his touch shocking and inflaming every part of her.

Feeling her writhe under him, Declan trailed his lips slowly along the swell of her breasts, dragging his tongue lightly across the curve of one pale mound, then the other. Elayne's breath caught when he moved his lips and tongue to her exposed nipple, and she rested her hand on the back of his head, twining her fingers into his full blond locks. He groaned from deep in his throat as her fingers played with his hair, and the need building inside made his mind reel. Releasing her other arm, he grabbed the front of her shift, freeing both her breasts in one fluid movement.

Exposed to Declan, Elayne had a moment of modesty and reacted to cover herself, but Declan stopped her hand.

"Nay," he said, lifting his head to catch her burning gaze. "Ye are too beautiful to cover yourself." Sitting up, he pulled her shift down further, unmasking more of her alabaster skin to him. His blood pounded though his body, and he shook his head in an unsuccessful attempt to gather his senses. He touched her jaw with one long finger, stroking the smoothness of her skin down to curve of her breast. Then reaching behind his head, Declan pulled his own tunic over his head, his blond hair standing out like a halo. His broad chest was chiseled, lightly furred with dark blond hair that spread from his belly to below his plaid.

"There," he said, his voice husky, "now ye can view me as well." Elayne lifted her hand to touch his bare skin, pausing just before her fingers touched him. A smile tugged at Declan's lips, and Elayne could not help but smirk in return. He wrapped his fingers around hers, pressing her fingertips to his chest.

"'Tis only fair, as I got to touch ye."

Elayne stroked the hair on his chest, then followed the hairline to his waist. He sucked in his breath as she tickled his skin and dipped her finger under the edge of his plaid. Declan stepped off the bed, unbelted his leather bindings, and unwound his tartan from his hips. The tartan fell to the floor, and he stood in front of her, unabashed in his full masculine glory. His blond curls stopped at his shaft, which pulsed and bulged forward, as though his body itself searched for her. Intrigued, she leaned closer to him, reaching her hand out again.

"My Laird?" She asked him, the smirk on her face growing, her eyes shining with curiosity.

"Aye," he whispered hoarsely.

She trailed a delicate finger along the length of his manhood, amazed at how it sprang under her touch. Declan's breath grew ragged as she brushed her fingertips back and forth, then wrapped her fingers around the full length. He sagged into her, grasping her hair, his control fleeing from him as her grip tightened.

"'Layne, please," he begged.

Elayne released him and stood. She reached behind her waist and untied her skirt, allowing it and her shift to fall to the floor. Declan crushed himself against her naked form, his rough hairs scratching at her soft skin. His hand clasped behind her head, and he kissed her fully, devouring her with abandon. Barefoot, she was nearly as tall as he, and kissing her was easy, effortless, their bodies fitting together as though they were molded as one. She wrapped her arms around his bare back, touching her tongue to his as the kiss deepened. His erection seared her belly, and he laid her on the bed, sinking into the furs. His deep hazel eyes burned into her gray ones, and her entire being quivered at the strength of his gaze.

"'Layne, are ye certain?" He honestly did not know how he would stop if she said nay. Fortunately, her eyes spoke what he wanted to hear.

"Aye," she said aloud, her whisper tickling his ear.

He kissed her again, licking at her lips and tongue with his. His rough hands lightly trailed along her breasts, down her belly to her woman's mound. His fingers parted her lips there, probing gently, exploring her virgin folds. Her breath caught when his finger skimmed just against her, her brain spinning as his finger delicately probed deeper. She felt she could not form any thoughts and her heart wanted to beat out of her chest.

Declan brought his hand back up and cradled her face.

"'Twill hurt for but a moment, my 'Layne," he told her softly, and shifted atop her. Haltingly, he slid inside her, feeling her adjust to his invading member. His consuming gaze never left hers as he began to move, first imperceptibly, then with more vigor. Elayne grimaced as he first entered her, a strange, sharp pain that pierced quickly, ebbing as Declan continued to thrust within her. She could not pull away from his sharp look as he feasted his eyes on her face. As the pain lessened, she reached her hand up to cup his face in return. Shifting to wrap one arm under her shoulder, he clung to her, and again kissed her long and hard.

The pace of his thrusts changed, coming faster and harder. Her mind spun out of control as he touched the very center of her. She closed her eyes as Declan's breath quickened, her excitement throbbing, rising to match his thrusts. He chanted "Oh, 'Layne" to her as his movements became frenzied.

He stiffened above her suddenly, groaning. Elayne felt him contract in her with a smooth warmth, and Declan collapsed on her, bearing her down into the thick furs. His rapid breathing slowed, and after a moment, he lifted himself up on one arm, peeling his damp skin from hers.

The intensity still shone from his face, searching Elayne's bright eyes for any sign of regret or shame. Her breath caught as she lost herself in his admiration. Unsure of what she was supposed to do next, she grasped the back of his head and kissed him with the passion coursing through her. He returned her kisses as he shifted to her side. The dimming rays of sunset lighted against his blond body hair, casting him in a shimmery glow. Declan brushed a lock of hair off Elayne's face, trailing his fingers along her naked body, across her breasts, along the side of her ribs and back up. She shivered in response, moving closer to him. He enveloped her in his arm, and they rested, enfolded together as day gave way to eventide.

***

"'Tis official, then, aye?" Declan finally spoke, breaking the calm afterglow. "Ye are not sorry for it, are ye?"

Elayne was not one to question her actions after the fact, and she expressed as much to Declan.

"'Tis official, aye," she agreed. "And nay, I am no' sorry. I ken what this opportunity was when my father proffered it." She turned her head to look at him directly. The need for open honesty overwhelmed her.

"I ken I made some mistakes earlier this year. And my reputation . . . I ken that I am called a harpy or a banshee. Not exactly wife material, aye?" Declan's body shook against her as he muffled a laugh. She screwed her face up at him. "Dinna laugh," she tried to sound offended, but the words came out in a giggle.

"I may have heard the word harpy used in conjunction with your name," he smiled at her, cupping her the swell of her breast in his hand. "Harpy of the Highlands, specifically. But as the leader of the 'beast clan,' I also ken what rumors oft amount to."

She gave him a gracious look in return. "Aye, I appreciate that. But I still understood what I was entering into with ye and what lying with ye today would mean. I ken I would wed ye, as long as ye wanted me. Of that, I did have concerns." At this, she cast her eyes away, almost shamed in the admittance.

Declan's body shook against hers again, and once more she faced him.

"What makes ye laugh so?"

"Oh 'Layne. I didna tell a soul this, not even Torin, ye ken?" Elayne nodded at his request, and her marked smirk curled up the side of her lips in anticipation of his secret.

"I had seen ye before. At the village, on my way back home from service to the Bruce. Your voice was loud and bossy—" Here she gave him a playful poke at his arm. "And I said to myself, 'That, Declan, is the type of woman ye need at *BlackBraes*. That is a woman who takes control.' And ye were so tall and powerful looking, your hair beautiful in a sark, shimmery halo around your face, no' like a wilting little lass. I dinna need a wilting lass. A strong, powerful clan requires strong, powerful leaders, in both the Laird and the Laird's wife, ye ken?"

Elayne nodded, her smile crinkling her eyes, and Declan continued. "So, I asked a merchant, 'Who is that loud woman?' The merchant barely flicked his eyes in your direction and advised I run far from the harpy, Elayne MacNally." At this, they laughed together, arms and legs entangling more.

"What shall we tell Bonnie?" Declan asked, his concern for Elayne's virtue obvious. "She is certain to notice your absence this afternoon."

"Well, we could tell her the truth, and make sure she attends the actual wedding," Elayne suggested. Declan rolled his eyes with humor. "I agree," she said. "Perchance that is no' the best idea. I guess we can tell her, and anyone else, that we needed to discuss the placement of the new young lasses, and how ye want handle my cousin's actions."

"That is a sound plan," Declan concurred, then rolled himself up, so he was positioned above her. "I thank ye for this, Elayne. A lot can happen with such a committed action as we just engaged in. Intimate relations outside of marriage can ruin a woman's reputation—" Elayne laughed behind her lips. Her smile encompassed her whole face, so different from the fierce mask she presented to the world. "Or rather what is left of your reputation, so I understand if ye want to keep your distance to prevent any gossip until we are rightly wed."

Elayne's eyes narrowed as she took in his. "Let me ask you this, my Laird. Would ye prefer that I kept my distance for the next fortnight?"

"To speak the truth, nay, 'Layne. It has been a long time since I have lain with a woman. I was no' what ye call a rake by any means, so I fear I was more than eager for your offer. Plus, I wanted ye. Since the moment I saw ye in the village, I wanted ye. I burned for ye the day you arrived. That eve in the bath, I was consumed with wanting ye. And I want ye now. Given the choice, I would have ye in my bed every night until we are wed, and every night thereafter."

Elayne touched her finger to her lips as though brooding over his words. When she looked back to him, her grin was wide and contagious.

"I should think we shall need to come up with a series of untruths to explain my continued entry into your chambers, then." She wrapped her arms around his shoulders as he moved forward to capture her lips once more.

Chapter 12: Conspiracy Theories

A listair's ride from *BlackBraes* was slow and introspective. As the horse hobbled along the rocky trail, Alistair considered his options. He could ride to clan Ross, follow up with his recent report on Declan and the Beast clan, or he could try to have MacNally intervene, provided the old Laird knew the truth about the local clans and Declan's allegiances. Of the two, a discussion with MacNally, while unpleasant given their last interaction, may be easier, and certainly a shorter ride. Unsure if he wanted to become embroiled in politics to a large degree, Alistair saw a greater appeal in approaching Laird MacNally himself. The man was fair and balanced, which was not a conclusion he could draw regarding Laird Ross. The squat, sweaty man radiated senseless villainy.

All too soon, Alistair arrived at the gate of *Akedene*, and he had to screw up his courage to request another conference with MacNally. His uncle did nothing to hide his enmity at Alistair's last proposal to undertake the MacNally clan leadership, so Alistair must choose his words carefully to even gain an audience with the Laird. Alistair, however, knew MacNally's greatest weakness was his only daughter, and presenting Elayne's current situation as precarious may just persuade MacNally to either retrieve his daughter before the wedding or speak out at the wedding itself.

Laird of Clan MacNally strode into the hall, the dark, muted tones of his plaid swinging against his large frame. James MacNally resembled nothing short of a bear in Highland regalia, a humorous image that tugged at the corners of Alistair's lips.

"My nephew," MacNally's voice boomed. "To what do I owe this pleasure?"

Alistair ignored his uncle's seemingly sarcastic tone. He bowed low in deference. Additional respect could only help his cause.

"My Uncle," Alistair began, hoping the reminder of familial ties would also work in his favor. "I come from clan Ross with deleterious news. When I left here last, I admit I was discomfited, so I sought release in the village when I heard rumors of the clan MacCollough. It is referred to as the 'Beast Clan,' is it no'?" James MacNally inclined his head, keeping a fair eye on his nephew, pondering the young man's intentions.

"I had heard that some eastern clans are no' pleased with the actions of the Bruce, consider him a false king after his murder of Comyn, and are working to undo his claim to the throne with the help of the English. And they are tracking those who colluded with the Bruce. The clans seem certain that the reign of Bruce is near an end. MacCollough is in their sights, as he helped Bruce escape from Methven, and they believe MacCollough is still in contact with the Bruce. They have designated him a traitor."

Here he held his sights on MacNally, implying a larger issue in play. When MacNally didn't respond, Alistair continued.

"I took the time to try to confirm these reports, and I learned a bounty is on MacCollough's head and on those aligned with him. I fear for Elayne, Laird. If she is seen as aligned with MacCollough, then perchance her life is in danger?" The half-truths poured easily from Alistair's lips, and he hoped his uncle would believe it all.

James MacNally rubbed at his beard in consideration.

"Ye do ken, Alistair, that I am Bruce's man? If what ye say is true, and I have heard nothing to indicate as such, then aren't I in danger as well? What will make Elayne any safer here?"

"As far as I ken, Uncle, ye didn't help the Bruce escape certain capture, and ye dinna ken where the man is at present. Ye are no' a target of their ire. MacCollough, Uncle, has done these things, and is viewed as a traitor, much as the Bruce is by many of the Highland clans. Uncle, please, I beg ye. I fear for Elayne's safety if she remained at *BlackBraes*."

MacNally permitted his nephew to talk, his mouth running away with him, and the more Alistair talked, the deeper he would dig his hole. James let him dig himself deeper.

"What would ye have me do? I have heard that Elayne seems to have found a home there, that she and MacCollough are to be wed in nigh a fortnight."

Alistair stood up taller, excited by his uncle's response. "We can go now, tonight, to rescue her. Bring her home where she is safe."

"And what of her reputation?" MacNally grizzled, his anger now starting to rise to the surface. "She already must deal with the suggestions that she is an iron-willed harpy that no man wants. What am I to do if she comes home and her reputation is further tainted, having lived in the MacCollough house?"

MacNally's anger reached full steam. His daughter seemed happy; he heard via messages from Senga that Elayne was adapting well, thriving even, under the chaos (*as Senga described it*) of the MacCollough clan. Elayne's own letters had tones of contentment he had never before encountered with his high-strung daughter. He was ecstatic that she was to wed, finally finding a place where she fit, where her out-spoken, boisterous ways were welcome, where a man, a Laird, loved her for those traits. That his nephew would try to rob Elayne of all that she was due infuriated MacNally all the more.

"Her reputation?" Alistair squeaked.

"Nephew," James MacNally spoke the word with threatening emphasis. "Again, you overstep yourself. I think ye have taken some information and manipulated it to your favor. There is no treason, since Bruce is still king. Once more, Alistair, I will ask that ye leave this house, go back to your mother's, and find your purpose in life. I promise ye, it is no' to be Laird of Clan MacNally."

With those final words, James pivoted in a swirl of plaid and left, sending Alistair off with a flick of his hand.

***

Alistair's head hung low as he leaned against his horse, weighing his options now that his uncle rejected his concerns. Ross' egregious plan to ride on all the clans that supported the Bruce was far beyond Alistair's limited purview. His was not a place in history, and he did not want to become embroiled in war — he did not wear the mantle of a warrior in the traditional sense. Alistair's greatest aspiration was limited to becoming Laird of his clan, which was not certain even if he aligned with Ross. Alistair's one idea was to convince Ross to attack solely MacCollough, a more manageable goal, and see where alliances fell after that.

The best option presently, at least to Alistair, was to speak up at Elayne's impending nuptials. If he could convince the priest that MacCollough was not a suitable husband for a lady, potential treason notwithstanding, he could stop the wedding in its tracks. If he were able to halt the wedding, perchance he could, with all nobility, step up and wed the now tainted Elayne, the brash loudmouth no man in his right mind would *want* to wed anyway. All his desires would come to fruition in one fell swoop: next in line for Laird, solidify his position with Elayne, and a wife to boot. The more Alistair considered this new development, the more appealing it became for him. The other option, permanently removing Elayne (and MacCollough, as Ross wanted), he desired far less.

Alistair's head lifted as he pondered these thoughts, and his ride home was one of new-found potential. He nickered at his horse, galloping toward his mother's house, and the idea inside him grew. Wee James could ride a message out to Clan Ross, asking them to bide their time as his plan would render MacCollough alone, in a lesser position that he had been previously, and ripe for the picking for Donald Ross and his English-sympathizing clans. Alistair could then take his time and decide which side — the Bruce or

the Comyn supporting clans — would rise as rulers of
Scotland. It was, Alistair thought, perfect.

Chapter 13: Wedding Interrupted

layne and Declan agreed their nightly trysts were better hidden from the manse if they kept to his chambers, as he did not have a nosy servant skulking about the corners. Even then, Bonnie and Senga ensured the house help scrubbed the room from top to bottom regularly, which sent the couple scrambling to search for any evidence of Elayne's presence in Declan's chamber. At night, however, his heather-scented room welcomed their passionate encounters. Newly dipped, dust-free candles cast a soft glow as the couple undressed each other, finding new ways to touch, kiss, and enjoy lovemaking.

One night, as Declan rode Elayne hard, both of them panting with enthusiasm, Declan paused and his eyes, full of mischief, twinkled at Elayne.

"My love, are ye adventurous to try something different?"

She crinkled up her eyes at him, "I am unsure how to respond, my Laird," she teased.

Grasping her hips, he rolled to the side and pulled Elayne atop of him, letting her ride him. She squeaked at the effort, and he smiled in return.

"Ye deserve to ride, 'Layne. I think ye would prefer to be in control." His words struck a note within Elayne, and she gave him her characteristic grin, which appeared so contrary when she was in her naked glory above him, his groin quickening within her. She would ride him hard, he knew, and love every minute of it.

She began to rock against him. Her hair fell over her shoulders and breasts, forming a private curtain around them, blocking the incandescent light. Declan reached for her full breasts, each thumb stroking a nipple as she undulated faster, grinding into him, her moaning matching his. Elayne's breathing came rapidly as her insides quivered and ignited from her loins up through her entire being. Her body throbbed, and she cried out his name over and over, her whole being quaking in effort and euphoria. She clutched at his chest as she came, rocking against his hips, her eyes closed as she called out.

Then she collapsed on the whole length of him. Her ragged breath blew against his chest, and he ran his fingers through her hair as she recovered.

"What was that?" she breathed at him.

"Did ye enjoy it, milady?"

"Is it like that every time? If I ride ye?"

"I dinna ken," he replied, "but I think it is like that a lot if ye ride me."

Elayne wiped at her face, rubbing away sweat and exertion, and rose back up over him.

"But my Laird," she said, quizzically. "Ye did not have your moment!"

"Aye, that is true, my 'Layne, but ye see," he told her as he rolled her on her back, pinning her under him again, "unlike a man, a woman can continue to enjoy her pleasure until the man finishes."

"Oh, aye?"

"Aye," he responded. "'Tis a benefit to being the woman in the bed, ye ken?" He delved inside her and she gasped, still sensitive and trembling after her orgasm. His thrusts brought continued moans as he plunged into her weeping sheath, his own orgasm building, tightening across his whole body. Declan gasped raggedly into her hair, chanting her name over and over as he came, pouring his seed deep inside her. He then took his turn to collapse atop her with his head on her breast, their bodies entwined where Elayne did not know where her body ended and his began.

As Declan regained his senses, they reclined on the furs, facing one another. Each rested a light hand the other, keeping their connection unbroken even after their ecstasy was expended. She twisted her fingers in his hair, completely satiated with the newness of their lovemaking. Elayne brushed a blond lock off Declan's forehead, and a slight smiled passed over his lips.

"Do ye think anyone knows what we are doing? Has anyone said anything to ye?" Elayne asked him, the excitement of their taboo interludes stirring inside her.

Declan shifted his head to kiss her down her neck to her breast.

"Is it horrible of me if I say I dinna care?" he spoke into her nipple. A burst of laughter bubbled from Elayne.

"Aye, my Laird, probably 'tis."

"I would have to say nay. I have heard naught from anyone to suggest our secret lovemaking plan to ensure marriage has been discovered. But," he paused pensively, his golden eyes searching over Elayne's face, "Torin did comment that I seem to be in a better mood lately. Perchance he was hinting something."

"To be certain," Elayne giggled at him, "that is exactly what he was suggesting."

"And ye?" Declan asked. "Has someone made an inappropriate comment about your possible nightly behavior?"

"'Tis Senga who concerns me. She is older, more experienced, has ken me since I was a babe, and I fear she may notice something in my chambers or in my actions that give me away."

"Ye can be quite stoic, my love," Declan said frankly. "Kings and courts would pay for leaders whose faces reveal as little as yours can." She tweaked his nose at this comment, but the humor shining behind her eyes and lips told him she felt flattered by the statement.

"That may well be, but Senga can read me better than most read nobility. I dinna ken that she disapproves, ye ken. She hopes for me to wed and this," she gestured over them with a long swipe of her arm, "is a wax seal on the marriage. However, just her knowing what goes on in your bed in the late eventide is disconcerting."

"Well, my 'Layne, soon we willna care who kens. I could take ye on the table in the main hall and none would look cross ways."

"I would no' want to ken what Senga would think of *that*," she replied.

***

124

Castle *BlackBraes* buzzed with activity the day of Elayne and Declan's wedding. The morning began *dreich,* a light, misty rain falling to the glen, creating a gray cast over the cool autumn day. Bonnie and Senga, elated at the weather, reminded Elayne that the happiest brides wed on rainy days. Elayne pursed her lips at this old wives' proverb, but if her days leading up to the wedding itself were any indication, mayhap the saying contained a bit of truth. While she was content as the daughter of the Laird at her father's house, her position here at *BlackBraes*, not to mention her burgeoning passion she shared with Declan, made her happy in a way she had not known since she was a child.

That celebratory disposition continued throughout the day as everyone prepared for the wedding. Senga and Elayne had spent the evenings sewing a gown, trimming the edges of her fine linen kirtle with shimmery yellow brocade. Her over-dress complimented the trim with tones of cream and yellow, contrasting smartly with her chestnut hair and the green and black MacCollough plaid that she would wear draped over her shoulder. The corset of the gown pushed her breasts up, creating soft, pales swells that peeked out from the plaid, making her waist even more narrow. Always during dress-making, Senga complained about Elayne's height, that she must use more fabric, take more time sewing, and she thought Elayne's waist too dainty for a braw Scottish lass. Nonetheless, even Senga glowed with appreciation when she saw Elayne in her wedding costume. She called for Bonnie so they both could appreciate and nod with approval. Elayne scowled back at being put on such a display.

Bonnie tapped at her chin. "Do ye have his *Lukenbooth*?" she asked, her brows creasing.

"Ooch, aye," Elayne reached into her trunk, pulling out a large silver heart-shaped brooch, a small emerald nestled in the center of the heart. "I had the smith create it for me, since I could no' find one for sale in the village."

Carefully handing it to Bonnie, Elayne watched as the lass admired the gift. Elayne and Senga had spent a fortnight playing matchmaker between the young women in the clan and the considerable availability of men, so far to no avail. Bonnie's subtle interest in the *Lukenbooth* made Elayne wonder if something changed recently. She caught Bonnie in a whispered conversation with Hamish earlier but thought nothing of it at the time. Mayhap affection was budding? After the wedding, Elayne would certainly focus more on playing matchmaker; 'twas one of the primary reasons for Elayne's marriage to Declan. She could not fail him in this endeavor.

Bonnie gave the brooch back to Elayne, who packed it in a soft cloth, ready to present the gift to Declan at the wedding ceremony.

"I ken Declan has the Oathing stone," Bonnie told her. "I heard Torin discussing the engraving with the smithy. It should be fair beautiful for your wedding."

Elayne only nodded, doubt briefly clouding her happiness of the day. She and Declan chatted about the wedding off and on in bed (the thought of which caused a light blush to spread over Elayne's cheeks and a warmth in her loins), yet now that the moment was nigh, bridal jitters crept in. Bonnie and Senga did not notice, as they were smitten with vision of her in her wedding dress. Senga gestured to Elayne to sit in order to coif her hair with one hand as she shooed Bonnie out the door with the other. Elayne perched on a stool, waiting for Senga to work her hairdressing magic as Bonnie stepped out of the chamber.

Loud voices drew Bonnie's attention further down the hall, and as one prone to eavesdropping, she did not pass up the opportunity to spy on her Laird. Perching just outside the wooden doorjamb, she leaned in towards the doorway but didn't have to. Anyone in the hall could have heard the conversation between Declan and Torin.

"She has changed everything, most of all, ye! The men of the clan *like* the clan the way 'tis. 'Tis been that way for years for us! No' with the frilly covers and worrying about dirtying scrubbed floors! I am no' a child to be reprimanded. And she is too loudmouth and bossy by half!" Torin's deep voice came out as a screech, adding irony to his assessment of Elayne. Declan, conversely, remained calm.

"I ken your concerns, but can ye honestly say ye were happier with itchy clothes, stinking beds, and poor food? She may be willful, but she completes what she sets out t'do."

"And what of all these new people? What—" he started, but Declan cut him off, practically laughing at this complaint.

"People? Ye mean the lasses? Christ, Torin, ye ken how our clan has shrunk since the time of my grandfather. A clan that does not breed dies out." His voice lowered an octave as he spoke his next words. "I ken why ye bristle at the idea. Ye live with the pain of it every day, that I can see in your eyes. But once ye find the moment is right, ye should be thankful that Elayne would try to find a lass to consider being with ye, the scruffy lout that ye are!"

Bonnie heard a final "Harrumph" from Torin and a scuffling sound. Then Torin's voice neared the door, and

Bonnie stepped away quickly as she heard Torin's final statement.

"That does not mean I like the harpy."

***

Dozens of people formed the wedding parade to the small church in the village where Father Fraser waited for them on damp stone steps. While the rain had stopped, the muddy road hindered their approach and splashed mud drops on their skirts and shoes. The rain and mud could not dampen the party's spirits, and Declan and Elayne were all smiles as they arrived at the edge of the village, near the kirk.

James MacNally stood at the front of the group, resplendent in his full plaid regalia, his greenish-gray eyes bright and his face beaming with joy for his daughter. After the past few years of Elayne's commanding personality limiting her marriage choices, James questioned if he would live to see this day. He clasped his hands in front of his kilt, rocking back on his heels, and cast a glance at Mari, her delicate blonde hair shining under her kerchief. Bringing his woman to his daughter's wedding was a bit of a risk. He was ready to have that conversation with Elayne if necessary, but he wagered his daughter would be too preoccupied to notice one extra guest.

Elayne's eyes touched her father's, and his beaming increased. She nodded her head and gave him a smirk, one that only his Lanie could give. He reached up to lay his palm over his heart and bowed toward her. His life was complete; his daughter was safe.

A large coterie of villagers added to the clansmen and women from nearby clans who circled the church awaiting the happy couple — whether to celebrate with them or to settle their disbelief that two of the most unmarriageable people in the Highlands were to wed, Declan did not know. Nor did he care to. With his marriage to Elayne, he would usher in a new era for his clan, cast off the disturbing mantle of his father and grandfather, and — he hoped — create a new, less beastly, reputation for his people. That Elayne was stunning, strong-willed, and adventurous in bed (that fact caused a knowing smile to pass from his lips to his wife-to-be) made his decision to wed much easier.

Elayne caught Declan's smile and blushed again. Whilst Declan focused on the future greatness of his clan, Elayne marveled at how far she had come since early summer. Her assumptions in regards to Ewan MacLeod and her embarrassment over behaving like a love-sick lass helped her appreciate the arranged marriage to Declan, his absolute acceptance of her, and her mostly smooth transition into Clan MacCollough. As she reflected on this last thought, of taking on Clan MacCollough as her own clan, she scanned the crowd, pleased at the outpouring of Highlanders who stood in witness to the event.

The sun parted the clouds in some sections of the sky, allowing bright shafts of light to shine down on the wedding party and excited onlookers. Dusky colors of greens, blues, and blacks made the event seem ethereal, even otherworldly.

In the far back, black tips of pipes rose over the assembled villagers. The crowd parted as she and Declan moved to the kirk steps to the pipes' melody, Elayne lifting her mud-stained skirts as she mounted the steps.

Her gown caught the light, casting her in a shimmery golden glow that matched Declan's eyes. Her plaid matched Declan's full Highland regalia, complete with a newly cleaned

kilt and his dress sporran. They presented as a picture of
Highland royalty, a stark contrast to the clan of just a few
months ago. His hair, however, did not comply with the
honorarium of the day, sticking out of his side plaits in blond
tufts, creating a halo effect around his head. *Appropriate*,
Elayne judged, patting her own dark coiffed hair with a
nervous hand.

Declan dropped her elbow and grasped her shaking
hand, both of them turning to face the crowd before presenting
themselves to the priest on the church steps. The clans people
cheered in acceptance. Father Fraser, himself radiant in a
cream robe and verdigris vestments. He smiled proudly at the
couple and raised his hands to quiet the crowd.

"Men, women, clans, are ye assembled here in the light
of God to witness the binding of Declan MacCollough and
Elayne MacNally into one body?"

A loud "Huzzah" spread from spectators. Father Fraser
lifted his Bible from the narrow table by his hip and raised it
high in the air.

"We begin the wedding of MacCollough and
MacNally, joining two clans. If any here oppose this union,
speak your peace now!"

Declan and Elayne were the only ones not surprised
when a hum of discord rippled from the villagers, both sets of
eyes giving a sidelong glance. Alistair marched forward, clad
in his own full Highland dress plaid. Elayne dropped her head
and had to bite the inside of lip to keep from laughing out of
turn.

"Hear, hear!" Alistair yelled to make himself heard. "I
oppose this union!"

The crowd craned and turned to see who dared to call
out opposition to the wedding. MacNally immediately

stiffened, recognizing the voice of his nephew. Cursing under his breath, he pushed Mari behind him and stepped forward, blocking Alistair's path and holding his hand out at his nephew's approach.

"Lad," James growled, "Nephew. Ye dinna want to cause a scene here. I ken your grievances. Save your words and await time with me to discuss your concerns."

"Step aside, *Uncle*," Alistair spat out. "I have a right to air my concerns here. The priest and good people assembled," he gestured toward the villagers and other clansmen, "may want to hear this information. It may save some of these very people."

"Alistair!" MacNally commanded. "Ye will no' do this here."

Alistair moved to lay hands on MacNally when the priest, putting two fingers in his mouth, whistled. Declan and Elayne flinched at the piercing whistle. The crowd's attention diverted from Alistair and the Laird to the ear-splitting sound the priest made. Father Fraser held up his hand and addressed everyone.

"My kin! Dinna block this good man. He has come to make his voice heard, and in the sight of man and God, he will speak his peace."

The priest reached his pale hand toward Alistair. The lad gave a haughty glare at MacNally as he approached the priest and the wedding couple on the steps. He paused at the bottom and dropped to a knee on the damp ground in deference to the priest's holy station.

Elayne rolled her eyes at his attempt to pander to the holy man. Declan, conversely, was on edge, his jaw set. They had anticipated an action like this, hence their passionate interludes over the past fortnight. But to see Elayne's presumption come to light and watch his wedding day unravel before his eyes set his ire aflame. Having a man appear and question what Declan had claimed reminded him too much of his father's overbearing ways, and he would not let such a slight stand. Elayne sensed his tension through his tunic and placed her hand on his arm, trying to calm his internal storm.

"Thank ye, father," Alistair continued, "my grievance is that my own cousin is set to marry a man too far below her station. Not only that, but a man who is set to be tried and hanged for treason! I would no' have my good-cousin attached to such a low man. I oppose this marriage for the danger it presents my cousin and my clan as a whole."

A rumble of shock and confusion spread through the crowd and across the priest's face.

The priest probed further. "My good man, what is this treason of which ye speak? MacCollough is renowned for his assistance to King Bruce. No accusation of treason rests upon his head."

"In that ye are wrong, father." Alistair rose, speaking loudly to both the priest and the people gathered. "Ye should be aware that many of the northern clans are aligned with Comyn and Argyll and their English backers. The English have already chased the Bruce into hiding, and they are, at present, working to re-establish the English crown in Scotland. The clans are searching for those who remain loyal to Bruce, to flush them out, to hang them for treason. I have it on good authority that MacCollough is at the top of their list."

MacNally, no longer rooted to his spot under order of the priest, grasped the neckline of Alistair's shift and yanked him back, off his feet. He pulled the young man under his fierce gaze.

"What is wrong with ye, lad? Are ye daft? There is no treason. Bruce is still king, keeping the English at bay. Words like those ye are speaking smack of treason against the king, and ye are in the presence of men who support the Bruce. Would ye like to spend the eve in watching the walls of MacCollough's dungeon?"

At this, Elayne moved forward, but Declan halted her with a small touch to her waist. She raised an eyebrow as he stepped in front of her, leaning close to the priest.

"Father Fraser," he whispered into the priest's ear. "May my bride and I speak with ye inside?"

The priest's eyebrows rose, but he nodded, escorting the Declan and Elayne inside the kirk, away from the curious stares of the assembly and the angry gaze of James MacNally. Leaving Alistair in the angered hands of his own uncle, the priest closed the door and regarded the couple.

"Aye, Declan, ye have my full attention."

"Father, ye will have to forgive both my bride and I for our indiscretions. Forsooth, we must be wed, in the eyes of man and God." Declan's golden gaze flicked to Elayne. "As I already have carnal knowledge of this woman."

Elayne knew, under normal circumstances, she would be mortified to be addressed thusly. Today, she was unable to hide the grin that pulled at her cheeks. It was all she could do not to laugh within the sacred walls of the church.

"Lady Elayne," the priest direct his heated attention to her, and she rubbed at her face to hide her inappropriate response. "Is what this man says true? Does he have carnal knowledge of ye?"

"Aye, Father," she responded, and unable to help herself, she added, "And I have carnal knowledge of him."

Declan guffawed, then covered his mouth and coughed to hide it, but Elayne could see the humor in his eyes. The priest did not find the situation humorous, and his alarmed pale face whitened even more. He held a hand to his chest as though his heart would stop.

"My children! Do ye ken what ye have sanctioned?"

Declan and Elayne grinned at each other.

"Aye father, we ken," Declan admitted.

Father Fraser fanned himself as though he might faint under such information, casting his eyes heavenward, searching for guidance. Taking a deep breath, he bowed to Elayne, speaking softly.

"If what your cousin states is true, ye may be putting yourself in danger in this marriage. Are ye certain ye want to wed this man?"

"Firstly, Father, my cousin is a liar and seeks power for himself," she told him frankly. "He has ulterior motives for the speech he gave on the kirk steps. Regardless, since we have carnal knowledge of each other, we have no choice. And since I asked the Laird MacCollough to have carnal knowledge of me, I am fairly certain I want to wed him."

The priest whitened even more and physically swooned. Declan put his arm around the suffering cleric, patting the man's arm. Using the edge of his green vestment to wipe the sweat from his forehead, Father Fraser breathed quickly, almost wheezing. Declan grinned at the over-dramatic priest.

"So, father, are ye ready to wed us?"

***

The assembled crowd turned *en masse* when the heavy wooden doors of the church opened. James held Alistair by the neck, keeping him in place. Elayne stepped out first, followed by Declan who escorted her properly, his hand on her elbow. Then Father Fraser trudged out, years of wear and distress marking his features. Wiping his face with his vestment again, the priest raised his hands to the congregation.

"Ladies and gentlemen, clansmen and women, after much introspection and prayer, I have concluded that this man and woman shall be wed in the sight of God this day."

He flicked his hand toward Alistair, and James pushed him to the back of the cheering crowd and resumed his place of honor, beaming once more.

The priest guided Elayne and Declan to join hands and commenced the wedding ceremony. Elayne reached into the folds of her skirt and produced the *Lukenbooth,* placing it in Declan's palm. He traced it over with a finger, and for a moment he wondered if his mother gave a gift like this to his father. As of late, his thoughts kept returning to the past, and he didn't care for how those memories erupted unbidden. He blinked a few times to bring himself back to the present. Elayne had removed his old battered brass one and, taking the silver and emerald wedding gift from Declan's hand, she pinned it to his tartan where it reflected the green and black of the plaid. She patted it in approval as the priest continued.

"Now, Declan, do ye have a ring?"

Declan reached into his sporran and pulled a small golden circlet from its depths, hints of green embedded in it. He had the same thought as she, using emeralds to accent the wedding jewelry. He slid it on her finger. Father Fraser then wrapped their hands in a strip of MacCollough plaid and reached behind his small table to bring out the engraved

Oathing stone. Placing their wrapped hands atop the stone, Declan recited the vow as the priest directed, his voice serious and gruff:

> "I vow you the first cut of my meat, the first sip of my wine,
> from this day it shall only your name I cry out in the night
> and into your eyes that I smile each morning;
> I shall be a shield for you back as you are for mine,
> no shall a grievous word be spoken about us,
> for our marriage is sacred between us and no stranger shall hear my grievance.
> Above and beyond this, I will cherish and honor you through this life
> and into the next."

Elayne repeated the words, heady and breathless. Father Fraser raised his palms high over the wedding couple's heads, intoning to God that He bless the union, then nodded toward Declan.

"Ye may now kiss your bride."

Declan drew Elayne in close, pressing her to his full length and kissed her wholly and deeply in front of the cheering crowd. She grasped his face with her hands and kissed him just as wantonly. Now that they were wed, such a show would not cause gossip, and they allowed the kiss to deepen unceasingly to the jeering of the villagers

When Elayne finally pulled away, Declan wriggled his eyebrows at her, then faced their audience.

"As Laird and Lady MacCollough, we welcome all to the keep for our celebratory feast!"

The cheering increased — the carousing atmosphere fitting to the MacCollough men. The congregation tossed late flowers and dried grasses over their heads as Declan and Elayne rushed through the crowd, Elayne's hand clasped tightly in his. Just as he intended to thread his arm through his bride's and properly escort her back to the castle, he lost her amid the swarm of people. He craned his neck, searching for her in the chaotic throng of clansmen and women.

Only Elayne's screeching voice reassured him that she was unharmed, and for a moment a wisp of pity crossed him for whoever was presently at the receiving end of her tongue-lashing. He followed her voice, shoving celebrators to the side as he moved toward the far side of the crowd. To his vexation, Alistair had his fingers wrapped around Elayne's wrist, yet failing in his attempt to drag her outside the village again.

"Cousin, ye are daft, and I would ken! Ye must leave now and dinna return to this place or I will see ye thrown in the dungeon myself!"

Alistair ignored her pleas, trying to pull Elayne farther away, not realizing Elayne had rooted herself and was unmoving. He also did not notice that Declan, Torin, and Laird MacNally followed Elayne's voice directly to him. Alistair smacked her face.

"Shut your mouth, ye braying bitch! I will no' have ye halt my plans!"

Fueled by anger, Declan rushed forward to strike Alistair. Physical violence reminded him of his father, a man regretfully on his mind far too much this day as it was, and Declan reacted out of instinct. Before his fists could land on the young man, to everyone's surprise, Alistair's most of all, Elayne slapped him back, the echoing strike leaving a pronounced palm print on his cheek. He dropped her wrist to put his hand to his face.

"What the hell —" he began, when she stomped toward him. Alistair found himself shirking back from his cousin, a woman, no' more than a lass, and he was horrified with himself.

"Dinna strike me, ever. Ye are worthless tripe, a rabble rouser, and ye must take your lies and trouble making elsewhere. Ye are no' longer welcome in this clan."

At that, Declan did step in, seizing Alistair by the throat, lifting him up on his toes. Fear set into Alistair's eyes as he gurgled in protest.

"In my house," Declan said, "we dinna strike those we claim to love. Ye have presented false charges of treason against me and my clan, which now extends to my good-father's clan, and ye expect us to let ye leave? I shall have ye skinned for the insult to my wife, if nothing else."

Elayne stayed Declan's arm with a light touch, and Declan released her cousin's neck. She leaned in close to Declan, speaking only to him.

"We canna kill him, my husband. He may be worthless, but he is my kin. It would assuredly cause a rift in my father's clan."

Declan evaluated her request. His anger dissipated, the tension leaving his body. He did not agree with his wife's request, but she was correct in her assessment. In truth, the lad did not do much damage to the day, and Elayne slapped him back, for Christ's sake.

"Ye are a bossy wench, wife, ye ken?" he told her.

The right side of her mouth shifted up in a sly smile, and she responded, "Aye, I ken. More's the pity for ye."

With a rough shove, Laird MacCollough sent Alistair to the ground. "Get ye from my land. This is your final warning. If anyone sees ye return, they have my permission to kill ye on sight."

Alistair scrambled toward the trees, but the last word was his as he shouted over his shoulder:

"Ye will regret this, MacCollough!"

Both Torin and James MacNally lunged toward the trees, but Declan raised his hand to halt them. "Let him flee. I doubt he will return."

He cast a quick glance at his new wife who stood in statuesque defiance in the village glen.

"Lady Elayne's smack made sure of that," he quipped.

***

Torin walked behind the couple as they led the wedding parade back to the castle. MacNally walked next to his daughter, and Torin's gorge rose every time he thought of his dearest friend and Laird wedded to this atrocious woman. This harpy who struck a man, who didn't let her husband defend her, was not the choice Torin wanted for his oldest friend or his clan. His mood darkened as they walked, a stark contrast to the celebratory mood of everyone else. He trudged across the glen like a petulant child. The deed was done, and he could do naught now. If the cousin's accusations could not prevent the marriage, any protest he made would surely fall on deaf ears.

Bonnie, Senga, and the young lasses of the keep had hurried back as soon as Declan and Elayne shared their wedding kiss, racing to prepare foodstuffs for the feast. Senga brought in dark hydrangeas, fuchsia, and hardy late roses to brighten the hall with festive colors and scents. Bonnie and her lasses dashed from the kitchens to the hall, their hands full of platters and cups. A wild boar the clansmen caught just yesterday rotated on a roasting spit outside the gardens, its aroma drawing tenants and villagers. Duncan offered to work the spit and carve the pig, labor which suited him well.

Like Torin, the large russet man shared no joy on this wedding day. Not only did Duncan not care for the loudmouthed woman newly aligned with his Laird, as a result of MacCollough's entanglements with her clan, his Laird was accused of treason. A senseless claim, true, but an accusation, nonetheless. And now his Laird's hall was overrun with clansmen who had looked down their noses at the uncivilized "Beast Clan." Duncan's mind spun with these thoughts, and the ale he steadily drank throughout the day only made him worse. At least alone in the gardens, with only a split pig (*no' a harpy*, he happily thought) for company, he could find solace.

He leaned against the cool stone wall of the keep, pulling his plaid around himself to ward off the chill. Autumn was destined to come hard and cold this year, Duncan observed, noting that many of the leaved already abandoned the trees. A loud banging jarred him from his reverie. The kitchen door burst open, and one of Bonnie's lasses hurried to the smoldering pit, a large wooden platter under her arm. He stayed back in the shadows, watching with dry humor as the lass juggled holding the platter, wielding the large carving knife he left on a tree stump, and keeping her skirts from trailing into the fire. The prospect of having to extinguish an inflamed young woman did not appeal to Duncan, so he sauntered over to her. She jumped in surprise when he spoke into her ear,

"I dinna think, lass, that the dinner guests want scorched flannel with the roasted boar."

"Oh, milord!" the diminutive lass squeaked at him. "I did no' see ye there."

She bowed briefly, then flicked her pale hair away from her face as she handed the knife over to him. Relief sparkled in her soft blue eyes.

"I am glad that ye are present, milord!" she exclaimed. Duncan could not recall ever meeting such an excitable creature. She flitted like a plover. "Miss Bonnie asked that I bring in the pig, but I can no' imagine how to do such a task. This pig is fair larger than any I ate 'afore!"

Duncan forcibly bit back a smile. In spite of his sour mood, this little creature engaged him, and that is how he found himself carving large sections of roasted pig loin out for her platter. Then, and he could not believe he was actually doing this, Duncan carried the platter into the main hall for her. She chatted the whole time, asking him a few probing questions, and while he sought to retain his gruff exterior, he found himself answering, conversing as amiably as she. He wondered what was wrong with him.

Her name was Kaleigh, her father was a MacKenzie who lived near the borderlands of Clan MacCollough. She told him she came to MacCollough land because she was the oldest of seven and wanted to spread her wings, which was too difficult for her in a small tenant croft. This adventure, as she called her work at Castle MacCollough, was her only chance to travel from home. Her father worried for her, and Kaleigh indicated she was not pleased at his appearance at the wedding.

"And ye dinna fear coming to the clan of wild men?"

Kaleigh scoffed at his question. "I was certain it was a joke. And look — 'twas a joke. The keep is clean, Mistress Bonnie and Lady MacCollough seem to have a well-run household, and Laird MacCollough has his strong hand on the lands. I have no' seen anything that makes me think this is a land o'er run with wild men."

Duncan laughed under his breath. *Just wait,* he thought.

***

When they finally entered the hall, Duncan noted that the clans were not as unified as Laird MacCollough wanted to believe. As much as the Laird would have wanted this marriage to show all the Highlands that Clan MacCollough turned over a new leaf, complete change and acceptance would be a slow process. In the hall, a few of the MacKenzies, Kaleigh's father included, sat near a large assemblage of MacKenzie clansmen and women, separate from Declan's men and MacNally's entourage, which did not bode well.

Duncan oft thought the MacKenzie's responsible for the "Beast Clan" moniker. He could no' say such to MacCollough, who wanted to garner favor with his border clans. Yet, the MacKenzies routinely complained about MacCollough behavior, oft blaming reiving and mischief on their bordering neighbors, pointing their fingers directly at Duncan. While they weren't always wrong, Duncan despised their arrogance. He would go out of his way to avoid any MacKenzie present this day.

MacNally and his people sat at the front tables with near Elayne, drinking and cheering (*I canna blame the man,* Duncan thought), with only a few of Elayne's family representing the clan as a whole. Her crazed cousin Alistair was, not surprisingly, absent. After witnessing her cousin's ravings at the kirk, Duncan was convinced Declan or Laird MacNally strung the lad up by his ballocks, especially since Laird MacNally surely panicked at the prospect of his banshee daughter returning to his nest. As for the MacColloughs, his clan gathered near the back of the hall. Lines were drawn, and Duncan hoped that all parties involved behaved, not for the new Lady of the clan but for his Laird MacCollough, whom Duncan respected.

As for Declan, his conversation with other clansmen was distracted by the appearance of Duncan, holding a platter of meat, escorting a blonde lass into the hall. *'Twas a day where wonders would never cease,* Declan thought, wanting to hold his breath that the pleasant feasting this eve may continue. He tilted his head to the side, catching Elayne in a sidelong view. Her hair piled high on her head, surrounded by a crown of greenery, was fitting as she held herself regally. Elayne could rival any queen of the realm. His eyes flicked down to her burgeoning breasts swelling above the plaid of her gown and felt himself harden, his breath quicken. Tonight, when she lay in his bed, it would not be out of wedlock, not hidden. Tonight, he would lay with his wife. Declan had to force his eyes away from her to engage the rest of the hall.

As the clansmen in the hall devoured the food and drink, raucous talk and laughter filled the hall to the rafters. Elayne and Declan maneuvered around the tables, celebrating with their guests, many of whom never imagined either Elayne or Declan wed. With the doors to the hall open to the yard, the strong, lingering melody of pipers filtered in, a cacophony of joy emanating from the entirety of the keep.

Both Declan and Elayne knew the mood was too good to last.

What began as a low rumble from the far side of the hall gained momentum as the sound reached the newlywed couple. The rumbling became stomping and anger, and before Elayne could react, fists flew between the MacKenzie and MacCollough clansmen, knocking men back over tables, upending food, shoving men and women to the side. Bonnie, Senga, and Kaleigh scampered toward the kitchens, and Declan scrambled to the fray.

Torin and Duncan fought back to back against the rising tide of affronted MacKenzies. Each throwing gigantic fists at oncoming clansmen, they kept many of the MacKenzie men at bay, laying them low or landing punches that threw them back over benches and tables. One MacKenzie leapt at Duncan, knocking him off his feet, and several other MacKenzie clansmen piled on. Torin spun to assist when Declan reached the fight and began pulling men off Duncan.

Declan received a punch to the back of his head for his effort, and Torin returned the gesture. Declan managed to push several men away from the brawl, drawing his sword. As Torin turned to help his Laird, one of the MacKenzies punched his mid-section, bowling him over.

Declan grabbed the offender by the back of his head. "Halt!" he hollered at the top of his voice, just as an ear-piercing whistle startled the whole hall into a standstill. Expecting to see the priest, he instead saw Elayne. His wife stood on one of the ale-stained tables, fingers in her mouth just as she had observed the priest do earlier in the day. Once she had the attention of the hall, she gestured toward Declan.

"Husband? Ye were saying?" she asked.

Granting a slight nod to Elayne, Declan regarded those remaining in the hall with an irate glare.

"What is the meaning of such disrespectful behavior in my hall on my wedding day?"

Torin wiped blood from his swollen lip. "Laird, these men insulted the integrity of your clan, again naming us a beast clan of wild men, calling us uncivilized, and —" He cast a glance at Elayne, assured his next words would strike a wound if nothing else, "and claimed that joining our clan to a feral harpy would no' change that."

"Nay!" one of the MacKenzie clansmen yelled back. "'Tis your wild men who offended us! We tried to have a civilized meal to celebrate your nuptials, yet your men did no' treat us with respect. They spilled food and drink on us, on our *women,* used coarse language in their presence. How can your men no' ken how to behave at such fine event? 'Twas as if they were already drunk — how can this be so early in the eve?"

Rubbing his hand over his face in frustration, Declan did not know how to handle such chaos. The MacKenzie man all but admitted to naming his clansmen uncivilized as Torin indicated, so he trusted Torin's words about how they addressed his wife. Yet Declan also knew that Torin and his men lacked manners, which many found offensive. Every action appeared to undermine his desire to change the perception of his clan, to be respected, to grow it into something esteemed. Conflicts like this hindered all that he worked for.

Declan spied Laird MacKenzie, who had not participated in the fray. Deciding to choose discretion, he bowed to the man. "Laird MacKenzie, my apologies if my men offended any of your clansmen with their rough ways. Ye ken we are working towards something greater than my father's legacy, but that will take time. Would ye please resume your celebrations with us?"

The MacKenzie's eyes flicked from his own man's to Declan. He adjusted his blue plaid and spoke.

"I appreciate your apology. However, I dinna ken that 'twould behoove us or ye to remain here. Too much animosity passed this night. We will take our leave. Ye have our good tidings toward your marriage and may ye and your new *wife* find success in changing the legacy of your clan."

Neither Declan nor Elayne missed the inflection of word "wife" by the Laird, and Declan's visage darkened. No longer joyful, his light eyes narrowed, and his chin jutted forth in anger. Elayne watched from her vantage point on the table, almost enjoying that the man wanted to call her a harpy, or worse. She was accustomed to worse.

Stepping close to the MacKenzie Laird, Declan drew himself up, his large chest dwarfing the other man. MacKenzie shuffled back, and the air in the room hummed with anticipation. Even Elayne wondered if Declan would break the implied cardinal rule of the chieftains and strike the other man, which would only lend further credence to the Beast Clan label. Declan's fists, however, remained by his side, and he spoke as civilly as he could muster.

"I will no' permit someone as low as ye the opportunity to apologize to my wife. I ken what ye think. I strive to make amends as a bordering Laird, but ye willna let the past of my father go. That is on ye, no' on me. I will ask ye now, as a civilized man, to leave my lands."

The MacKenzies left, including Kaleigh's father. Kaleigh watched from her space near the kitchens but did move to leave with them. She had felt welcomed and happy since coming to MacCollough land and was not about to let drunken sots ruin this adventure for her. Her eyes remained on the scene in the hall, Duncan in particular, to see what would happen next. No other clansmen or women joined the MacKenzies. The now subdued atmosphere of the hall could end the celebratory night, and Kaleigh thought that a disappointment for her, for the clan, and for the newlywed couple.

Stepping to the large wooden doors at the front of the hall, Declan disappeared outside for a moment, then returned, followed by the pipers. He hopped up onto the table where Elayne still stood, wrapped his arm around her waist, and kissed her soundly. His time with the King taught him diplomacy. The hall erupted in applause, and the merrymaking resumed. The pipers filled the hall with melodies, and some Highlanders pushed the tables away from the center to make room for dancing. Several of the men stomped toward the middle, in time with the pipes, while the rest of the room watched them dance and resumed eating whatever food remained on the tables. Bright colors swirled, music carried on throughout the night, and even with all the chaos, for the first time in a long time, Declan felt pride in the clan he led.

Chapter 14: Small Gifts

Before the night grew too long, Declan thanked the crowd, bid them good eve for both himself and Elayne, moved to escort his bride up to their chambers. A few clansmen joked that the couple needed an audience to confirm the marriage was consummated, and Elayne paled at the suggestion. She already had to endure letting the priest (who had not looked her in the eyes for the rest of the day) know of her "indiscretions" with Declan; the thought of the entire clan finding out was mortifying. Fortunately, Declan laughed it off and, sweeping Elayne up into his arms, marched up the rest of steps, surprising both Elayne and the cheering crowd.

The quiet of their chamber was a welcome respite to the boisterous noise below. Notes from the pipes flowed into the room from the window, a light sound in the otherwise still night air. Elayne flopped onto the bed in relief. Her new husband attended the fire, banking it for the evening, allowing the chill of the fall to envelop them. He then flopped on the bed next to her.

She turned her head to face him, and as he gazed back, they both began giggling uncontrollably. Slowly their laughter died out, and as they wheezed air back into their lungs, Declan reached for Elayne's hand.

"Well, my *wife*," he started with overt inflection, "What say ye that we consummate this marriage?"

"Aye, my *husband*," she returned the tone. "We dinna want anyone to suggest the marriage is no' legal."

Declan leapt off the bed, bringing Elayne with him. He clasped her face in his hands and kissed her forehead, nose, and each of her cheeks.

"First, I have to thank ye, wife," he said in his husky voice. "Tonight, was the first night where Clan MacCollough enjoyed a civilized feast, good food, good kin, and music, much like what I saw in other clans when I was away with the Bruce. Tonight, I felt like a true clan Laird, and I owe so much of that to ye."

"My Laird, methinks ye would have attained this, regardless. Ye are quite the force to be reckoned with."

"Ooch, Lady 'Layne," Declan responded, "that is the highest compliment coming from ye." His eyes squinted with his smile, and he kissed her full on the lips.

His tongue sought her mouth, tracing the outline of her lips, licking her décolletage, teasing his tongue between the cleavage of her breasts. Quivers of excitement rushed from her breasts down her belly to her woman's mound. She grasped Declan's head, pulling it up to kiss him back, their tongues dancing. His hands moved to her breasts, kneading them over her gown. He then wrapped one arm around her, grasping her derriere and pressing her to him. His arousal was strong and stiff beneath his tartan, and she reached her hand to rub his erection under his kilt.

Breathing heavily, Declan thrust her away from him, tugging her gown away from her kirtle. Elayne shrugged her gown off her shoulders to grant him easier access, and he freed her breasts from the golden fabric. Cupping the mounds in his hands, he bent to lick the nipple of one breast, then the other. Elayne covered his hands with hers, letting her head fall back as she moaned, his lips sending rivulets of pleasure through her.

When he lifted his head, she caught his plaid in her hands, pulling it from his chest. He lifted his shift over his head in one swift move, then tugged at Elayne's kirtle, dropping it to her feet. Falling on his knees in front of her woman's mound, he kissed her dark curls there, then pressed farther licking between her lower lips, tasting her. Elayne cried out in surprise and Declan tightened his arms around her hips as she writhed under his mouth. His tongue and lips played against her velvety folds, exploring and tasting her as he never had before. Her cries of surprise became moans of enjoyment.

Declan pulled her down to the floor, atop their wedding clothing. He heaved himself on top of her, unable to wait any longer. The anticipation of the night destroyed his control.

"I can wait no' longer," he panted, pressing his manhood as deep into her sheath as he could. She was warm and wet and ready as he moved inside her, trying to thrust harder with each movement. Elayne clung to him, her nails grasping his shoulders, marking him. Her hips rose to meet each thrust of his. Declan dropped his head, so his forehead touched hers and plunged harder, panted harder, the folds of her nether lips pulling him closer to his climax.

Elayne's insides convulsed as he rubbed against the most intimate part of her. Pleasure and excitement flooded her entire being, and she cried out his name. His hair tickled her face as he called out to her in return.

"Now, Elayne! Now!" And he thrust once more, shuddering inside her. His whole weight collapsed on her breasts, and there they rested in a mix of sweat, lovemaking, and the cool fall air. The piper music played on to the beat of their breaths.

***

Declan rolled to his side, pulling Elayne with him. She rested her head on Declan's heaving chest which was still overwrought from his exertions. She faintly gleamed with sweat, enjoying the chilled breeze that passed through the window slit. Her hair spilled across his blonde chest in a river of dark, and he rested his hand on her head, holding her close as though he were afraid to let her go. In that quiet, Elayne had a sense of completeness never before experienced. With no need for commanding, edginess, or stubbornness, she melted into him, her breath mimicking his, sharing his warmth. How she arrived at this place, with hope and passion for the future after a lifetime of crazed existence, she knew not. All she knew was warmth, peace, and love in this singular space on the floor of Declan's chamber.

She shifted her head to catch Declan's eyes, half closed moons on his face. He too appeared content, the stress and chaos from the wedding feast gone from his visage and from his mind. Using the tips of her fingernails, she traced the nipples on his chest then trailed up through his blonde fur to his neck and traced his jawline.

"I have a gift for ye, husband," her whisper broke the quite of the eve.

"I already received a gift from ye, aye?" He waggled his eyebrows at her suggestively.

She patted his jaw with a gentle tap. "Nay, husband, not that type of gift."

Elayne rose from the floor, her skin dimpling in the cold air as she peeled herself off his heated skin. Declan's eyes roved over her elegant form, soaking in as much of her as he could before sleep overtook them. Too often over the last week, he desired to rip her clothes from her in the hall in midday, bystanders be damned. He could not get enough of her. In his chamber (no longer his chamber, *their chamber*), after they loved each other long and hard, she often strode around the room in her raw skin. Declan wondered if she knew how that drove him to the brink of madness and did it on purpose, Nay, he didn't wonder — he was certain she did.

Dropping to her knees, she reached into her trunk, which Senga had removed to this chamber earlier in the day and pulled out a gift wrapped in cloth. Elayne returned to Declan, who immediately put his hands on her, rubbing her thighs, needing to touch her. She grasped one of his hands from her leg, smirked at him, and placed the unwieldy gift into his hand.

"What is this?" he asked.

"Open it, my Laird."

He pulled the wood case from the cloth and peered at the falcon etching on the lid of the box. The box was empty when he opened it.

"What is it for?"

"It's a keeping box, for ye to keep important trinkets — your *Lukenbooth*, ye ken? Or if ye have documents that ye want to keep from prying eyes."

"Prying eyes? Yours?" Declan grinned back at her.

"Aye, mine, or any others. Whatever ye want to keep in it, 'tis yours. I just saw it at the market, and it spoke to me. The color, the falcon, it seemed to want me to gift it to ye."

Declan's smile fell from his face. "But I dinna have a gift for ye."

"Don't ye now?" she asked as her hand slid between his legs to his cock.

Declan stayed her hand. "Let's move to the bed."

***

His failure at the wedding weighed on Alistair's shoulders. He had been convinced that the priest would listen to him, as a representative of clan MacNally and a close cousin. How could he have failed to stop the wedding? MacNally himself contributed to the complications; the old man could not wait to see his daughter wed, and who could blame him? To rid himself of his obnoxious daughter was undoubtedly a blessing for James MacNally. Alistair had not considered MacNally would remain so committed to this union once he knew of the disparity among the clans and how the powerful Ross Clan considered MacCollough a traitor. It seemed that Alistair's estimations were largely misconstrued.

Now he needed another avenue to solidify his position in the clan, and unfortunately, it appeared that Elayne's demise was the only option. The MacColloughs would lose any sense of civility, the border clans would unite against them, and MacCollough would become easy pickings for Ross and his comrades. These actions, Alistair hoped, should be enough for Alistair to fall in line for Laird of Clan MacNally once James died. The MacNallys could then be aligned with the stronger clans of the Highlands. Perhaps this could still work out for him.

What would make his plans work best was the brash Elayne herself. As a strong-willed harpy, she oft rode out on her own with nary a maid to accompany her. She walked the market without escort, leaving herself exposed. He must bide his time, reside nearby — perhaps he could find an abandoned croft? — until the next time Elayne was alone. He rode into the frosty night air to find a place to camp for the next few days, until an opportunity presented itself.

***

James MacNally stayed the evening in the MacCollough keep, Mari warming his bed. While he didn't think Elayne's wedding day was the appropriate time to inform his daughter of his relationship with Mari, he also didn't want to keep Mari from this celebration. He was fairly convinced that if Elayne did not find issue with Mari, then he would court Mari for marriage. Too many years had passed since his wife Gillian died. He hid his consorting with women and did not pursue marriage in any form, out of deference to his daughter. Now that she was wed and his relationship with Mari lasted several tests (keeping the relationship hidden not the least of them), he was in a position to claim his own happiness.

For so long, his Lanie's happiness remained his only ambition in life. She was hot-tempered and willful, and he acknowledged that her status as a single child and lady of the keep contributed to those character traits. Over the last several months, since the fiasco with the MacLeod clan, Elayne had become a different person. With Declan, she appeared a contented person. Her face, how it shone throughout the day, how it alighted whenever she looked at Laird MacCollough, was so different from the taciturn, stubborn young woman she had been. James could not have asked for more — Elayne was happier than he had ever seen her.

As Lady of Clan MacCollough, and with his clan joined with the MacCollough clan, she was well positioned. Declan's behavior and treatment of her indicated he was a strong man of solid character, one who could easily lead both clans as one when James' time was done. James and Mari would depart with the rest of the clan in the morn, and he needed to have a private discussion with Elayne before then.

For the first time in decades, James MacNally felt a sense of inner peace and contentedness for the future. He wrapped his arm around Mari's waist, pulling her closer to him under the blankets, and relaxed into his slumber.

***

James found his daughter in the kitchens early the next morning, directing porridge and fruit to the tables for guests to break their fast. Milk and honey flowed freely. The jovial noise of the kitchens and hall continued the celebratory atmosphere of the previous night.

"Lanie," James called out. Elayne rose from stirring the porridge pot on the hearth and hugged her father.

"Good morn, Father. I trust ye slept well this past eve?"

"Aye, Lanie, that I did."

"Were ye wanting some porridge and honey 'afore ye left?"

"That would be divine. Could we take it somewhere a bit more private?"

His nerves started to get the better of him. He was perturbed that a strong Highland Laird like himself quivered in fear at the prospect of speaking to his own daughter. Whether it was his daughter or the legendary Elayne that touched his nerves, he would not venture to guess.

Elayne escorted her father to an empty table in the hall. James allowed his daughter to sit first and sat next to her. He blew on his porridge to cool it and bide his time until he could summon the words to inform his daughter of Mari and his possible future plans.

"Will Mari be joining us for this conversation?" Elayne asked as she spooned porridge into her mouth.

James MacNally choked on his bite and spat it out, porridge dripping in his salt and pepper beard as he stared at her. Elayne could not halt the smug smile that played at her lips, and she purposefully took another bite of honeyed oats.

"What—? How—?" MacNally stuttered. How did she know?

"Did ye truly think ye could keep your relationship a secret? Father, do ye no' ken how the house servants' gossip?" Elayne shook her head at him in mock condescension. "Do ye think I would no' have ye find love somewhere, only focus on me and pine for mother? What style of monster do ye take me for?"

MacNally's mouth hung agape. He wiped the porridge off his beard with his sleeve and gathered his wits.

"So, ye are no' angry at me?"

Elayne turned her intense gray gaze on her father. "Nay, Father. Plus, I am no' home anymore. I wouldna want ye rambling around the keep with naught but servants and clansmen getting ye into trouble. Ye would take on the title of Beast Clan!" Elayne laughed at her own joke.

Her force of will had not changed, James noted, yet she appeared so much more light-hearted in how she applied it. This marriage definitely suited Elayne well.

When the time came for Mari and James to leave, Elayne hugged them both goodbye.

"Take care of my father," Elayne commanded to Mari, who nodded in response.

Over the rest of the day, other clansmen departed. The hall emptied, and quiet settled on the manse. Declan held his hand out to Elayne.

"Time to become an old married couple, aye?"

Chapter 15: Unintended Information

T ell me about your youth," Declan probed one night as they lay entwined in each other, naked skin on skin. His fingers trailed over her hip up to her breast and back down as they curled into one another. Elayne ran her fingers over his face, scratching at Declan's beard, pondering his question.

"Well, my mother died when I was a lass, ye ken. My father raised me, giving me full run of the household. He had no' other bairns, so I was spoilt, I guess."

Though she hated to say the word aloud, it was a truth she could not ignore. She had grown up as the spoiled only daughter of a powerful man.

"I learned to read when most cannot," she continued. "I have been riding since I could walk. But it also came with responsibility. As the only woman of the house, lady of the manse duties fell to me at a young age. My labors included writing letters, helping in the accounting of rents, cleaning and household management, and preparing herbals for those who fell ill. I imagine that is why I became such a loudmouth," she snickered, embracing her impugned image in the clan and the western Highlands in general.

Her finger followed along his jawline, then she pressed her lips there, working toward his mouth. They touched tongues, and a shiver of excitement flared from Elayne's belly to her Venus mound making her open and wet, though they had just coupled and now lay spent and clammy in bed.

"And ye, my Laird Declan MacCollough? What of your childhood?"

Declan's previously open and lively face closed; he lost the slight smile he wore while Elayne spoke and kissed him. Suddenly distressed at his reaction, she traced over his lips with her finger.

"My apologies. Perhaps I should no' have asked."

He pressed her fingers against his lips, kissing them, his eyes never leaving hers.

"Nay, 'Layne. 'Tis only fair that ye ken what ye married into. I knew much of your history 'afore we wed, 'twas no secret. Ye are open and have nothing to hide. My past, ye see," he paused, choosing his next words delicately, "my past is something that should remain hidden. My past is the reason I wedded ye. I wanted something more than I had as a child."

Propping herself up on her arm, Elayne's breasts pulled from under the plaid and she placed Declan's hand over her swollen mounds. Cradling his head with her other arm, she pulled his face to her breast and cuddled him.

"Tell me. I am strong enough to help ye carry that weight."

Declan was silent in the air of the night. Elayne's skin dimpled in the cold, and her nipple hardened under his hand.

He moved his palm and kissed her exposed breast, licking the hard nipple. His honeyed gaze shifted up to her, and he shifted up to regard her unusually guileless face.

"My grandfather lost his wife, my grandmother, early, like ye. But unlike your father, my grandda did no' handle it well. He let his sons run wild, while the keep and lands began to fall into disrepair. He took his anger out on others, including his sons and tenants. Clansmen and their families began to leave seeking calmer horizons. My father and his brothers were stuck here, like deer in mud. My da was the oldest, so I imagine he felt the need to somewhat guard his younger brothers against their father."

Declan turned to observe at Elayne directly, trailing his hand from her breast to her neck and back down. Now that the floodgate opened, his pained words poured forth in a rush.

"When my grandfather died suddenly, my father had only just wed, and he found himself Laird of a clan that was spiraling out o'control. And he did no' care. More tenants left, mostly men with wives and families, until mostly only men, unwed men remained. *BlackBraes* then earned its unfortunate title of the clan of Wild Men. My mother had no' help with the running of the keep, and after I was born, I was told she became withdrawn. Mayhap she was sad, lonely. My father certainly did not treat her well, and when I was nigh on two summers, she disappeared. I was told she left, but I heard rumors she died. I dinna ken what happened to her."

The sadness in his voice tugged so heavily at her heart that tears formed in her eyes. She blinked them away, enthralled with the story of the sad little boy that was her husband's childhood.

"I left. When I was sixteen, I traveled alone to the lowlands to stay with some distant relatives, then joined

Robert the Bruce's banner when I was nineteen. By twenty-one, I was a favorite of the king, and by twenty-seven, when my father died, Laird of a clan I had nay seen in ten years. The moment I returned, I ken I needed to take drastic measures to upend the destruction my crazed father wrought on the people here."

"What was her name?"

"Her—? Who? My mother?" he asked, eyebrows raised. Elayne nodded. "Davina. Davina Mary MacKenzie MacCollough."

Elayne had no response. How did one respond to such a story of heartache and abandonment? Having no words to soothe him — by nature, she was not the type of woman who had such words — she grasped his head with her hands, drawing him to her, and kissed him with all the emotion she could muster. If he had no solace in his childhood, he would now find solace with her.

***

Declan's story of his mother stayed with Elayne throughout the next few days. She lost her mother to a fever as a young child — she had security in the knowledge that leaving was not her mother's choice.

But for Declan, having lost a mother in such an inauspicious manner, not knowing if she still lived or not, affected him deeply. While she could not erase the scars on his heart, she knew this could be an opportune moment for her to flex her less-than-desirable character trait as a strong-willed harpy (a name that she had heard less of since she first came to *BlackBraes)*. Elayne wanted to try to locate Declan's mother, or if not the living woman, at least her final resting place.

Elayne sat in the solar at the unmilled table, quill and parchment at the ready. She wrote several copies of the same letter in her delicate script. Each one would arrive by messenger to a different location: two nearby convents, the larger church in Edinburgh, and the larger MacNaughten family clan further south. The four letters read the same:

Dear Sir (or Mistress)
As the new Lady of Clan MacCollough, I am
Endeavoring to locate the Mother of my new Husband, Laird
Declan Ian MacCollough. She perchance left the Clan
MacCollough neigh 26 years past. Her given name is Davina
Mary MacKenzie MacCollough. If ye ken the Whereabouts of
said Mistress, or of those who may have such Information,
please send a Messenger back to Lady Elayne MacCollough of
Clan MacCollough.

I thank ye in advance for your Aide.
Lady Elayne MacNally MacCollough

She called for Senga, who met her in the solar.

"Senga, call for Rory. I need messages sent, and I prefer that Declan no' ken until a later time. Can ye and Rory keep this unspoken until I hear back from these missives?"

Senga took the letters in her hands, nodding to Elayne. She left silently, focused on the gravity of her task.

Whether or not Declan wanted to see his own mother after all this time did not concern Elayne. If given the opportunity, she would want a moment with her lost mother. He had a right to know his mother's whereabouts even if she yet lived; more importantly, his mother deserved to know her son, now that the father was gone. That her actions could have any unwanted repercussions did not cross Elayne's mind.

***

Duncan's recent interest in Kaleigh ran contrary to how he presented himself to the men of the clan, contrary even to how he presented himself to the Laird. He had a middling concern that someone may uncover his gruff countenance to find a lovesick puppy under his skin.

His actions of late even surprised himself. For the longest time, the widow in the village or a whore passing through served his masculine needs well enough, and like the other men in the clan, he dismissed any frivolous prospects of love or marriage. That attitude was the clan approach until Declan returned from the King's war, changing all their ways. Declan's command to tame the clan bristled his haunches — after years of rough ways, to civilize a whole clan of men was no small feat and most of the men, Duncan included, did not welcome such a change.

And then to bring Elayne MacNally, of all women in the Highlands, to the clan, and wed her? Many a mug of ale was consumed to wash away that information. And no one wanted to listen to her, even if Declan commanded it. In hindsight, some of her actions did have sound consequences. Meals are now hot and well-prepared. The full, content belly provided a strong argument in favor of the woman. The stink in the manse had dissipated, and the whole of the clan enjoyed a measure of comfort absent until Elayne's appearance. The mere presence of more women contributed to a more favorable environment, possible only because Elayne provided a measure of reputability to the clan that fathers would trust. And with those lasses came Kaleigh.

Duncan sighed heavily, hanging his head in defeat. The person he despised the most had brought to him the person he now arduously desired. He surrendered himself to Elayne's machinations.

"Kaleigh, will ye join me in the gardens?" Duncan poked his head in the doorway of the kitchens, his eyes scanning furtively to ensure neither Senga nor Bonnie observed him.

Elayne's dark head bowed near Bonnie's lighter one on the far side of the kitchens. Kaleigh ducked out the door before they could be exposed and joined Duncan on the far side of the gardens near the stables.

"I wanted to make sure ye felt no' effect of discord on the wedding feast."

"Aye, why do ye ask?"

"Well, your father was present, and that could nay have made the best impression. Ye had said ye thought the rumors of Clan MacCollough were false, and now ye ken they are nary a joke. Does that change your mind about the clan or residing here?"

Kaleigh's lips tightened as she spoke. "Aye, that night it did!" Her hands fluttered to her chest like those of an elderly widow who witnesses a moral atrocity. Duncan coughed to hide a laugh at the impression.

"But then it calmed. The Laird and Lady Elayne just seemed so . . . " She studied the horizon, selecting her words. "Jubilant, even after it all." Her blue gaze returned to Duncan, and she peered into his soul. "I want that. I want to have that look for my clan, for my man, for my family, even amid such bedlam. This clan, Miss Bonnie, and Lady Elayne made me feel secure even after that, with my father's Laird causing such commotion. I was no' treated differently."

She paused for a moment, placing a dainty hand on Duncan's arm.

"Do ye see me differently as a result of that eve? Is that why ye ask?"

At this, Duncan burst out in roaring laughter, his whole body shaking uncontrollably. Kaleigh sat back at his reaction, removing her hand until Duncan covered it with his, keeping it on his arm.

"Ooch, dear lass! I was afeared of the same thing!"

Kaleigh's face screwed up in confusion. "Ye were worrit I would be treated differently?"

"Oh, nay, nay. Ye are too dear and likable, Kaleigh. 'Tis difficult for anyone to *no'* like ye." Kaleigh's face softened, and it washed over Duncan as soft as a summer breeze.

"Nay, lass. I was worrit ye would feel differently about us, the clan." At this admission, Duncan's tone changed to a more serious one. "I ken what others say about the clan. Christ, I believed it myself. I did no' want to change, either. Now, I see what you see — what Declan and Elayne have, how the whole of the clan celebrated even after the commotion at the wedding feast, and I realized what our clan has been missing. We deserved the horrid name, but now?"

Duncan leaned in toward Kaleigh, taking in her sweet scent that reminded him of golden hay and warm bread, "now, I think we have the chance to rise as a great clan in the Highlands. I canna believe it to hear myself say it. Just days ago, I would no' have agreed. Now, we have the beginnings of a strong clan. We have strong leadership, alliances, and even the support of the Bruce! What more could a man want in his clan?"

"Aye," Kaleigh cleared her throat. "What else?"

"Ye, lass." Duncan's dark eyes narrowed, his ruddy, burning gaze consuming her. "I have wanted ye since I first say ye ready to stab that split pig with a tiny kitchen knife. Ye came to a strange clan, wanted adventure, and got it. A lass like ye, I could see by my side."

Duncan reached behind his plaid and withdrew a floral ring, bright fuchsia, dusky heather, scarlet hydrangea, woven together with care. He held it out to her, haltingly, the first time she had seen him uncertain — naught more than a schoolboy with a youthful crush. Kaleigh could not stop the grin that pulled at her lips or the blush that heated her cheeks.

"Did ye make this yourself?" she was impelled to ask. This time, Duncan suffered the blush that stained his cheeks above his coarse beard.

"Aye. But I had to ask Bonnie to assist. What I ken of flowers would no' fill a spoon."

Sandy waves flowed through Kaleigh's light hair as she shook out her locks then placed the flower crown with slender fingers.

"Ye want to court me?" Kaleigh confirmed.

"Aye, if ye would allow."

Duncan did not miss the azure sparkle in her eyes, "Well, I will allow it, but ye will still need to talk to my father," she told him. Duncan's eyes rolled heavenward, dread filling his chest.

"We will have to see how that goes. Methinks the man does no' think much of me."

Kaleigh nodded in agreement. "Oh, I ken he doesn't."

Chapter 16: In Sickness and in Health

One brisk morning, a message came to Elayne that a crofter was ill. Her first thought was to have Bonnie or Kaleigh join her as she rode to the croft, but everyone busied themselves, preparing the keep for the cold winter presently nipping at their toes. The long-ignored kitchens were still not stocked to capacity, much to Elayne's aggravation. The neglected gardens only produced so much, and she feared a harsh winter could starve many in the clan.

Declan was also hard at work, hunting and bringing in larger crops with other tenants and often absent from the manse, not returning until after the evening meal. With the new clanswomen at the keep and Declan's desire to grow the clan, ensuring the clan was fed topped their concerns. Elayne spent most days imprisoned in the kitchens with the other women, baking, storing grain, salting meat, and trying to preserve the crops from the late harvest. Too much time inside made her stir-crazy. Perchance a trip to take herbals and preserves to a crofter served a secondary purpose — an opportunity to enjoy the beauty of autumn before winter kept her inside all the more.

She packed her bag with necessities, including an indulgence of sweet berry spread, then wrapped herself in a heavy gray cloak and ventured out into the damp day. Torin grudgingly helped her saddle her mare, Blath, cautioning her against the chill, and secured her bag to the saddle. Reigning Blath to a trot toward the crofts close to the village, she lifted her face into the misting rain, enjoying the sensation of the drops on her face and hair after her long confinement indoors.

The tenant's cottage sat amid a small cluster of cottages, close to the village. She knocked on the coarsely-fashioned door, until an elderly man appeared in the doorway, coughing wetly. Elayne feared the cough may have settled in his chest but hid her concern under a slight smile.

"Aye, Greer MacCollough," Elayne greeted him. "I ken ye are no' well. I can hear your cough. Do ye want an herbal to ease the coughing?"

"Aye," Greer MacCollough croaked, coughing more. Spitting into a cloth, he moved aside to permit her entry. "The good Father has been coming over the past few days, but he can no' come every day. Ye are a welcome sight, lass."

Inside the croft, a low peat fire flickered and warmed the small room. Elayne pulled a tin cup from the wall, added herbs and water to the cup, then hung it on the crochan hook over the fire to steep the ingredients. Greer sat heavily on his bedding, coughing more, and Elayne frowned, her unease for his health mounting. Not only was the air growing colder, but the man lived alone, which worried Elayne as well. She made a mental note to send someone to check on the old man every day that the priest was otherwise engaged, else he would perish and naught would ken.

She made sure he finished the drink, then helped him lay back into bed, covering his frail body with the coarse cloth. She clicked her tongue to herself as she finished these ministrations. While Elayne had no guarantee the man would have had a wife under other circumstances, she viewed Greer as a victim of the lack of women in the clan. Had he a wife, Greer would not be alone in his illness, fretting over visits from the priest. Elayne sighed heavily as she left the croft, fastening the wooden door behind her.

Misting rain became a steady drizzle as Elayne gathered the reins of Blath, relieved to leave the heavy, sick air of the croft and head back to the keep. She grabbed the pommel of the saddle to mount her horse when something struck the back of her head and all went black.

***

Unfortunately for Alistair, several MacKenzie clansmen encountered him in the copse of trees, trying to pull Elayne atop his horse. Alistair once again cursed his rotten luck.

"What have we 'ere?" the shortest of the sodden, blue-clad men inquired.

Alistair rested Elayne's limp body on the ground, and twisted around, wiping his sodden hair from his face. Three MacKenzie men, probably hunting in the damp morning fog, stood before him. Each clutched a weapon, obviously on edge near Alistair, who did not respond.

"I said," the short man stepped forward, "what are ye doing 'ere?"

"'Tis no' your business," Alistair puffed. His plans had already gone so awry that he had to employ this last resort and attempt to do away with Elayne, and now these men had interrupted even this. Alistair clenched his jaw. Was there no action he could take successfully?

The taller clansman leaned toward the short man, whispering into his ear and pointing at Elayne. The short man nodded.

"I would wager that the lass there, she would be the Lady MacCollough, daughter of Laird MacNally?"

"'Tis no' your business," Alistair said again. He reached for his horse when the short man clutched at his sleeve.

"Ye are no' leaving," the short man confirmed. The other two MacKenzie Highlanders leapt on Alistair, bringing him to the ground where he struggled in vain. The tall MacKenzie punched him twice so stars leapt about his head. Then the short man and his clansman started dragging Alistair through the muddy wood. The tall MacKenzie bent low to hoist Elayne into his arms and followed the others toward the MacKenzie castle.

When they arrived, they shook the rain from their plaids as they unceremoniously dumped Alistair at the foot of the MacKenzie Laird. One quizzical eyebrow rose as the tall man stepped to the side, placing Elayne gently on a bench near the blazing hearth.

"The new Lady MacCollough? What has transpired here today?" He reached down and lifted Alistair's head by the hair for a better look at his face. "Christ, 'tis this her cousin? The crazy lad who tried to stop the wedding?"

"Aye," the short man began. "He had the unconscious Lady wi' him and did no' want us to see. It seemed rather nefarious, so we decided to bring the man and the Lady to ye."

At that, the short man kicked Alistair in the leg. "What do ye want to do with them?"

Laird MacKenzie rubbed his brow in consternation. He was not on the best terms with MacCollough since the wedding. The man may blame MacKenzie if he returned with Elayne, especially in her current condition, no matter what tale he told the new Laird. MacKenzie had also heard rumors about Alistair's ambitions, not only regarding the clan MacNally but also his encounters with Clan Ross. Secrets did not keep long in the Highlands. He grimaced inwardly; Christ, he hated daft Donald Ross and all his English-sympathizing cronies. MacCollough, for all his failings, was a devout follower of the Bruce.

James MacNally, an old friend and ally of clan MacKenzie, looked the best choice. The man was nothing if not fair, and he should best know how to deal with his injured daughter and wayward nephew. MacKenzie made up his mind; he would send a message to Laird MacCollough, and they would ride for Elayne's father.

***

Laird MacKenzie himself rode with his clansmen, Fergus and Hamish, to MacNally lands, the strident daughter of the Laird thankfully silent in the cart behind the horses. He only hoped the lass eventually awoke, loud mouth and all. MacKenzie did not want to bear any ill tidings to MacNally, least of all the death of his daughter. The injury would be enough to infuriate James MacNally, and MacKenzie was grateful that he had a finger to point in regard to Elayne's current unconscious state.

The target of that blame rode on the horse behind Fergus, bound and gagged. MacKenzie did nay want to listen to *that* MacNally either. Fortunately, the odious lad rode willingly, nay thrashing about. The muddy road and the drenching rain slowed their pace, flinging muck everywhere, and MacKenzie grimaced at his present situation. He should be warm, by his hearth, a mug of mulled cider in hand and a hot meal on his plate. Instead, he was cold, wet, and coated in mud, all because Alistair MacNally was too big for his britches.

MacNally's manse appeared in the distance, the subtle light from narrow windows serving as a beacon to guide them through the steadying deluge. A MacNally clansman met them at the gate and led them to the stables where Fergus unceremoniously dragged Alistair from the horse into the straw. MacKenzie directed Hamish to lift Elayne, no small feat given her height, and carry her to the MacNally keep. MacKenzie inhaled deeply and led the way, ready to take the brunt of MacNally's fury.

The giant man himself met the MacKenzies in the main hall as Laird MacKenzie shook rainwater from every crevice and fold, stamping mud off his boots. James MacNally's face clouded in rage, roaring when he realized Hamish held his seemingly lifeless daughter, snatching her body from his arms.

Elayne first groaned then squeaked at the disruption, and she began to shiver in her sodden dress. Two servants shoved a low bench near the hearth, and James lay her upon it. She opened her dazed eyes, and MacKenzie exhaled in relief. MacNally spun back to MacKenzie.

"What is the meaning of this? Ye bring me my daughter nearly dead?" His eyes caught his bound nephew behind Fergus. "And what of this?" MacNally howled, his rage uncontrollable.

"James, old friend. Calm yourself. I will tell ye all that has transpired this day." MacKenzie's serene tone attempted to cool MacNally's hot head. He wiped at his damp clothes again. "Could we have this discussion as my men and I dry ourselves by the fire, mayhap with a cup of warm mead?"

MacNally's eyes narrowed as he took in the scene in his hall: his daughter barely alive on a bench, his nephew in shackles behind MacKenzie's men, the Laird himself trying to speak calmly and sensibly. He jerked his head toward the hearth and helped the servants drag some benches and blankets over as one young lass scampered for the kitchens. The chatelaine entered carrying a long robe, and draping it over Elayne, assisted the lass up to her chambers, proclaiming that a hot fire and a warm bed was all the lass needed.

After Fergus removed Alistair to an empty chamber upstairs, MacKenzie took the time to warm himself from his soggy ride and began to share the tale of what came to pass with Elayne and Alistair that day. He had completed most of the tale when a crashing sound came at the door.

"'Twould be her husband, methinks," MacKenzie commented.

Chapter 17: Do Ye Care for Me?

At dusk, a rowdy cacophony announced Declan MacCollough's arrival, with Torin in tow. In his fear and concern, Declan didn't notice the rain that had soaked the two of them to the skin. MacNally met them in the hall, just as MacKenzie's intent earlier, hoping to calm MacCollough before he reached Elayne. Or Alistair. MacNally could only imagine the outrage Declan would have for Alistair after all his irrational actions. And then to injure Elayne? Nigh, effort to kill his lass? MacNally barely contained his own fury. He placed his hands on Declan's shoulders, halting the man as he stormed in like a bowder.

"Dinna try to stop me, James," MacCollough growled at him. "I will kill the man, though he be your nephew. Not for the aggravations he caused me, but for the danger he poses to my wife."

"Declan," MacNally began, "Elayne is awake. Ye should go to her first."

MacCollough's nostrils flared as he collected himself. After a deep breath, his anger cleared a bit, allowing him to focus on what was important. Elayne. She needed to be his primary concern.

"Aye, James. Aye. Take me to my wife." He spoke with an air of desperation. "Please."

MacNally nodded once and led Declan up the dank stairway to Elayne's room. James swung opened the door to her chamber, then fastened the door as he left Declan and Elayne alone.

Elayne rested on the bed, a cloth draped over her forehead and her eyes opened in a squint when she heard someone enter the room. Declan rushed over and knelt by the side of the bed, holding her hand.

"'Lane," he whispered. "Are ye well?"

She squeezed his hand. "Aye, my Laird," her voice raspy. "'Tis nay but a bump on the head. Alistair is not much of a fighter. The miscreant could barely harm a wee hedgehog. He had to wait until my back was turned, the jackanape."

Declan pressed his hand to her forehead. Worry plagued his soft, fair features; his hazel eyes watered. She lifted her hand to his face, his beard rough against her cupped palm.

"At least he did nay rob ye of your voice," he told her wryly, and her face softened.

"'Twill take more than a knock on the head to quiet my mouth, to be sure. In truth, Declan, I am fine. My headache is nearly gone. I just want to go home and forget this day."

Declan placed his hand over hers and kissed her palm. "I will take ye home, 'Lane. But first I must deal with your cousin."

Elayne traced her fingers over Declan's features.

"Nay, my Laird."

Declan pulled back sharply. "Nay?" He bellowed. "How can ye say that? I have a right as a husband to have my vengeance on the man who tried to kill my wife!"

"I ken your anger, husband. But he is still my cousin, my father's nephew. He death shall cause much discord in my family. I have spoken to my father, and Alistair is to be banished to the Isles. He leaves on the morrow for the coast, forever marked as an exile and a traitor."

Declan looked slighted, as though Elayne slapped him instead of speaking to him.

"Elayne, ye can no' ask me to let the man live."

"Nay, I am telling ye. I can no' kill my own blood." She lifted her pained gray eyes to his own incensed hazel gaze. "I may be a bitch, but I can no' hurt my kin and clan that way. I will no' have harm come to Alistair. Do ye ken?"

Declan's silence was deafening, and Elayne reached for his face again.

"If ye —" and she stopped.

"If I what?" he probed softly.

She glanced away, shifting her eyes to the fire. "If ye care for me at all, ye will no' ask me to have my cousin killed."

Declan placed his fingers under her chin, lifting her eyes to his once more.

"If I care for ye? How can ye ask that?" he asked in an injured voice.

"I ken I am a difficult woman. I ken that marriage to me was no' your first choice, that ye were desperate. I ken what this arrangement is."

"Do ye think I would have wed ye if I did no' care for ye? Do ye think we both are so desperate that we can nay account for our emotions, if no' our passions?"

Elayne had no answer, trying to avert her eyes from his intense scrutiny. Her head throbbed in time to her heartbeat. She was not ready to broach this topic with him, yet the consequences of the day dictated otherwise. Declan's demeanor unnerved her more than the first time she had lain with him. Long used to keeping her emotions under a veil, Declan's words made her insides quiver.

"I ken our marriage was an arranged one, and perchance 'tis too soon to ken where our emotions lay, but never doubt, my Lady 'Lane, that I do care for ye. Mayhap more than ye ken." Declan kissed her hand again as Elayne blinked back tears.

"Come, my Lady Elayne. If ye feel well enough, ye should be present when I bid your incorrigible cousin adieu."

***

Elayne declined an audience with Alistair for both herself and Declan, mostly out of regard for her cousin's safety. Declan fluttered around Elayne as though she were an invalid, clutching at her on the stairs as they descended to the hall where MacNally and Torin awaited. Declan nodded to Torin, who soundlessly removed himself to gather their horses.

"Surely ye do no' want to leave in the rain, with my daughter just recovered?" MacNally queried. "'Tis late. Remain here this eve and ride home in the morn."

Declan deferred to Elayne. She shook her head. "Nay, father. Thank ye for your hospitality, but I desire to rest in my own bed this eve, at *BlackBraes* with Senga, Bonnie, and Declan to care for me. Ye have your hands full with Alistair."

Always the willful lass, James dipped his head to acquiesce. And she was nay wrong — Alistair still aboded at *Akedene,* and if Declan stayed the night, Alistair may well be a cold body by morning. James could see the outrage seething under Declan's skin when Elayne spoke his name, like naming the devil. Sending Declan home, regardless of Elayne's desires, was the most shrewd decision.

James embraced his daughter, holding her close. As fractious of a woman as she was, Elayne was still his little girl and injury to her affronted him as a father. He released her to Declan, clasping his forearm to say goodbye. Declan wrapped his plaid tightly around Elayne, making sure to cover her riot of dark locks. They stepped out into the rain, Declan supporting her delicately as they approached the stables. James relished the sight of his daughter and her attentive husband before resigning himself to his dealings with his nephew, and then later his sister, who reminded him too much of Elayne.

Alistair rested on the floor of an empty chamber in the upper hall, indignation stamped on his face. He wallowed in the failure of his plans, of his position in the clan lost to an uncivilized outsider, of his embarrassment in front of his uncle. His dirtied plaid hung limply on his wearied frame, pooling around him in a sea of mockery. James almost felt bad for the lad, but then the acrimony over his actions resurfaced, and MacNally had to restrain his own hand from killing his nephew.

"Ye are fortunate Declan escorts Elayne back to *BlackBraes* as we speak, 'ere he should kill ye had he resided here this eve." MacNally's large frame filled the doorway. "I ken why ye perchance felt the need to take some of these actions. Ye are the nephew of the Laird, no' the son. Ye wanted power and esteem but lacked the opportunity for it. Ye see MacCollough as an interloper to the clan. Perchance ye even wanted to try and tame the wild Elayne MacNally. Regardless, ye made the wrong choice in attempting to kill my daughter."

James knelt by his silent nephew, leaning close to speak to him harshly.

"On the morrow, ye will leave this clan." Alistair snapped his head up, his mopish, tawny hair covering most of his eyes. He flicked his head to clear his vision, his hostile green eyes burning hatred toward his uncle. Had he any saliva left, he would have spat at James' face.

"Aye, ye are banished, my nephew. I dread telling your mother, who will certainly despise me for years, though I will assure her it was a superior option than your death, which is what Declan and I would prefer. Ye and your mother can thank Elayne for this largess. The self-same banshee ye attempted to kill is the very woman who saved your life."

James lightly slapped Alistair's cheek, then grasped his chin to force him to look James in the eye.

"Ye shall leave in the morn with naught but the plaid on your back and the coin in your purse. Ye will cross the Minch for the Isle of North Uist and dwell there, as best ye can with some distant MacDonald relatives on your father's side. And ye will never, so long as I walk this earth, set foot on mainland Scottish soil again."

He smacked Alistair once more for good measure, then departed the room.

***

Alistair had limited time once he learned of his fate. The Isles? If MacCollough's clan uncivilized, the Isles were the gateway to hell. He had heard the men were little more than wolves and women less than that. He shuddered at the thought.

Inside his sporran, he located a small, rolled parchment. Tearing off a portion, he crawled over to the hearth and dug through the old ash to find a stick of burnt wood. He shaved one side to a point against the stone and scratched a quick message to Donald Ross, sealing the missive as best he could.

Now he needed a fool to deliver it, and immediately Young James came to mind. The lad desired to do right, but it never seemed to work in his favor — he must share the same luck as Alistair. The catastrophe at Clan MacLeod with Elayne last summer only highlighted the lad's missteps. He was the perfect patsy to deliver the message. Alistair was sure to see the lad before his ship sailed as MacNally employed Young James in the most inane of tasks. Sending Alistair to the coast would surely fall under that banner. His bad luck had to take a turn after this.

And he was correct. The following morning, a few clansmen, wee James included, rode with Alistair to the ships in the early morning fog. His plaid barely kept him warm, and he dreaded the icy boat ride to the isles. The misty sun rose over damp hills of the glen behind them as they slogged through the mud to the coast. After a few hours, he maneuvered himself near James and signaled his attention.

"Lad," Alistair spoke in a loud whisper. "Lad, I need a favor. Ye ken I have aligned with Ross in hope to bring down the MacCollough?"

James barely nodded, uncertainty painted on his youthful face. His still-hairless chin set hard as Alistair continued.

"Lad, I dinna want any harm to come to Elayne, though ye may have heard different. But Ross may move against Clan MacCollough if he hears I have no' been successful in my attempt to stop the wedding. If he does, then our cousin Elayne is in danger. If ye care for your cousin, and your uncle, please send this message to Ross. Ye can read it if ye prefer. I try to tell him to no' move against the MacCollough. It could well be the message that saves Elayne's life."

Alistair waited to see if the lad would bite. Youthful indiscretion won out, just as Alistair planned. Young James fingered the missive from Alistair's bound hands and tucked it into his sporran. Alistair struggled not to smile as James wordlessly rode ahead.

Too soon they were at the coast and the small village of Gairloch. Ian MacNally spread around enough coin to find a small crew ready to sail over the frigid, rough Little Minch to Lochmaddy — the last bastion of human existence before the vast oceanic expanse to the east. Alistair sighed heavily as he was transferred, still bound and freezing, to the captain of the small brilinn. At least he wasn't sent to St. Kilda's, that barely populated rock in the middle of the sea, a minor silver lining amid the inhumanity of the past few days.

Alistair settled into the craft, pulled his damp plaid tighter around him against the icy spray of the sea, and watched the coast of Scotland proper disappear.

Chapter 18: Civil Disagreement

Clan MacCollough, BlackBraes

Bonnie and Senga met Elayne at the door and ushered her up the stairs to her chamber. The cold ride in the rain chilled her to the bone, and Bonnie helped their shivering lady undress as Senga warmed stones in the hearth. They put Elayne to bed with wrapped hot stones at her feet. Her eyes slammed shut as the women closed the door.

Declan managed to keep his outrage under wraps until he located Torin in the stables, wiping their horses dry with handfuls of hay. He approached the large man with a quiet step.

"Why did ye wait to tell me the lass had gone?" He spoke in a bitter, low voice, trying to keep his fists at his side. Torin did not face him and instead focused on brushing the horse.

"I had to hear from Bonnie that Elayne rode out on her own and did no' return for the noontide meal? After ye yourself prepared her horse to ride, knew when she left, and that she had not returned the horse?"

He seized Torin by the collar of his tunic, forcing Torin's eyes to his. Declan blistered with fury which he did not temper well. His whole body shook like lightening ready to strike, that much Torin could see.

"Why did ye do this?"

Torin dropped the soggy hay and stepped back from Declan, squaring off.

"I support ye in all ye do, Laird. But this marriage to Lady MacNally —"

"MacCollough. Lady MacCollough," Declan corrected sharply. Torin sighed in exasperation.

"Aye. But we dinna ken this woman, really. She is willful and overbearing and just had an unpleasant experience this summer. How do we ken she is no' in this marriage for what it can bring her? Hell, she and her father could nigh smell your desperation to bring what ye call 'civility' to this clan, and ye trust her?"

"Desperation?" Declan questioned.

"Aye. Do ye ken what the woman wants with the man who was second place to the MacLeod?"

Declan seethed. "Second place?"

"She needed something to redeem her reputation, and here ye were with open arms and this crazy idea because ye want something greater for this clan, and ye didn't even *ask* what we wanted."

Declan remained silent, Torin's words mollifying his own ire. 'Twas better to let the giant release his contentions.

"I am supposed to be your right hand, and ye did no' even consult me. And ye want me just to accept her, want us to accept her?"

"Aye, that I do," Declan finally answered. "At first, perchance 'twas desperation. With the Bruce, I saw what it was to have respect as a clan, to have allies instead of border clans who think us wild nuisances. To align with the MacNally's and have a strong willed woman like Elayne who could scare most clans people into action, I saw as an advantage. And perchance, aye, she was desperate for us as well."

"Her desperation almost makes her actions worse. We are not what she wanted. Who is to say she will remain loyal to our clan?"

"Thus far she had given me, us, *our clan,* no' reason to distrust her. All she has done for our clan is clean up *your* messes, make *your* food, and try to provide leadership as the Laird's wife. Why do ye question her loyalty?"

Declan rubbed his forehead, exasperated with his oldest friend. "As my seneschal, I hoped ye would understand what I am trying to do here. Ye have seen our clan, that we are no' the size or strength we used to be. Have ye looked at the parish records at the kirk?"

Torin's face screwed up in puzzlement. "What records?"

"The ones the priest keeps at the kirk — birth, death, marriage. The death records far outnumber the marriage and birth records. A clan that does not populate dies out, and I would no' have that for our clan. Or for you, Torin."

"Dinna bring me into this argument, Declan. Ye have no' right to speak of it."

"Aye, my old friend, that is true. But can ye deny children and growth of this clan for others? For me?"

"And what of that growth? Ye claim your wife is loyal. If such is the case, then why has she no' quickened yet? She

seems to be like the fairy folk, working magic against ye —
especially since the clan knows ye fucked her before ye were
wed —"

Declan's fist flew into Torin's face before Declan
realized he moved, his fury fueling his action. Torin caught
the punch on the side of his face, which threw him back into
the farrier's bench. Torin stumbled and readjusted himself,
rubbing at his bruised jaw. He then hurled himself at Declan,
his fist making contact with Declan's face, bloodying his nose.
Torin wrestled Declan to the ground, smashing his face again,
this time glancing the punch off the side of Declan's.
Wriggling to the left, Declan managed to move his knee up
under Torin's chest, chucking him onto his backside.

Declan scooted back to recline against one of the stalls,
shaking his head to clear it. Torin's punches landed like anvils
on his face, and Declan needed the moment to collect his wits
before speaking. Torin sat on the other side of the stables,
panting.

"I will leave ye here 'afore either of us say or do
something we regret," Declan told him. "When ye come back,
ye will apologize to me for your offenses to Elayne, and I will
apologize to ye for my offenses."

Declan struggled as he stood, gaining his footing as his
head spun, and stumbled out of the stables into the night rain.

Torin remained where he was and spat a wad of blood
onto the hay-covered ground.

***

When Declan entered his chamber, he found Elayne
sleeping deeply. He tiptoed around the room, undressing, then

186

slipping under the warm furs with her. Her steady breathing relaxed him, lulling him into a troubled sleep.

He awoke just before she did, dim light peeking from around the tapestry at the window. The sound of rainfall abated, but a wet chill still clung to the air. As he removed himself from the bed, he felt a hand on his arm. He turned back to Elayne, now awake and looking none too happy at his swollen, bloody face.

"Declan!" She sat up quickly and soupçon of pain crossed her face. She put one hand to her head and her other on his cheek. "What happened to your face?"

"Ooch, naught to worry ye, 'Layne."

"Naught to worry me? Are ye mad? Who did this to ye?"

Declan looked at his feet, ashamed that his conversation with Torin ended in blows.

"Who? A MacKenzie? Duncan? Torin?" Declan's eyes shifted at the last name, and Elayne grimaced in reply.

"Well, if 'twere Torin, ye are lucky to be alive," She observed flatly. "Now, will ye tell me what led him to use your face as pounded armor?"

"We could not find a meeting of the minds. I did no' leave 'afore anger got the best of me, so much of it 'twas my own fault."

"Ye should have asked Bonnie or Senga for a poultice. The swelling is quite bad, my Laird."

"Aye, I ken. I canna see too well out of my left eye, or breathe too well out of my nose."

He made an effort to grin at her, his face appearing even more misshapen. Elayne rose from the bed and stepped gingerly to the water basin, wetting a cloth and pressing it to his face. The chilled water relieved some pressure from the swelling as she wiped blood off his nose, mouth, and cheek.

"'Twould appear he pulled his punch. Ye still have your teeth, and your nose is no' broken. He must no' have been too angered at ye."

"Pulled his punches?" Declan squawked, his eyebrows high on his forehead. She laughed lightly at his reaction, rinsed the cloth, and continued her ministrations.

"Ye should apologize," she admonished.

"Aye," Declan agreed. "I plan on it as soon as we see each other again."

Declan clasped her around the waist and pulled her close. She lowered her face to kiss him gently on his battered lips, then he guided her back to bed.

"Ye should rest one day more, at the verra least. I will send Senga up with vittles to break your fast."

Elayne assented, already feeling worn from her small labors with Declan. She climbed back under the covers and closed her eyes. Declan silently left the chamber so as not to disturb her.

***

Two days later, Elayne resumed her normal schedule. She had heard whispers of the fight between Declan and Torin, and the castle gossip itself was a further testament to that disagreement. She joined the other lasses in the kitchens, noting the keep was in more disarray than it had been for the last month. In the kitchens, she found Bonnie and two of the other young women busying themselves with the midday meal.

"What happened to the hall?" she asked, nabbing a floury lump of dough to knead.

"What do ye think?" Bonnie responded, an edge in her voice.

"Are we no cleaning?"

"We did," Bonnie responded. "I think some of the men came back to dirty it on purpose. Many clansmen are no' pleased with the idea of being civilized."

"What men?" Shock spread on Elayne's face. It only took a few days to lose all her traction?

"Who do ye think?"

"Duncan? Torin? Certainly, nay, Ian or Hamish!"

"Nay, milady," Bonnie tossed the bread dough with ire, sending flour everywhere. "Duncan has been busy as of late," she gestured out the kitchen door to the gardens.

Bonnie continued speaking as Elayne peeked her head out the door, leaving flour fingerprints on the stone. Duncan walked the gardens with Kaleigh, holding a large basket of vegetables and greens. Elayne smiled to herself — *leave it to the gentler sex to calm the savage beasts,* she thought.

"Torin has been noticeably absent, but the other clansmen are wreaking havoc on the clan on his behalf. Laird MacCollough is busy enough trying to keep the tenants, stables, and lands in order. I did no' want to concern him with the keep." She paused in her assault on the bread dough, meeting Elayne's eyes. "Perchance Torin may be a position to accept an olive branch from his Laird's recovering wife to make everything right?"

Elayne stood still in the middle of the kitchen, flicking her eyes from Bonnie to the kitchen door to the bread, evaluating Bonnie's words. Deciding to action, she wiped Bonnie's flour mess from her hands.

"Nay, ye are correct." Elayne lay her hand on Bonnie's sleeve. "Bonnie, ye are a confidant for certain. We should no' worry Declan with such minor concerns. Gather Kaleigh, and have Duncan enlist a few men to help ye straighten the hall," she called over her shoulder as she exited.

She walked stiffly and made her way through the misty air to the stables. Not finding Torin with the horses, she marched behind the stables to Torin's croft, rapping at his wooden door. Hearing grumbling from inside, she stepped back as Torin flung open the door. His immense size filled the doorway.

"What do ye want?" he asked coarsely. Animosity covered him in a dark cloak.

"Well, that is no' quite the welcome I anticipated," she responded.

Torin didn't answer but glared at her from under his bushy chestnut brows.

"May I come in?" she asked, trying to keep her voice light.

"Nay."

She pursed her lips together. "Then will ye join me in the fine Scottish air out here?" She gestured to a bench adjacent to the cottage.

He grumbled again, but tramped over to the bench, sitting heavily. She perched on the remaining edge of the bench, resting her back against the wall.

"I ken ye dinna care for me overmuch," she began. Torin "harrumphed" in response. "But I think we need to come to a union, no' for me but for Declan."

She turned to Torin, placing her hand on his. "I ken ye dinna trust me. I am trying my best to show ye that I am no' the conniving harpy my reputation has presented. Aye, my previous actions earlier this year bordered on madness, yet I used my shame for growth. I saw my marriage to MacCollough as an opportunity, aye," she paused as Torin grumbled again.

"But no' as an opportunist. Instead, as a chance to do something great, maybe find someone to care about and who can care for me. Perchance to even disabuse the Highlands of my miserable notoriety. I think I have found that here. I ken many of ye dinna want to change your ways, but MacCollough has large dreams. If I can help him achieve those dreams, I will. Can ye understand my motives here?"

Torin remained silent. Elayne took his reticence favorably as he no longer grumbled.

"For the sake of your lifelong friendship with Declan," she continued, " can ye understand his motives, and perchance support him? Even if it means trusting me just a bit? If ye can trust me, I will prove to ye that I am worthy of that trust. Can ye do it for Declan and his desires for the clan?"

"I dinna agree with what he wants for the clan. Who is to care if we are civilized or nay?"

Elayne pondered before speaking, trying to understand clan life from Torin's perspective. "I ken your feelings. Change is frightening. Yet, would ye rather have allies at your back if something goes awry with the English or the lowland clans? To maintain the loyalty to the king? Declan's idea for civility means respect from other clans. And it means growth of the MacColloughs. Surely he told ye of the lower number of clansmen over the last half century?"

Torin nodded imperceptibly. "Aye. I looked at the parish records. It is as he said. We are nearly half what we used to be." Torin hated to admit it.

"I am glad that ye looked for yourself. Then ye will no' have doubt about my words. Without civility, men will nay want their lasses to wed into the clan, and the numbers will continue to falter, the clan will weaken. And what of ye, Torin? Do ye nay want a woman —"

"Dinna speak of a woman to me," Torin interrupted, his voice gruff.

Elayne watched him from the corner of her eye, remaining quiet to allow him to speak his peace. When Torin spoke again, his tone was slow and pained.

"I had a woman — we were hand fast, ye ken? — and she carried my babe, but then the babe stopped growing. My woman sickened and died."

Elayne again gave him a moment of silence out of respect for his dead love.

"That I ken." Her words were soft. "It leaves a scar on your heart, long and jagged. Mayhap it is not ready to heal, and that is acceptable. The heart needs whatever time it takes to heal. Fortunately, when scars form, we are stronger for it. As a warrior, ye ken this well. And once the heart is well healed, it will be strong enough to open at the right moment with the right woman."

"And what are ye doing to grow the numbers of the clan?" Torin bit out, accusingly. "Ye have no' quickened yet with the Laird's child. Surely ye are no' trying to prevent it?"

Elayne blushed at his words, a rare occurrence for her. While a spike of anger at the suggestion lit through her, if she wanted to build his trust, she knew the time to bond with Torin was upon her.

"Ye ken I am an only child, aye?" she began.

Torin shifted toward her. "Aye."

"Well, my mother was slow to quicken, and lost a babe 'afore she had me. She quickened once more after me, but lost the babe, then died shortly after. From heartbreak, my father claims. As a motherless daughter, I ken your fear of love. I also ken I may be slow to quicken as well, as my mother was. 'Tis nay certain, but Senga says it sometimes happens that way." Elayne stared straight ahead, controlling her emotions with her uncompromising demeanor.

"I did no' ken. My apologies, milady."

Elayne waved her hand, dismissing the sentiment. She turned and patted Torin's hand, sensing perhaps they had made a breakthrough.

"Can we come to a reconciliation, then? Ye dinna have to like me, but can we work together for Declan and the clan as a whole?"

Torin nodded. "Aye, milady. We can."

Elayne stood and placed her hand on Torin's rough beard, peering close into his eyes.

"I thank ye, Torin."

She stepped away from the bench, marching back toward the keep, disappearing in the foggy light of day.

Chapter 19: Megalomania

Clan Ross, Balnagown Castle, near Cromarty Firth

Young James' arrived at clan Ross the day after Alistair's boat departed for the Isles — *Good riddance to bad rubbish,* Young James intoned — stopping 'afore the road to the Castle Ross, fingering the parchment Alistair had put into his safekeeping. Opening the sepia paper, he reread the message, trying to decipher the words for any manner of code. After Alistair's antics regarding Elayne, doubt tickled Young James' mind. His distant cousin had a long history of buffoonery, and Young James hesitated to trust Alistair's intentions. Surely the message could no' be as simple as it read? Try as he may, Young James could not discern any mal-intent in the brief missive.

Laird Donald Ross,
The Endeavor is at an end. The Lass is trule Wed to the
MacCollough, and they are bringing stability to an Unstable
clan.
Alistair Lee MacNally

The scrawled message was too simple, too short.
Perchance 'twas only due to the size of the parchment?
Alistair must have torn it from a larger piece, given the jagged
edge at the bottom. That answer seemed too easy, but reading
the missive once more, Young James could find no treasonous
message; at worst the words did nothing more than let Ross
know that Alistair was done with his preoccupation of
MacCollough and his new wife.

At best, perchance the message would do more good.
Alistair's conclusive words could temper Ross' continued
movements against the Bruce and Scotland, which may assure
life at Clan MacNally.

Young James looked to the east, covering his eyes as
he faced the rising sun and the route to Clan Ross. The bright
sun struggling to warm the chill off the morning climbed high,
an omen of fortune for Scotland. James made up his mind and
continued on eastward into the blinding light of sunrise.

Castle Ross emerged from the mossy foothills, an
imposing dark fortress against the serene beauty of the
surrounding flora. Young James' steed picked its way across
the rocky path to the keep, as though the horse dreaded this
visit as much as Young James. Ross' greed for power under
the English crown was no secret in the Highlands, considering
his strong connections to the lowlands, but these ideas made
Young James dizzy. He did not have a mind for politics,
lacking diplomacy himself. The intricacies of politicking were

often lost on him. His desire to avoid politics, mayhap extend peace for Scotland in the north, confirmed his decision to deliver Alistair's message.

Two armed Ross clansmen met Young James at the gate, waving him off his horse. He slid down and surrendered the tired horse to them, asking after Donald Ross as third clansman led Young James into the depths of the imposing stone structure.

"Wait here," the man grumbled, leaving James and disappearing into bowels of the keep.

Laird Ross appeared soon after, his brow furrowed at the sight of Young James.

"Gillivry says ye are here with a message from Alistair MacNally? Did he send ye?"

"Of a sort," Young James stammered, his unease rising as bile in his throat. "The MacNally nephew has been banished to the Isles for crimes against MacNally's daughter. Alistair requested I deliver this missive directly to ye."

Young James held out the rolled parchment. Ross snatched it from his grip.

"Did ye read it?" he growled. Young James nodded.

"Aye. The lad indicated I should do so to ensure he was not trying to plot further against his clan. The message is brief and direct."

Ross unfurled the parchment, squinting to read the scrawl on the paper. His eyes cut to Young James and back to the message.

"Ye are correct, lad. This missive is direct. To ease your mind, the only suggestion is that we refrain from any further action on Clan MacCollough. I find this to be sage advice."

Relief visibly flooded Young James' body. He had not realized he had been clenching his chest, and at Ross' words the strain released. Ross snorted at Young James' discomfort, clapping a narrow hand on the lad's shoulder.

"Would ye like to stay and rest a bit, lad? 'Twas a long ride from the coast, to be sure. Ye can take a meal here, rest your horse, then ride for MacNally after ye repose?" Ross' eyebrow rose at the question, and Young James, overwrought from his dealings with Alistair and his travels to clan Ross, accepted the offer.

Donald Ross waved his hand and a kitchen maid materialized, a steaming bowl wrapped in a cloth clutched in her dainty hands. Ross seated Young James at the table. The maid returned to the kitchens to bring out milk, honey, and mead, but Young James barely noticed as he dug into his porridge. Ross excused himself, signaling for Gillivry to follow as he exited the hall.

***

The heat of the fire in Donald's solar permeated the room with an oppressive fever that matched the demeanor of Donald Ross himself. The diminutive Laird paced the length of the fur laid before the hearth as he fanned the air with the mysterious parchment. Gillivry feared the MacNally lad could hear Ross' vile lamentations and kept flicking his head over his shoulder, as though he could see through the hefty door. He initially hoped the Laird would eventually pace near the window and pull the tapestry aside and allow cooler air to relieve the perspiration dripping down his back, but considering Ross' exclamations about MacNally, he was grateful for the sweltering, enclosed room.

"The lad is the most miserable excuse for a man in Scotland! How can he fail in so many different ways?"

Gillivry wisely kept his own thoughts to himself. Ross paused by the writing desk and collapsed into the chair, dropping the message onto the desktop. He tapped it with his bony finger and turned his glaring gaze to his clansman.

"But the lad is no' completely useless, eh, Gill?" His lips curled into a smirk, contorting his whole face into a mask of grotesque lunacy. "His words may hide his true intentions. He did manage to send us a valuable piece of information. Do ye ken what that is, Gill?"

Shaking his head, Gillivry maneuvered by the window to move the tapestry and permit the outside air to refresh the suffocating room. The invigorating air wafted over him, helping him focus on Ross and his intrigues. But no amount of fresh air would help cool the heat in his head from Ross' machinations. The man was singularly focused, and dread crept into Gillivry to hear Ross speak on what amounted to treason in a Scotland still ruled by the Bruce. What began as a way to prevent any collusion between the MacCollough and the Bruce and find the Bruce through MacCollough had grown into something more sinister and fanatic as Donald Ross' compulsion to destroy the Bruce and his allies became irrationally focused on Declan MacCollough.

"This," Ross tapped the paper again with his sweaty finger, "is a message only I would decipher. While he makes it seem that any attempt on Elayne would no' be fruitful. But the next line," his smirk grew into a grin, "tells me that MacCollough can be had. If we can separate the two, get MacCollough off his own land perchance, the clan will no' come to the aid of Elayne. We can destroy the keep, using his bride as leverage to force his hand regarding the Bruce. Then we dispose of the MacCollough, and the inconstant clan will dissolve completely. And thus will be the end of Clan MacCollough. Fair retribution for the one who helped the traitorous Bruce escape and retain his crown on Scotland."

His wiry fist pounded the desk, sending his parchment quill flying. Gillivry retrieved the quill from the floor, returning the brown fluff to its place on the desk. His mind reeled at the recent change in his Laird; what had been a side interest in perhaps holding MacCollough accountable for the Bruce's escape from Comyn's allies had intensified into a maniacal obsession with the man and the downfall of his backward, inconsequential clan, and Scotland as a whole. Gillivry feared where Ross' mania would lead them. The root of these compulsions seemed to be the wayward Alistair MacNally, and to Gillivry, the MacNally nephew's exile across the sea was a just punishment.

Ross placed his face near Gillivry's, who recoiled at the odor of ale and haddock of the midday meal on Ross breath.

"We have 'im, Gill," he sneered, pushing Gillivry toward the door. "I ken how we will achieve this. Get ye gone. Retrieve Mac and Seamus. We have some work to do here."

Chapter 20: Come Together

Torin found Declan not far from the stable, pitchfork in hand, chucking hay into a small cart. The mist had parted, rays of sunlight cut through the cool Highland mist, and a fine layer of sweat and grime covered his best friend.

He took a moment to admire Declan. This man had so much working against him, even his clansmen and seneschal, yet he still worked for all of them, gave himself to a possibly loveless marriage for them. And what had Torin and the others done to thank him? Nothing. Nay, worse than nothing; he and the others conspired to antagonize his efforts. *What a fine betrayal*, Torin thought, and realized that perchance he evaded serious consequences from his Laird, with only a punch to the face for his behavior. This apology would take all of Torin's fortitude, but it was a well-deserved apology. Torin had much to atone for with his Laird.

Declan's grunting and the sound of the pitchfork clanging off the cart covered Torin's footsteps, and Torin exaggeratedly cleared his throat to gain Declan's attention. Declan threw the pitchfork atop the cart and spun on his heel to face his seneschal. He had an inkling of why Torin stood before him, large as he was but still resembling a sheepish lad.

Torin cleared his throat again, this time to prepare himself — apologies did not come easy.

"My Laird," he began. "I owe ye an apology for my words and behavior earlier regarding your wife. Ye love her, and I overstepped my bounds. I hope ye can forgive me."

For Declan, the apology was arbitrary; he had already forgiven Torin before he left the barn the day of the fight. He knew his dear friend's words came from a place of concern, but he needed Torin to understand. This apology was that moment.

However, Torin's use of the word "love" disrupted Declan's thoughts. He liked and cared for his wife, was passionate for her, but love? Would he ever feel love for his strange wife? He was uncertain she would ever love him, and admitting such to himself broke him a little. They had never discussed love, only how they mutually benefited each other, and Declan did not know how to begin that conversation with Elayne.

Moved by the weight of Torin's words, Declan embraced his friend, clasping him hard around his back. Torin stood stoically and regarded Declan with a quizzical expression.

"And I owe ye an apology, Torin. Ye only have mine and the clan's best interests at heart, and I should nay judge ye too harshly."

Torin clapped Declan on the shoulder, nearly knocking Declan off his feet.

"From this moment forward, we must present a united front. I will endeavor to keep ye abreast of my actions and decisions, if ye swear the same. It won't always happen in such a way, but we must trust in the other. Can ye swear that loyalty to me? And to Lady Elayne?"

Torin grumbled at that last request, rolling his eyes. "Aye," he answered with difficulty. "But I willna say I like it."

Declan lifted the pitchfork from the cart and waved it at Torin. "Get ye busy in the stables 'afore I have him shoveling hay wi' me here."

***

By the time Declan found an uninterrupted moment with Elayne, it was late in the evening, well after the eve tide meal. He took care not to press her while she recovered from her head injury, but today she reappeared in the hall, once again taking up the mantle as the Lady of the Manor in her most aggressive manner possible. He did not doubt that Torin's apology today resulted from Elayne's force of will.

She was clad in only her shift when he entered their chambers. Elayne's dark hair fell down her back in burnished shades of chestnut, sorrel, and copper as she brushed the long locks. The cool, almost cold air made her nipples poke against the cloth, and he hardened at the sight of her.

"Wife, it has been days since I have had ye," he said, pulling her up from the low stool and carrying her to the bed. Kissing her full on the lips, he pulled her shift down, exposing her breasts, licking one pink tip then the other. She cradled his head, purring like a contented cat at the shivers his tongue created.

"I dinna think I can be gentle with ye tonight," he admitted, and she responded by pulling his head back to her breasts. His tongue flicked along each nipple, then lathed between her swollen mounds to her belly, then lower to her nether lips, tugging her shift down as he went.

His fingers followed his tongue, her skin tingling with excitement. Her desire for this man heightened the more he touched her, and when he used his fingertips to spread her nether lips apart and licked between them, she gasped.

"My Laird!" she exclaimed, her hips rising.

He silently pressed Elayne back on the bed with one hand, his mouth otherwise occupied. He continued using his tongue on her most private parts, licking the folds of her intimate areas with the tip. His tongue probed inside her, then licked back up to the button that sent rivulets of euphoria buzzing through her entire being. He then sucked on it, and she cried out in ecstasy as her whole body quivered. Probing inside her with a finger, he felt her wetness and almost spilled his seed under his kilt. It had been too long since he bedded his wife, and he needed her. *Now.*

Declan ripped off his tartan and rose over her, his thick cock entering her hard and fast. She cried out again as he sheathed his cock to the hilt, pressing as deeply as possible, and it still wasn't deep enough for him. He intended to move slowly, prolonging their pleasure, but his manhood did not agree, and he began to ride her harder and faster, his breath matching his pace. Her hips shifted to meet his, tremors of pleasure rippling through her. She twined her fingers into his hair, gripping him as her orgasm consumed her.

He thrusted as his wife cried out. Declan's own groans started deep in this throat, and he cried out to Elayne and God as he came over and over, pulsing inside her, filling her with his seed. He held himself above her for a moment, enjoying his orgasm and the sensation of her fingertips trailing across his chest. Then he finished and collapsed next to her. His breathing filled her ears as she recovered, a film of passionate exertion covering them both.

"Ye were needy tonight, husband," she told him as she stroked his hair. He placed his head on her breast and savored her touch.

"Aye, wife. 'Tis been far too long without ye."

She laughed at him. "Claims the man who told me he was celibate for nigh a year 'afore our first bedding."

His body shook as he joined her laughter. "Well, I grew accustomed to finer things."

Declan sat up, feeling more full of energy now that his cock was spent. He gazed into her eyes and ran his fingers through her hair.

"I rudely interrupted your ablutions. Can I finish helping ye brush your hair?"

She purred at the idea. "Ooch, aye. That would be divine." She nodded her head toward the hearth. "My brush is on the mantle."

A wooden box, similar to her wedding gift to him only with a fleur-de-lis carved on the lid, sat next to the brush. A small piece of parchment poked out from the lid, and he recalled her words when she gifted him the falcon-carved box on their wedding day: *if ye have documents or the like that ye want to keep from prying eyes.* Glancing over his shoulder, he saw Elayne sprawled on the bed like a sultry cat, her eyes closed, and he reached for the parchment. He cursed himself for being nosy but justified his curiosity with the fact that, as her husband, he should know all that happened in his lands. He was unprepared, however, for the message he read.

Lady Elayne MacNally MacCollough,

Your desire to Find your Husband's Mother is a Noble one. Unfortunately, none of our Clan have Knowledge of any Davina MacKenzie MacCollough. I shall inquire elsewhere and send a Message if I learn of her Location.

Your most Humble Servant,
Sister Mary Ellen Argyll

Declan recoiled in turmoil. His pride that his wife was so invested in his life and his history was tainted by anger of her taking such a step without his knowledge, to find this woman who abandoned him. Having locked those aching emotions away for so long, to read a reference to his mother in his wife's belongings raised his ire. Uncertain how to respond, he grabbed his claymore and wrapped his plaid around his hips as he opened the chamber door.

"Declan?" Elayne asked, when she heard the door hinges squeak, only to receive a slammed door in response.

***

The misty autumn evening prickled Declan's skin as he heaved his sword over his head. Using a set of movements — overhead, side thrust, upward thrust — he worked through his vexation at his wife's actions. He knew she had a willful side, accepted it even, but this time her actions targeted him.

As he swung his claymore, his thoughts ran over his appalling familial relationships and his vexation that Elayne could not understand why he desired to remain separate from his past. Her mother did not willingly leave her; her father was not a monster. She could not conceive of the hurt that comes from such a childhood, or the pain of the reminder when he saw her letters.

In this moment, the loudmouth willfulness and household management she brought to him and the clan for him fell away in frustration at her betrayal. Petty? Perchance. But why did she not tell him of her intentions? To what end was her pursuit of his estranged mother? That bruised part of him he thought he locked away surfaced because of Elayne's actions. He hacked at the tree with all the strength and aggression flowing with the blood in his veins.

Working his body in the moonlit harvest evening, however, did little to calm his fevered mind. His bare skin became drenched in sweat as he parried and thrust closer to a laurel, hacking the poor tree until bark fell from its trunk.

"It will nay recover if ye continue with your attack," Elayne's voice carried on the night air.

She stood near the edge of the garden, moonlight shining bronze reflections in her hair. Wrapped in a plaid she took off the bed, she stood closed and stoic, much like when she first came to *BlackBraes*. Declan halted his movements, the veins in his arms pulsing as he clenched his sword hilt but did not respond.

"My Laird, will ye tell me why ye left our bedchamber so abruptly?"

He kept his back toward her, fondling the hilt of his blade.

"I can see why some dinna care for ye, Lady 'Layne."

His words burned in her head and heart. Until this night, they worked so well together, Elayne could almost imagine her reputation was not well-earned, that her husband respected her eccentricities. To hear him say otherwise was a blow, and she did not reply.

"Ye are willful, and ye take action ye often ought not take. Like looking for a woman who is dead to me."

Half-dressed in the open air, he appeared the wounded warrior his broken voice painted. Declan spun on his heel, his furred chest prickling in the air, his hair in wild array. His body glistened with perspiration, illuminating the chiseled curves of his heaving chest. Her eyes followed his muscles to the definition of his waist where his tartan dipped low and his golden hairs flowed in a trail under his kilt. Passions fought within her as she gazed upon his form that rivaled the gods of old. That she could feel both a heated passion and an angry passion for him at once mystified her.

"Well, then, my husband, 'twould appear we are well-met," she bit out.

"What do ye mean by that?"

"I ken my reputation as a willful harpy who always must have her way. I have grown accustomed to it, accepted it. Ye even welcomed that iron will when ye welcomed me into your home and wedded me. But ye dinna see that ye are cut from the same cloth."

Declan's eyebrows furrowed. "What —?"

She held up a slender hand to silence him. Her will won out, and his jaw snapped shut.

"Did ye not have your will imposed on the whole of the clan when ye decided they were too wild? That ye wanted to be an esteemed clan in the eyes of the king? Did ye ask anyone, even your man Torin, what he wanted? Nay, your will was the only one that mattered, so much so that ye brought me, someone many in your clan despised, and commanded them to respect me. Ye do what ye want, when ye want, yet ye fault me for the same crime? 'Tis the soup pot naming the kettle black."

He lifted his rigid chest and inhaled sharply. Her words stung him to the quick, but years of discretion, first with his father, then with the king, tempered his response. One more deep breath passed through him before he replied.

"I ken your words. Ye may be correct. We both share a force of will which can cause much discontent." He ran his fingers through his hair, making it stand on end. "Ye should no' have written after her," he told her in a softer voice. "My past is a wound I have since sewn up, and I no longer wish to engage."

He hung his head, stepping closer to Elayne. His rage had burned hot and also burned out just as quickly once his wife was in his view. In a moment of clarity, he understood she was trying to help, unaware of the depth of his tormented youth. Declan's anger came from a dark pit of childhood hurt, and Elayne received the brunt of that hurt. His words stung her, the impassable look on her face spoke more than words, and he needed to assuage that pain.

"I apologize, my wife. My words came from anger, and I did not intend them."

"Nay, ye did, husband," she responded, the lilt of her voice surprisingly soft. "As I did my words. But I ken why ye spoke them. I was unaware of the extent of injury your mother caused, even after your tale of her. I did no' put myself in your position, where memories of childhood perchance are painful. My childhood was not, and if I had the chance to see my mam again, I would take every opportunity to do so. I should nay have put that presumption on ye."

Her willful traits had become familiar to him; he adopted those when he cleaved to her in marriage, knowing full well that her fractiousness might one day impact on him. Declan stabbed his sword into the damp, spongy ground, reaching for Elayne. She did not move forward (*always stubborn!* Declan thought), but she did not step away when he embraced her, warming her through her plaid. These last few days had tried his sensibilities as a man, as a Laird, as a husband. He was uncertain how many more misunderstandings he could take. Taking a wife was an effort for which he was not well prepared.

"We may come from different places, my 'Layne, but our hearts are stout. I can see why ye took the actions ye did, and I should no' fault ye for them."

The intensity in her eyes as she narrowed them at Declan colored her next words. "Should I continue my search for your mam, then?"

Declan could not answer, instead lifting his gaze to the heavens, as though he hoped God Himself would answer that question for him. Elayne took his meaning.

"Ooch, aye, then. I will destroy my correspondences when they arrive. I will no' be the cause of more pain for ye," she paused, "if I can avoid it."

He had to chuckle at her final words, encircling her in his strong embrace, his cooling sweat leaving a film on her cape. Elayne lifted her plaid, trying to cover him from the night air, and Declan grabbed the cloth to secure it around the two of them, trying to protect them from all the ills of the day.

"Look at us, my love," he told her. "Down here in the cold, wet garden, freezing and fighting, when, had we both been less bull-headed, we would still be abed, naked, and warm."

He stepped from the tepid warmth of the plaid, grasped Elayne's hand, and escorted her back into the keep to their chambers. Elayne followed, her mind spinning. *My love,* he had said. Was it an endearment, or did he mean something more?

While his harsh earlier words echoed in her mind, could it be possible, for as much as she knew herself to be a brash harpy, a supposedly unlovable woman, that she found someone to love her?

Chapter 21: Hope Springs Eternal

Bonnie, Elayne, and the kitchen maids toiled feverishly in the kitchen, bubbling pots of steamed fruits and vegetables contributing to the oppressive heat as they stored the boiled food in ceramic pots under wax seals. They needed to hasten, and even with the doors to the kitchens open wide, their shifts clung damply to their skin, their hair sopping from the effort of completing the task.

"Shall I retrieve the next basket from the gardens?" Bonnie asked of Elayne.

As the new castle chatelaine, she should not have to ask. The oddity of asking for permission instead of just retrieving the basket prompted Elayne to flick her eyes to the door. She could just see Hamish as he labored at the end of the garden, pulling more vegetables for storage. He had removed his tunic, and his fair back glistened in the pale sun. A smile tugged at Elayne's mouth in amusement, and she licked her lips to hide her expression.

"Aye and take a moment to catch your breath and cool yourself from this heat. We dinna want ye passing out 'afore we finish."

Elayne took the stirring spoon from her, booting Bonnie to the side with a sway of her sweat-soaked hips. Bonnie did not hesitate and raced for the gardens, whether more for the fresh air or the man digging in the dirt, Elayne could not guess.

The muscles under the skin of Hamish's pale backside flexed as he dug in the dirt with a small spade, releasing the vegetables from their resting spots. Turnips erupted from the earth, their purple dermis reflecting the sunlight, while late season peas dangled on their vines, awaiting a quick tug. Hamish grabbed several turnips by their teeming green stalks, flinging them into a half-full basket. When he glimpsed Bonnie sauntering down the path between plantings, he stood tall, stretching his back, his slender muscles twitching with exertion.

"Good day to ye, Hamish." She gave him a small wave as she pulled at her shift, trying to force the refreshing outside air against her skin. The back of her neck, where her hair drooped, was already drying, and she was grateful for the reprieve from the sweltering kitchens.

"And to ye, miss," Hamish responded, flashing shockingly white teeth in a smile that lit up his face like sunrise. That smile first caught Bonnie's attention when she came to castle MacCollough and kept her returning to his company. Regardless of his work, he always shared a bright smile with her, one that reached his twinkling eyes and melted her insides.

"The lady needs more vegetable for the storage pots. Ye have dug up most of the gardens, but there are still more? I see ye are still digging?" She gestured to the dirt-caked spade in his right hand.

"Ooch, aye. Did ye ken turnips will grow where ever they planted? They want to grow nigh to the woods! These are fall turnips, so they will be more hardy than summer ones and should keep well for the winter, so I'm trying to get them all up."

"How do ye ken so much about turnips?" Bonnie plucked some of the upturned turnips and tossed them in the nearby basket.

"My da. He had four sons, and one of us had to help mother in the gardens. They selected me. As it worked out, I have a bit of talent for agriculture and enjoyed having my hands in the dirt."

He held out his soiled hand as evidence, his nails nearly black with fresh earth. Bonnie took his hand in both of hers, brushing at the loose dirt.

"Too bad I dinna care for turnips overmuch," she told him, her nose scrunched up in distaste. "Well, my mam did say a little dirt nay hurt anyone." She turned her face up to his, her eyes crinkling as she played coy.

"And we do have peas," he joked. "May I help ye bring the baskets to the kitchens?" he asked, not removing his hand from hers quite yet.

"Ooch, aye, not that ye would want to. It's like the de'il himself has set up house of hellfire in the kitchens!"

"Well, I think we should walk slowly, to bide our time 'afore entering the kitchens of hell."

Bonnie laughed out loud, tucking the smaller of the two baskets under her arm. Hamish scooped the larger basket into his arm and ushered Bonnie back to the kitchens.

Elayne glanced to the kitchen door as they returned. Evidently, Hamish preferred blondes, just not the one she expected. Her heart swelled seeing the pair engaging comfortably, a look of joy upon both their faces. Elayne's marriage may have been one of convenience and opportunity for both herself and the Laird, but happiness greeted most of her days since meeting Declan, and she wanted that for the lasses under her province. She could now confirm the shared goal of growing and strengthening the whole of the clan was well underway — and thus she could forgive Bonnie's slow gait back to the inferno of the kitchens.

***

Elayne's excitement over her observations in the kitchen erupted when Declan entered the chamber that evening. Her scribblings slid to the floor as Elayne rose from her writing table in a sweep of plaid, rushing to Declan before he fully closed the door.

"Wife! What is this?"

She grabbed his hands, pulling him off his feet and all but shoving him onto the bed. Lifting her skirt, she straddled him, her face alight with merriment.

"Husband, our plan has commenced!" she exclaimed like a giddy little girl. Declan could not stop from smiling up at her.

"What conniving are ye raving about?" he asked.

"Bringing women to the keep. Ye feared the clan would not repopulate, that it lost far more numbers in the last decades than it gained. We have started to correct that ill!"

Declan pushed himself up on his elbows, his face against Elayne's full breasts, but his quizzical eyes were on her face only.

"What do ye mean, 'Layne?"

She pushed him back down on the bed, leaning over him so her dark hair formed a private curtain around them. Her teeth glinted in the dim light.

"I have it on good authority," she spoke in a solemn tone, "that two women, maybe more, have a love interest each with a MacCollough man."

Declan's eyes widened at this women's gossip, and the smirk that came to Elayne's face contradicted her serious speech.

"Which women?" Declan sounded like a nosy lass. "Which men? Nay Torin?" he suggested.

Elayne's effervescent mood fell a bit. "Nay, my husband. Torin has many scars on his heart, and it may well be awhile 'afore he is ready to love again. However," her face brightened again as she shared her news, "one of the men is Duncan."

"Duncan!" Declan surged forward and bumped his face into Elayne's breasts. She giggled and shoved him back down.

"Husband! Ye must behave until I tell ye *all* the news. Aye, the austere Duncan himself. Bonnie is a fair informant, and she has confided in me that the previously aloof Duncan has found the bonny Kaleigh MacKenzie to his liking." Elayne wagged her eyebrows at Declan.

"Ugh, MacKenzie?" He flung a hand over his eyes in mock indignation. Elayne giggled again.

"There is more, husband!"

"Ooch, my 'Layne, I dinna think I can take much more."

"Ye ken young Hamish, he of the gardens?"

"Aye?"

"Well," Elayne drew out, playing with Declan's patience. "Bonnie could nigh leave the kitchens quick enough to join Hamish in the gardens."

"Bonnie, our chatelaine?" Declan's eyes nearly popped out of his sockets. Elayne nodded.

"The same one," she proclaimed. "If these encounters bode well, perchance we shall have more weddings verra soon."

Declan's mind reeled in disbelief. A few scant months ago, the hope for his clan's future was unscalable mountain, and now it was a molehill. His dream of growing his clan to one that would make the Bruce proud was within his reach. He had his wife to thank for much of this success, he knew.

"Ye seem overly joyous, my love," he said. Once again noting his word choice, she let it pass and reached her hand below his waist to the bulge under his plaid.

"I would think we need to celebrate, my husband," she said in a husky voice, kissing him full on the lips.

Chapter 22: Fallen Angels

Sunrise came slow to Clan MacCollough as Declan walked toward the John the Smithy, anticipating the need for additional cutlery as winter came and more clansmen and women ate at the keep. The MacCollough gardens had been abundant this summer and fall, ensuring anyone lacking vittles for the winter would eat. Declan also needed arrow tips for the late fall hunts to fill the larder with meats before the weather changed.

John had just begun to fill the water pail when Declan stepped into the entry, which dwarfed against the giant who was John. His hair touched the top of the domed ceiling, and the bellow was a child's toy in John's hands. The fire in forge roared to life as he worked the bellows, prepping his work area.

"My Laird!" John's voice boomed larger than the man himself. "What brings ye here this day?"

Declan presented his list to John, emphasizing the need for expediency, when Torin burst in, sweaty and breathless.

"Declan," he panted. "Please, ye must come now."

Declan bowed to John, who returned to his work at the forge. Declan followed Torin outside, grabbing the man's hauberk.

"What ails ye, man? Have ye gone daft?"

"Declan," Torin began, his voice low. "We must go to the kirk now. I have Duncan there already."

Torin's urgency curbed any further questions as they marched to the church. Duncan's fierce stance at the doors did not inspire hope as to what he should find inside. They entered the sanctuary, and Declan's eyes watered as the foetid smell of decay assaulted his senses. He blocked his nose with his sleeve as they advanced through the sanctuary until they arrived at the first pew, where the body of the priest reclined on the bench.

He could be sleeping if it were not for the sword run through his belly, a swath of gray fabric around the exposed hilt. What blood Declan could see had congealed days ago into viscous crimson puddles on the priest's chest and below him on the stone floor. Nothing appeared out of place or disrupted. He found no other marks with his cursory glance over the body, suggesting theft or torture were not motives. The priest appeared to be killed for the sheer pleasure of killing. Crossing himself, Declan fingered the fabric, and faced Torin.

"This plaid? The sword? Who is responsible for this atrocity?"

"I ken this plaid. 'Tis clan Ross," Torin answered.

"Ross?" Declan responded disbelieving.

"They align with Comyn," he explained. "Perchance they are angered at your relationship with the Bruce? For all

218

we know, they aligned with Elayne's cousin, prompting his mad behaviors. 'Twould seem this is a message?"

"A message? Of what?"

"There's more."

The crucifix set in the window cast its shadow down on the decaying priest, as though Christ himself protected the man in death. Declan could not tear his gaze away. What more could there be? What could rival the assassination of such a devoted man of God?

"What more?" Declan whispered harshly.

"The old widower, Greer MacCollough."

"Elayne went to aid him the day she went missing. What of the man? Does he ken who committed this grievous act?"

"If he does, he is not telling," Torin responded in cryptic tones. "The priest here was also aiding the man, ye ken?"

"Aye, every few days or so," said Declan, his brows drew together.

"Come with me," Torin sighed. Declan's chest tightened as they left the priest's body under the cautious eye of Duncan.

They arrived at Greer's croft, and the heavy silence that weighed over the cottage spoke tones loud enough for Declan to hear.

"Nay," he breathed.

"Aye," Torin whispered back as they entered. "Since the priest has been dead for nigh on three days, 'twas over three days since anyone checked on old Greer. I suspect the poor man died a day ago."

The odor in the small croft was more manageable than the stench in the church, but the smell of a dead body always disturbed the senses. Declan once again covered his nose, crouching near the body sprawled on the bedding at the rear wall. Filth covered every surface, and Declan had a moment of deep respect for his wife, who ventured here of her own volition for no other reason than to care for a dirty, sick man. With no one else to care for him for the last several days, the need for food, water, and care wreaked havoc on his old bones. His body appeared ravaged by illness.

The man was elderly, so death was close at hand for him regardless, but the man did not deserve to die sick and alone. Declan understood the larger, unwitting impact of Ross' actions. That clan did not kill one but two, and the ramifications of these crimes assailed Declan's sensibilities. On the heels of such good news from Elayne, to the abject horror of the death and destruction caused by Clan Ross rattled Declan's mind. He wavered in the old man's croft, wanting to cry, to kill, to curse God all at once, and as a result, could do nothing. He stood frozen next to Greer's decimated body, trying to collect himself, when Torin clapped him on the back.

"Come my Laird. We need to figure out how to bury our dead when the priest is one of the bodies. Do ye ken another priest?"

Declan clasped his head in his hands to calm the tumult in his brain. He did not react to Torin's question.

"Laird?" Torin tried again.

"Aye," Declan croaked. "Aye, I ken a priest. I will see to it."

He fled the tomb-like croft, gulping the fresh air once outside.

***

The messenger rode for MacNally land as though the devil himself chased at his heels. Declan had entrusted Niall to not stop until James MacNally was in his sights. Slogging through the muddy road to clan MacNally, Niall all but fell off the horse as he arrived at the gate, screaming for Laird MacNally.

James MacNally's frame filled the doorway, his face dark, his jaw set in a hard line. Niall stumbled over his words as he struggled to deliver the message until MacNally waved a broad hand at Niall's efforts.

"Slowly, lad," MacNally's voice boomed in the hall. "What is the urgency?"

Niall slowed his breath, gaining control of his faculties. "Laird MacNally, we have had a calamity in clan MacCollough. Our godly priest has been murdered! And an old man he cared for died afterward. But we no' have a priest for funeral rites. Laird MacCollough would ask that ye extend your priest to us in our time o' need."

MacNally's brows knitted as he shook his head at Niall's message.

"Halt your words, man. What do ye mean, the priest has been murdered?" He advanced toward the lad, his burning gaze sharpening on Niall.

"I dinna ken. I only ken the priest is killed, and MacCollough asked for your assistance."

"Aye, lad." MacNally moved decisively. "I shall retrieve our priest, and we shall ride for MacCollough soon." He pointed in the direction of the kitchens. "See to the kitchens for some nourishment 'afore we depart."

Niall bowed and scampered off, desperate for warm mead and bread after the cold slog through the overcast glen. The warmth of the kitchens would be a welcome reprieve.

MacNally hurried for the stables, bellowing for Ramsay to prepare the horse and sending the stable lad to the church for Father MacNally. James MacNally's mind reeled with the news from the lad, and his stomach lurched to his throat, fearing for his daughter once more. As of late, he doubted the decision to wed his daughter to the MacCollough. Perchance Alistair's speculations held more than a shadow of truth?

Pushed his skepticisms aside, he focused on the urgent matter before him. Hefting his own saddle on his stallion, MacNally twisted his head toward the stable doors as the stable lad scampered in, followed by a breathless Father MacNally. Ramsay saddled a horse for the priest, then helped him onto the beast. He was checking on Niall's horse when the lad sauntered in, a bannock in his mouth.

"Come, lad! Time's a wastin'! Get ye on your horse!" MacNally bellowed.

Niall tossed the half-eaten bannock into a pail and mounted in one nimble move, and the trio left, leaving a trail of mud and trampled grasses in their wake.

***

Declan's relief in the fresh air was short lived. After sending young Niall to MacNally's with a request for a priest, he then had to deal with what to tell the clan, how to pursue the crime against the priest, and how Elayne would feel about Greer, whom she attended a short time ago. The stress of this untenable situation pounded at his temples. Declan massaged his hands over his head, his hair standing up like an unkempt wildcat. He stood at the door of the kirk, Duncan and Torin guarding the entrance. A few clansmen and woman ventured near out of curiosity, but a stern look from Torin sent them scuttling back to the village.

"Laird," Duncan began.

"Aye, I ken, Duncan. Give me a moment to piece this out."

The sallow sunlight pushed past the clouds and alighted on his face as he looked up to the heavens, awaiting a command from God himself. When God didn't answer, Declan turned back to his men.

"First, we must bury our dead. We will have to announce to the clan that it appears Father Fraser was a victim of evil at the hands of another clan, perchance Clan Ross, and that old Greer died from sickness yesterday. 'Twill be of no service to us if we ignite passions by suggesting that Greer's death resulted from the priest's murder." Declan paused, inhaling before his next command.

"Father MacNally should be here shortly. We will prepare the bodies, lay them out in the kirk for a day, and if he agrees, MacNally can have the funeral on the Lord's day. Torin!" The immense man leaned in to Declan. "Keep the weapon and the cloth hidden. I would have it when I consult with Laird MacNally about our next step. Once we can discern Ross' motives, we can then move appropriately, preferable after conference with the Bruce. Until then, we must bide our time. Let us back to the keep to retrieve what we need for their shrouds."

Both nodded, then Torin returned to the foul air of the church to arrange the priest's body as Declan and Duncan made their solemn march back to the castle. The sun lost its battle with the clouds, and a bleak autumn rain began to fall, a fitting setting to the harsh reality of the day. They worked their tartans over their heads, but the coverings did little to keep them dry. By the time they reached the keep, they were wet and despondent.

News of the horrors in the church traveled faster than they did, and the mood at the castle was as gray as the rain that fell like tears from God. The silent kitchens and empty hall furthered the disheartened mood — the servants off in their solitary places, in shock, in sorrow, in grief. Declan found Elayne in a subdued pose on a stool by the window, staring absently into the evening as the soft rain wet her gown. She did not turn to him when he entered.

A sparse fire did little to warm the room, but Declan pulled a chair near the hearth. The chill pervading his body had less to do with the dank chill in the air and more with his mood. He was a man who had witnessed violence — what man who ever served a king during war had not? — but his own men, innocent men, a goodly priest and a sick old man, curdled his wame. The shivering continued even as the feeble heat of the fire thawed his skin. Despair hung in the room in a dark tapestry, covering everything in a shroud of loss. Death, though an accepted part of life, still came with formidable harshness, wielding its sharp scythe without mercy, and sadness shrouded the entire clan.

They sat apart in encumbered silence for a long while, waiting for time to make sense of the unnecessary death and devastation that accompanied it. Elayne finally dropped the tapestry in front of the window, ending the war waging between the frail heat of the fire and the cold of the rain. Her now-sopping dress dripped onto the floor, the dark fabric contrasting sharply to her pale skin. Declan stood to help her undress.

"Ye will catch your death from a chill, love, and we have had too much of that this day."

Elayne remained motionless as Declan worked the stays, untying the kirtle from the back. Dropping to the floor in a sodden heap, Elayne stepped away from it, lifting her shift over her head. She neared the fire, permitting the heat to warm her goose-prickled skin. Declan first stripped off his braes and tunic, then unfurled his plaid and moved behind Elayne. He pressed what remained of his body's warmth against her back, enveloping them both in the green and black tartan. They remained entwined that way, trying to make sense of the somber affairs of the day.

Chapter 23: Two Funerals

Pale sunlight settled on what remained of the changing leaves and brush, casting the world in shades of copper, gold, and crimson, the lustrous colors a stark contrast to the drab mood of the funeral. For the wake in honor of the two men, the earthly remains of old Greer and Father Fraser reposed in the church's sanctuary for two days. Differing clansmen and women shared the chore of watching over the dead until the bodies could be interred properly in the cramped cemetery behind the church.

The morning of the burial mass, Kaleigh and Senga arrived early to the sanctuary, accompanied by Father MacNally, to finish wrapping the bodies with the shrouds the women of the keep had sewed the evening before. The quietude of sorrow permeated the whole of the clan — from the keep to the village to the church. As the women worked, only the clanking sounds of the guest priest preparing the host for the upcoming mass disturbed the solemn atmosphere of the morning.

Several clansmen ventured to the church before the mass began, digging earnestly in the cemetery to prepare the graves. Fortune smiled upon them as the earth churned up easily. Clansmen dreaded winter funerals, when digging up frozen earth was not only time-consuming and back-breaking work, but also led to the aggravation of several broken picks and shovels. The misty rain of the last fortnight, however, favored them, and the depths of the graves deepened with ease.

Elayne dressed in her darkest gown, plaiting her hair in a burnished braid around her head. She draped her forest plaid about her head and shoulders, tucking the edges in tight. The sunlight, sparse though it was, may have been welcome on her face, but the solemn nature of the day cast such petty thoughts aside. Old Greer and Father Fraser would never again experience the joy of sunlight on their skin, and the guilt over those thoughts remained close.

Guilt wracked her from morning till night that her marriage to Declan was the root cause of the animosity against their clan. She and Declan were well and truly wed — there was no reason for someone to kill the priest. What purpose did it serve? They had not yet spoken on it, but after the funeral, Elayne was convinced Declan wanted to converse with her father regarding the implications of these last few days.

Declan, too, wrestled with guilt. He, like Elayne, questioned the reasoning behind the priest's murder. They banished Alistair, who was well on his way over the icy sea to the Isles. Relations with the MacKenzies took a turn for the better, minor skirmishes subsiding after the wedding. They had even helped rescue Elayne. And what quarrel could Ross have with MacCollough? To what end did killing the priest of a small, insignificant clan serve? These questions rolled around Declan's head, over and over, and the strain of it all showed on his face.

Together, Declan and Elayne joined the parade of her family, the house servants, and clansmen and women leaving the keep toward the church, a dark line of sorrow and despair against the bright colors of autumn.

***

Father MacNally understood the needs of his congregation and kept the funeral mass brief. He intoned the grace of God, offering the two faithful souls up to His keeping. He then asked for blessings not only for the men and their families but also for the rest of the clan. Father MacNally stood at the head of the two bodies where light filtering through the casements cast a sallow glow on the shrouds as though the light of God Himself was lifting the souls of the men.

After the final "Amen," most of the congregation filed out to the churchyard as Declan and his men carried the bodies out of the sanctuary to where two freshly hewn coffins awaited. Lowering the shrouded bodies into the coffins, clansmen then carted the caskets through the maze of decaying crosses to their final resting places.

While some villagers did not return to the castle, most of the clansmen accompanied their Laird to partake in a meal of mourning and remembrance. For the clan, many of whom had not experienced vicious bloodshed in several years if at all, these deaths reminded them too well that Death was always near, ready to knock on their doors and bring an unpleasant end to their happy time here on earth. Solemn moments of death demanded the solace of companionship to shrug off the mantle of mortality, as least for a short time.

***

MacNally's entourage, including his own priest, were to leave the on the morrow, prompting Declan to request a short audience before James departed. Out of deference to his wife, Declan invited her, as well as Torin, in an unpleasant conversation on the events leading up to the demise of the priest.

The cramped solar lacked sufficient seating, so Torin gestured to MacNally and his daughter they should sit in the cushioned chairs. He and Declan stood, which, exhausted though he was, suited Declan well. Declan was a pacer anyway, Torin knew, not that much space remained in the room for pacing.

"I assume ye want to discuss the horror that has passed?" MacNally ventured. Declan rubbed his eyes with his palms, trying to focus his thoughts.

"Aye," he croaked. The weight of recent events fully settled on his young shoulders, and the robust man struggled not to collapse. Declan directed his fatigued gaze to MacNally.

"Do ye ken any reason for Ross to move against us?"

MacNally shook his head. "Nay, lad. Are ye certain 'tis Ross?"

Declan and Torin exchanged a knowing glance.

"Aye. They left us a message." Declan reached over to the writing table and uncovered the tartan which had been wrapped around the sword that sent the priest heavenward. James MacNally grumbled hard in his throat.

"Aye, 'tis a message." MacNally agreed. "Nay, lad, again, I dinna ken their motives. I shall return home and inquire. I recommend ye do the same with your border clans."

MacNally flicked his eyes toward his daughter, who sat tall and haughty in her cushioned chair. "I trust I made no mistake in letting my daughter wed ye?" James' words left nothing to conjecture.

MacCollough clenched his jaw as Elayne screeched out in offense. "Father! What are ye saying? That we can no' care for ourselves?"

"Nay, lass," James started, facing her, his voice softening as it did when trying to placate her. "I just —" MacNally looked to MacCollough in desperation.

"He is just worried about ye and wants to assure none of my history is a cause for this event, or possible future brutality against the . . . . clan."

The deliberate pause was not lost on anyone in the solar. Elayne's chin rose up as she prepared to launch her verbal attack at her father, but Declan placed his hand on hers. Elayne restrained herself, sitting back into her chair, her face tight.

"I ken your meaning, James," MacCollough responded. "I am naught but a fierce supporter of the Bruce as ye are. Unless Ross is somehow angered at my loyalty, I dinna ken any motive for retribution against me or mine."

MacNally scratched as his beard. "Perchance it is tied to there. There are rumors —" Elayne scoffed, and MacNally cut a hard glance in her direction before continuing, "that the Ross clan may not support the Bruce as we do. Perchance your verra attachments to the King are the cause for these aggressions. Again, let us make inquiries. I shall be in contact with ye soon."

At that, the man rose like a bear and exited the room, followed by Elayne and the MacCollough men. MacNally's men loitered in the hall, ready to depart. James MacNally gathered Elayne into his barrel chest in a hug that nearly suffocated her. Releasing her, he turned to Declan and grasped his arm, then pulled the man close to whisper into Declan's ear. Declan nodded, and MacNally rounded up his men, leaving with them in a raucous procession to the yard where their horses awaited.

"What did the man say to ye?" Elayne demanded. Declan gave her a wry smirk.

"He let me know what the repercussions would be if any grave danger came to ye."

"Ooch, ye mean more than already has?" she countered lightly, sauntering toward the kitchens before he could respond.

***

MacNally's ride back to his lands was pensive and uneventful. His men held back, including Father MacNally, each lost in his own thoughts, most likely each questioning his mortality. Death fair nipped at their heels, and the purpose for it escaped James MacNally.

Once he entered the main hall, he warmed his chilled bones at the crackling fire raging in the hearth. James curled his hands into fists several times, flexing his fingers, trying to work the stiffness and pain from his knuckles. Each year, each winter, the cold seeped deeper in his bones, reminding him that his time on this Earth was limited and Death waited on no man, even great Lairds. He rubbed his hands together and walked to his study, dreading the writing awaiting him.

The only way to learn why Clan MacCollough was on the receiving end of such violence was to send out inquiries to other allied clans. MacNally readied himself for a long evening of writing for however long his pained joints allowed. Perchance another clan knew why MacCollough's clan found itself in the crosshairs; mere cattle reiving did not invite such savage bloodshed, no matter how valued a ragged Highland cow may be.

James unfurled a rough parchment onto his table when his young nephew and namesake peeped around the door, trepidation stamped across his dismayed features. The Laird sighed heavily, not relishing where this conversation might end.

"Uncle, mayhap I would have a word with ye?" Young James asked.

"I think 'twill be more than one word, nephew," James MacNally grumbled. He gestured to a stool by the table. "Have a seat."

The lad stepped into the chamber and perched himself on the edge of the stool. He was wound tighter than a ball of twine, every muscle clenched. James sat up taller in his chair at his nephew's behavior.

"Well, lad, what brings ye to me?"

Young James picked at the seam of his trousers, unable to look his uncle in the eye.

"I had heard ye, back at Elayne's new place," the young man stammered. "Ye and the young Laird seemed, uh, puzzled. Over the deaths of the men, ye ken?"

James MacNally pursed his lips together in a tight line, apprehensive to hear the remainder of the lad's tale.

"Well, I thought on it, Uncle, I did," Young James explained. "I thought I was helping Elayne. I don't ken for sure, but I may ken who attacked them."

The Laird scratched at his beard, his cutting stare never leaving Young James. The lad was unaware of the plaid found on the sword — mayhap his information could provide insight to the egregious killings on his son-by-law's land.

"Aye?" he prompted.

"Ooch, it happened when Alistair left. He wanted a message delivered to Clan Ross, and he asked me to bring it. I did no' think it was nefarious, as he told me to read it. What could he hide if I read it, ye ken?" The words fell from his lips in a jumble. "It was a plain message. I thought it may help the Elayne and her new clan, so I delivered it."

Outrage simmered under James' skin like meat in a pan — bubbling and spitting. In a futile effort to remain calm, he cleared his throat a few times before responding to his naïve nephew.

"In Clan Ross, whom did ye deliver the message to?"

"Ooch, the Laird, Uncle. Donald Ross," Young James responded innocently. James gripped the edges of the table, knowing if he let loose the table, those same hands would be around the neck of his nephew, and what would he tell his dear sisters then — having banished one nephew only to kill the other?

"And what, my nephew, did the message read?"

"'Twas a simple missive, Uncle. Alistair told Ross that their endeavor has ended as Elayne was wed. That the MacCollough clan is stable now."

The pieces of the mystery slowly assembled in James' mind — Alistair's lowly ambitions, Ross' haughty ambitions, Ross aligning with the English, MacCollough's assisting the

Bruce in escaping from Ross' clutches, and his Elayne as a pawn. The plaid left behind made more sense. If Alistair encouraged Donald Ross in his twisted endeavors to eliminate the Bruce, he wanted to use MacCollough to do it. In a way, Alistair was naught more than a puppet than Elayne. James MacNally shook his head in frustration.

"I wish ye had told me all this sooner, lad. I do. But that can nay be changed now. I must think on this information. On the morrow, I will need ye to send a missive to MacCollough. He should be here to discuss this news, and then we can plan our next move."

James dismissed the lad with a wave of his hand and sat back heavily into his chair. *When did it all become so complicated?* he asked himself. While life with Elayne had not been easy, her willful indiscretions paled at the prospect that his daughter may be a pawn for power by a senseless Laird with grandiose ambitions.

He crumpled the parchment in his hand, ignoring the shots of pain that flared through his fingers. Quitting the chamber, he rushed up the stairs to Mari, desperate to lose his disgruntled thoughts between the thighs of his woman.

Chapter 24: In the Name of Love

The mood in Clan MacCollough remained under a subdued cloud for days following the funerals. The night after her father left, Elayne had wandered aimlessly throughout the keep, her thoughts rambling and her anxiety screaming. Declan had stayed far from her during the burial preparations, sleeping in the hall and not in their bed. She hoped that might change when her father departed, but that night Declan again slept with Torin and his other men in the stony chill of the hall instead of warming her in their chamber.

Deep in her heart she understood why he slept in the hall — his actions came from a place of fear, a desperate fear he attempted hide. If a man is willing to defile the sanctuary of a God's house with a crime that mimicked Cain himself, what would stop that man from invading any man's home to do the same? Declan was nothing if not a leader and protector for his clan, and if that meant remaining in the hall to safeguard it, he would.

But these thoughts did not ease Elayne's troubles at all. She missed her husband and wanted him back in bed with her. While her meandering mind encompassed her attention, she did not realize someone had come up behind her until he spoke.

"Ye can nay sleep this eve?" Declan asked. Elayne started and turned to the sound of his voice.

"Ooch, Declan!" Elayne raised her hand to her chest. "Ye startled me. I thought ye asleep in the hall."

"Aye, I thought I would be as well." His shoulders slumped, and Elayne's heart ached at the broken sight before her. The guilt he carried over Father Fraser and Old Greer was unmistakable, and Elayne was at a loss of how to comfort him. His dingy shift hung on his frame, as rumpled and disheveled as the rest of him. She rested her palm on his chest, then reached her arm behind him and pressed her cheek to him.

Suddenly he was pulling her hair, raising her face to his own, his lips on hers, forcing them apart to assault her tongue with his. A small squeal of bewilderment escaped her as he pushed her against the wall, the rough stone cool through her shift. His rigid cock pulsed against her hip. Her breasts ached as his hands kneaded her smooth orbs, his breath ragged in her ear.

"Now. I need ye now."

He clutched her hand and dragged her to their chamber, kicking the door shut behind him. Declan's fingers looped in the neckline of her gown and dragged it down her body, exposing her for his view. His eyes roved over her naked skin, consuming her. He moved to push her to the bed, but she held her hand against his chest, halting him.

Elayne clutched his chin, forcing his burning golden gaze to hers. She grabbed his tartan, throwing it to the ground.

Twining her hand in the material of his tunic, she yanked his mouth to hers, and forced her lips on his, biting, matching his fervor. He crushed her onto the bed, ripped his tunic over his head, and lowered himself into the furs, nestling himself between Elayne's inviting thighs.

"Come to me, Declan," her whisper beckoning him, his erection throbbing against her.

His need for her engulfed him. Her nails sank into shoulders, marking his skin, as he thrust into her velvety warmth, hard and fast, to the hilt of his cock. Declan slowed for a moment, letting a shudder overtake him. A guttural moan rose from deep in his throat. He reached behind her head, entwining his fingers in her hair as he began to ride her, stroking her delicate folds. His thrusts were as desperate and wild as his moaning, as though he could not fill her enough. Her hips rose to meet each exquisite plunge; her legs wrapped around his hips to pull him in deeper.

As he worked her damp cleft, pumping and gasping, his cock touched every nerve ending, and swells of ecstasy coursed through her. Elayne called out to him over and over — as a prayer or a plea, it did not matter. He felt her flexing against his cock as she reached her moment. His whole body clenched, every sinew tight with exertion as his balls contracted up through his belly, rapture surging through him, and he came hard into her. His groans dissipated as his hips finished pumping. He dropped his forehead dropped to hers, perspiration from his efforts tickling her breasts as the small drops trickled down her full mounds.

Declan's whole weight collapsed on her. His lips found her nipple, kissing one, then the other, before he shifted to her side, keeping one hand tight on her breast.

The encounter was fleeting and frenzied and unlike their previous beddings. Satiated, the release of his seed in Elayne also released the burdens he carried for days. Elayne traced his ear with a delicate nail, playing with his hair as he regained his senses. He cleared his throat, but the hoarseness of his voice persisted.

"I hope I was no' too rough with ye." He sounded almost apologetic.

"Ye were fine husband. I ken that ye may have needed something more this eve."

"Aye, but as a lady and my wife, 'tis inappropriate, no?"

Elayne did not stifle the laugh that swelled up in her. "If ye canna bed your wife that way, what is the use of a wife?"

Declan's whole body shook the bed as he laughed with her. "Ye do continue to surprise me, wife."

Her nipples formed hardened peaks as her skin cooled in the evening air. Declan circled one with his fingertip, making it stand up more and trailed his finger to the other nipple. Her whole skin prickled, and he flipped the coverlet over them, bracing them against the growing chill. Enveloped in the bedding, the warmth of his skin radiated to her, and she nestled closer to him, relishing his heat. He burned like the blacksmith's fire every night, and she found herself sinking into his heat nightly, a heat she missed when he slept below with his men.

"Are ye staying in our bed this night?" she asked, unabashed.

"I was hoping to, my love, if ye will have me."

Elayne burst up onto her elbow, gazing into his fair, exhausted face. Her pragmatism ascertained what her heart and mind had missed before. Alistair nearly stopped their wedding, wanted to kidnap her, and now another outsider threatened his clan. Her own father feared that she was the next target. Both his grandfather and father lost their wives and, as he witnessed the abject state his clan fell into in the aftermath, Declan harbored an irrational fear that something may happen to her. He dreaded his clan would revert to its base behaviors if he let that happen. Elayne's understanding of his precarious nature crystallized as she gazed into his fragile hazel gaze. He was afraid for her. He was afraid he could not protect her. *Is that what love is?*

She averted her eyes, reclining back into the plush furs.

"Ye say 'my love'," her words hesitant and measured.

This time Declan propped up on his side toward her, the intensity of his gaze capturing her sidelong glance, searing her to her core. The smirk he gave her, however, conveyed more than words could. Her heart skipped a beat, and she grinned back.

"And ye have said it 'afore," she continued.

"Mm-hmm?" The sound came through his closed lips.

"Well —"

He waited. He would not make this easy for her, and she raised one slender eyebrow in aggravation.

"We are little more than an arranged marriage," she explained. "Is love something ye wanted? Or something ye can state with certainty?"

Her busy mind flitted over their similar pasts — her mother's death when she was young and his mother's departure in his youth — and she could not align those episodes with the idea of love. Neither of them had a strong example of what love could be; how could he know? Did she?

"Nay," he spoke, his expression honest and open. "I can no' say for certain what love is within a marriage. But I ken that when I am with ye, a fire lights in my belly. I wake with a flame for ye that consumes me throughout the day, until my whole being burns for ye, a burning that cannot be satiated unless I am with ye. Then I want ye more. I want to ken what ye think, how ye feel. I want your body every moment, and the thought of losing ye strikes a fear in me deeper than I believed possible for one man."

Her heart fluttered as he spoke — his words were of the ilk Elayne never thought she would hear. Declan rolled onto his back, staring at the rafters of the chamber, inhaling the scent of her. He found her hand under the covers, entwining his fingers with hers.

"That, my 'Layne, is love enough for me."

They lay buried in the furs, skin pressed to skin, Declan's words hanging in the air. Elayne nudged closer, absorbing his warmth, trying to select her next words. Emotion ran thick through her veins. Other than the spoiled love of her father, Elayne had not known love before, and giving voice to romantic thoughts as Declan did eluded her. Against her will, tears welled in her eyes.

"Declan, I dinna ken if I love ye the same," she whispered. "I dinna ken my own emotions."

Declan's fingertip traced the tear that rolled down to her jawline. "Do ye care for me, 'Layne?"

"What? Of course, I care for ye! Would I be in your bed and building a clan with ye if I did no'?"

"Well, greater things have started with much less," he told her, nestling his face into her neck as she twined her fingers in his hair.

"I have no' doubt we will have a great love, my 'Layne."

***

Young James arrived before the midday meal, bursting through the yard, bellowing for Laird MacCollough. In moments like these, his relation to Elayne was evident; apples did not fall far from their trees after all.

Elayne, working in the kitchens with Kaleigh and Senga, heard his calls for her husband and rushed to the courtyard to quiet the lad.

"What is wrong with ye, James? Are ye daft? Ye are fit to scare the cattle from the fields with your belly-aching! Shush your mouth and speak like ye have some sense!"

Elayne grabbed the reins of his steed as he slid off the horse. Hamish had appeared from the side of the stables with Bonnie, both in state of disarray, their previous doings discernable from their disheveled hair and flushed skin. Elayne huffed to herself and held the reins toward Hamish.

"Hamish, take the mount to the stables for a rub down while I concern myself with my infantile cousin," she commanded, and Hamish jumped to obey. Elayne turned on Young James, and grasping his sleeve in her fingers like an irritated mother, she dragged him up the steps into the hall. Senga kept one ear near the kitchen doorway so as not to miss any of the conversation.

"Cousin Elayne, I can explain —" Young James started. Elayne did not let him finish.

"Ye best explain. My husband is labors hard and does nay need the likes of my cousin interrupting his work. How dare ye frighten the whole of the hall with your bawling?"

James darted his eyes throughout the hall, as though looking for someone to come to his aid.

"Christ, James! What is it?" Elayne's temper was palpable.

"Ooch, aye. I have a message from your father."

"My father!" Elayne squealed. "Is he well? What does he need from me?"

"Actually, cousin, he does no' have a message for ye. 'Tis for your husband. Laird MacNally requests him at the castle as soon as he is able." Young James held the crumpled missive out for Elayne. She snatched it from his hand and unfurled it. While Elayne read the words without pause, a grimace of disquiet crossed over her mouth. She then glared at her cousin, thrusting the parchment back into his hand.

"James, ye need to learn to control yourself. Ye had me worked up that something was amiss with my father! As for Laird MacCollough, he is working with the men to finish collecting crops for the winter. He shall return shortly with the men for the noontide meal. Ye can warm yourself here and deliver your message then."

She spun to the kitchens, forcing Senga to scramble back from the door, lest she be found eavesdropping and encounter Elayne's temper. As she resettled at the table, Senga smiled to herself. Elayne tamed a bit and seemed overall happier since her falling out with clan MacLeod and her arrival at clan MacCollough, which brought joy to Senga's heart. But the woman still had her iron will that emerged often, as Young James just learned.

Elayne joined Senga at the table to finish dispensing the meat and bannocks onto platters, returning Senga's smile with a one of her own. The steaming meat and broth warmed the kitchen, chasing away the frosty chill of the day, but not enough to justify the beads of sweat forming on Elayne's high forehead.

"What worries ye, lass?" Senga broached in her familiar, soft brogue. Elayne's steadfast shoulders slumped over the table.

"A missive from my father for the Laird. Evidently my father has suspicions as to Ross' motives in the deaths of the priest and old Greer." Elayne wiped sweat and exasperation from her brow with one slender arm. "'Twould appear that my erstwhile, banished cousin colluded with Ross in their wanton claims for power. My father has asked MacCollough to join him on the morrow to discuss the matter."

Senga's brow pinched with unease for the lass. "Are ye intendin' to travel with your husband, lass?"

Elayne shook her head, allaying Senga's fears. No one else in the keep might notice, but no one has known the lass as long as the old woman had. Senga knew Elayne's head injury ofttimes still pained her. Then the last few weeks had been rough on the outspoken young woman; slight blue half-moons under eyes hinted at her burdened soul. Though she seemed to will the sun to rise and set each day, Elayne had her breaking point, and Senga feared her ward was nearing hers.

"Nay, we have much to do here with the approaching winter, and my husband will share all with me when he returns from my father's." Elayne wiped her hands on a cloth, nodded at the platters spilling over with meat and bread, then gestured toward the hall.

"Shall we?" she asked.

***

MacCollough and his men tracked in more mud than was to be found in the glen. Determined to fill Elayne's larders, Declan commanded the men to traipse through all means of vegetation as they harvested the lingering late crops before they returned to fall hunting. Their mud-encrusted appearance attested to their efforts. As they returned for the midday meal, MacCollough noted the leaves that blew after them on the ground outnumbered those left on the trees, and the frigid air that morning hinted that an icy winter would soon show itself. He hoped they stored food aplenty for those in the clan, including those who had recently joined them.

Declan's first detour was to the hearth, where the crackling warmth of the fire chased the chills from his body, but was not loud enough to drown out Torin's chuckling behind him. As he spent his formative years further south with the Bruce, Declan's blood had certainly thinned, not that he would admit as much to his seneschal. God knew he was weary of the giant's merciless teasing about his thin skin. And the teasing would increase as the winter carried colder days on its back.

He moved toward the tables, and a swath of dark and bright attracted his eye. An inner delight fell over him as he watched his wife, her dark hair and pale skin clad in his clan greens and black, appear like a tall, woodland fairy. She toiled with Kaleigh and Bonnie to spread platters of steaming foodstuffs across the tables for the men. The women lingered over their respective love interests, their shining faces adding to the glow in the hall. Throughout his life, growing up in the decrepit castle, he never encountered such a domestic scene, and his brow creased when a man interrupted.

"Laird MacCollough?" the young man on his left spoke. Declan took a deep breath and turned his head toward the voice of Young James. Surprise replaced his sense of contentment, which was then overshadowed by foreboding. Every hair on Declan's body stood on end at the sight of his wife's cousin.

"Why are ye here, lad? Did ye no' just leave yesterday?" Declan's intense look never left Young James, who found himself unnerved and looking at the ground instead of at Declan.

"Aye, I have a missive here from Laird MacNally, regarding the death of your priest these days past." Young James' grimy hand held a curled parchment, the wax seal broken. Declan raised an eyebrow at the lad, who shrugged without guile.

"Your wife," was all he replied, and Declan nodded knowingly, taking the message from the lad. Of course, his wife would have read it first, since he was not here when James arrived. He tucked it in his belt-pouch to read after the meal, then dug into his rapidly cooling dinner.

***

Declan grasped his wife's elbow, ushering her to his small study where he read the message in her presence.

"What do you think, 'Layne? Ye ken your cousin well. Could he have enticed the Laird Ross, of all people, to such irrational deeds?"

Perched on the edge of her chair, she allowed her fingers to play with her tartan as she considered her husband's question. She had grown up with Alistair, who at worst was annoying. But his recent attempt on her life in his quest for power from clan MacNally spoke more loudly than his childhood antics. And to ally with a large, English-sympathizing clan in his pursuit of power? Elayne's eyes were wide, disbelieving.

"I ken he wanted to be Laird of Clan MacNally," she began, trying to arrange her thoughts into words. "He thought it was his right as the oldest male. He did not consider that if I wed, that my father would align with my husband's clan. Essentially my father placed his chieftain line through me, and Alistair disagreed. But to this extent? To fall in with Comyn supporters, attempt murder, and to decimate an entire clan? I should not have thought Alistair's thirst for power would override his prudence. How could such a plan succeed, just to place him as Laird of a small clan?"

Declan scratched at his golden whiskers, his perplexity matching hers. The memory of when they found the priest's body and Duncan's suggestion regarding Alistair falling in with Ross hammered in his mind. Elayne then asked the question he had entertained since the discovery of Father Fraser.

"Why would Ross work with Alistair? How could having Alistair as Laird benefit the man?"

Declan cleared his throat. Elayne was familiar with MacCollough's support for the Bruce, the same as her father, but perhaps she was unaware of how vile men could be in a quest for power. The little hairs on his neck twitched in remembrance of what he witnessed as a knight for King Bruce — depraved actions from both the Bruce and Comyn's men as the throne of Scotland was up for grabs. And women are oft not privy to these behaviors, no matter how loud or willful a woman may be, or how involved she is with the leadership of her clan.

"Perchance more is at stake than what he knows. Your father desires that I ride to him tomorrow where we can conference about the matter. As you read, he suggests involving clan Lee to the south to join us to learn more, to form alliances with MacKenzie if necessary. I may even have to contact the Bruce, if we agree that the Laird Ross' actions deem it so."

Elayne's eyebrows rose to her hairline at his words.

"So ye do ken where the Bruce is!" she almost cackled. His cheek twitched in return.

"Not quite, my love. I am not important enough of a man to have such knowledge. But I know how to get a hold of him if it is of import to the Crown. Ross' actions, if they lend toward a move against the king, fall under that banner."

Declan's chest heaved in a deep sigh, the weight of such a decision heavy on his conscience. He leaned forward in his chair, lifting Elayne's delicate fingers from her plaid, clasping them protectively in his.

"I will ride to meet with your father on the morrow. I will bring only Torin with me, as I will no' leave the keep unattended, or you unprotected."

He pressed in farther, capturing her lips in his. Her body responded in kind, squeezing his fingers and melting into the hardness of his chest. She placed her palm on his furred jaw and his intense gaze caught hers.

"No matter how strong willed ye are," he told her, "ye alone can no' keep off an invasion if I am no' here. Even if I must command the men to no' let ye die."

Elayne rubbed her thumb over his lips as he kissed the tip. "Ye may well have to make such a commandment. I have made progress with Torin, but much less with any of the others. We can no' have the keep exposed because their need to be manly will no' permit them to listen to me."

"Ye are making more progress than ye think," he responded, leaning forward to kiss her again.

Chapter 25: Unwelcome Guests

Another cold day was well upon them and hinted that winter hid around the bend. Elayne snuggled under the plaids and furs on the bed, burrowing closer to Declan, trying to absorb his body heat to ward off the chill. He followed her under the covers, trailing his lips and tongue over her neck and breasts, her nipples hardening for a reason other than the cold.

She moaned as she clasped the back of his head, holding him to her, basking in the waves of pleasure of his lips on her nipples. His mouth moved up to hers, kissing her fully. His fingers brushed against her breast, enjoying the shivers he sent through her. He moaned wearily.

"I would give near anything to stay abed with ye this morning, but my duty calls," his voice muffled under the bedding.

Elayne popped her head out of the covers and rolled atop of him, her hands tight on his wrists, her dark hair a fury of waves and snarls around her head. He laughed at both her appearance and her attempt to hold him captive. Declan flipped her over on her back, nuzzling his face between her breasts.

"Save this for me when I return, my love?" She shivered again, this time at his use of the word "love" — the sound of it on his lips nearly as captivating as his mouth on her breasts. She trailed a nail down his chest to his furry trail that led to his cock.

"Aye, ye get a pass this time, My Laird, but I shall be demanding when ye return to this bed."

"When are ye no' demanding?" he joked, flinching as she poked him in his belly. He leapt off her to dress, and she shrieked as frigid air invaded the bedding and assaulted her skin.

She saw Declan off as sunshine attempted burst through the clouds in its feeble effort to light the day. After dressing in her worn shift and dingiest kirtle, she wrapped a kerchief around her head to hold back the wisps of chestnut locks that escaped her braids. Elayne had planned a long day of work to further fill the less-than-impressive larders. Eager to take advantage of the dry weather, she sent Senga upstairs with a lass to air out the bed chambers while she shoo'd the other women through the kitchens to the gardens.

"Time to collect any last edible plant we can find. Bonnie, will ye find Hamish and have him collect his cart? No' much may be left, but we have yet to gather near the far edges of the gardens, and then we can send Hamish around to help crofters collect their from their gardens."

Bonnie strode off in the direction of Hamish's croft as the other women moved close to the higher grasses at the perimeter of the yard, poking at the cool, damp soil, unearthing beets, onions, and carrots. Kaleigh and Elayne picked at the trees that edged the yard, snatching every last little apple or ragged pear hiding in the few, lingering, fiery leaves. Even if the plants were not edible, many could serve as seed plants for spring planting or medicinals. Elayne lost herself in imagining the largess of the garden next year, once properly planted and cared for, when Hamish sprinted through the remnants of the harvest, a small cart trailing behind him, followed by a beaming Bonnie.

"Hamish, we shall have more to collect than we anticipated, but we are on the far reaches and nearing the wood. Ye shall run amid the women, collecting foodstuffs from the baskets and bring it to the kitchens, ye ken?"

Quite the amicable soul, Hamish nodded and turned his cart toward Kaleigh's basket of fruit. Dumping the fruit with care, trying to prevent bruising — *Good lad!* Elayne thought — he replaced the basket right under Kaleigh. Bonnie approached him with Elayne's basket, adding it to the orbs in the cart. With his free hand, he grasped Bonnie's and gifted her his brilliant smile before releasing her to tote the cart to the manse. Elayne's heart swelled at the prospects flourishing in Clan MacCollough.

***

Hamish worked as the solitary man amid the gossiping and humming women for most of the morning. He tracked deeper into the trees, looking for wild fruit, when an odd sensation sprung his hairs off his neck. Bird squawks and scampering sounds of small animals abruptly halted. In an attempt to appear nonchalant, he stepped his way back, lightly but quickly, to the gardens where the largest collection of women in Clan MacCollough assembled. He rushed to

Elayne, the cart tipping askew and his eyes hooded. Leaning close, he spoke into her ear under the pretense of handing her a wormy apple.

"There are men, far in the woods, many of them. Get ye women into the keep, latch the door. I will find Duncan." Abandoning the cart, Hamish set a fast pace out of the gardens toward the stables, praying Duncan was nearby.

The brief thought, *for all the good that will do us,* passed through Elayne's mind as she clapped her hands, hiding the fear that shook through her. The last thing Duncan would do is come to her aid. Elayne's gaze flicked to Kaleigh, *but perhaps he would come to hers.* And Elayne knew for certain he would provide reinforcement for his Laird's keep.

"Ladies! We have a kitchen full of vittles. Let us take care of that 'afore returning to bring in more!"

Bonnie raised a singular eyebrow at the overeager tone but remained silent as she hefted a basket onto her hip and marched into the kitchens with the other women.

Elayne swirled about after Bonnie crossed the threshold, slamming the door shut and latching it.

"Bonnie!" she commanded breathlessly. "Latch the hall doors, quickly! Then get ye upstairs to my chambers. All of ye! Bar the door once ye are there. Now!"

Without pause, the women dropped their baskets. They sprang into action, racing up the stairs as Bonnie and Elayne rushed to the hall. Bonnie bolted the doors as Elayne returned from Declan's study, a sword nearly as long as Bonnie in her hands.

"Lady Elayne!" Bonnie's eyes widened with surprise and disbelief. "Can ye wield such a thing?"

"Upstairs, Bonnie, now. Aye, I ken my way around a sword, a bit. My father did no' halt to any notion I got in my

head, including follies such as wielding a sword. I am no'
contender for a man, though, so get ye up to my chambers."
Elayne hissed the last words out as she swung the sword
toward the main doors. Locks of hair came loose from her
kerchief, and with her flushed skin and tightened features, to
Bonnie she was a warrior goddess.

Elayne, on the other hand, felt nothing like a goddess;
every nerve in her body buzzed as though she housed a hive of
bees in her belly. Her blood pounded in her ears, and the light
coming from the window slits seemed brighter than the dim
sun she appreciated earlier that morning. Try as she may, she
could not slow her heart racing in her chest. While she told
herself this was all for naught, just some drunk and lost
MacKenzies, the panic in Hamish's voice spoke louder than
his words.

She knew not what she could do when challenged by
Ross' warriors, whom she assumed was skulking through her
woodland. Elayne was her father's daughter; she did not have
to work hard to put the pieces of the puzzle together and know
that Ross' men laid in wait for MacCollough to leave. Their
intent now, however, left Elayne mystified. What purpose did
the man have to attacking with the Laird away, if 'twere the
Laird he wanted to harm?

A banging sound from the kitchens behind her made
her jump, the tip of the sword clanging on the stone ground
before she could raise it against her would-be attacker. Her
arms quivered as she lifted the sword high over her shoulder
as her father taught her years ago. At Hamish's shock of
bright red hair appearing in the doorway, her muscles turned
liquid in relief.

"Hamish!" she exclaimed, dropping the sword again.
Hamish's face screwed up in confusion.

"Lady, why do ye have a sword?"

"For protection. Christ's blood, Hamish. What is amiss?"

Hamish shook his head in apology. "My lady, 'tis clan Ross, I can confirm. The Laird himself rides, but they are none too quiet, and I heard them well before they came close to the keep. Our men are on their way."

"How did ye get in here? I latched the door." Her brow furrowed as she was sure she bolted up the kitchens.

He shrugged, a blush rising to stain his cheeks, and Elayne understood he had previously entered unnoticed, most likely to entertain the fair Bonnie.

"Aye, well, I climbed up the wall and dropped through the oriel at the top of the kitchens."

"Well, Hamish, I must say ye are stealthy as a cat. Let's hope none of Ross' men think to do the same."

"I dinna believe they will. I moved the metal drying rack under it, the spiky one."

Elayne nodded in appreciation of the thought, then returned her attention to the doorway.

"Ye said Ross' men? And their Laird?" The security Elayne experienced at Hamish's arrival was dissipating. "Do ye ken how many?"

Hamish pursed his lips. "Nay, but it did sound like quite a few." Understatement was not the red-head's strong suit. Elayne bit her lip, considering their options.

"Ye went off to find Duncan?" she inquired. Hamish had removed his sword from its scabbard, balancing it deftly in one hand.

"Ooch, aye. He was in the stables. He told me to return here, and he would arrive shortly to reinforce the hall."

Elayne pursed her lips. *Dinna hold your breath, lad,* she thought. She shook off the idea that MacCollough's men would not only let Ross warriors kill the MacCollough's wife but also invade the clan keep, then focused on the heavy wooden doors, awaiting whatever burst through.

***

The disturbance in the yard grew louder — the yelling of men, the clopping of horses' hooves, the clanging of swords. Beads of nervous sweat sprouted on Elayne's forehead. *Where were MacCollough's men?* She barely had time to wonder before a clash struck the doors. She ducked to avoid flying wood chips as a balding man tramped in as though he were lord of the manor, followed by several armed warriors clad in gray plaid.

The balding man was shorter than Elayne by nearly a head. Maintaining the sour look on her face, she inhaled herself up to her full height to peer down at him. She could not miss his crazed look or heated breath. The man appeared muddled with more than just the excitement of launching an attack. Elayne wondered if the man were right in the head, and his twisted half smile and squinting eyes confirmed her suspicions. Any sanity inside the man's head had snapped like a twig, and now Elayne and her husband's clan were in the sights of a raving fiend. Lunacy would explain Ross' actions against MacCollough.

Beyond the warriors in the hall, she could see a few more men on horseback entering the yard. *Where was Duncan? The other men? Would they truly let her perish at the hands of Ross? Did they detest her that much?*

She gathered her thoughts and, hefting her sword in front of her, addressed the diminutive man in the most assertive tone she could muster, one that was fortunately familiar to her.

"To what end are ye in my castle armed and uninvited? Remove yourself from this hall at once."

Donald's twisted smile took on a show of humor, and his belly shook under his tartan in delirious laughter.

"Ye think ye can command me? Who will aid ye in that endeavor? The men of MacCollough obviously want nothing to do with ye, otherwise they would be here to defend ye!"

Hamish shifted in his position next to Elayne. Donald Ross dismissed him with a flick of his hand. "This one lad will achieve naught against my men. Now," Ross pointed his finger at Elayne, the tip wagging like a flimsy stalk of hay. "The MacCollough may think he can help a false King remain on the throne. Keep the rightful nobility from power. But he is sorely mistaken, lassie. After we take his keep, we will take him, and he will lead us to where we can find the Bruce."

Realization dawned on Elayne — MacCollough, herself, her cousin were pawns in Ross' sick desire to remove the Bruce. And with his inability to find the King, the only person on which to focus his ire was her husband. *What would mad men no' do for power?* Her thoughts were disrupted by a larger raucous commotion erupting outside. A sudden flurry of green and black spilled into the hall from the yard, and from behind her, an avalanche of MacCollough warriors surrounded the room. Donald Ross paled at their presence, sliding back toward the safety of his own men. A sneer replaced the fear on his face.

"These men?" he guffawed, his words mocking. "These men hate ye, Lady MacCollough. They despise what ye have done to their clan, emasculating them! These men will nary defend the likes of ye."

Duncan stepped from the throng of MacCollough warriors, grasping Elayne's arm. She did not know if she was relieved or frightened at his presence. Was he here to defend her, or turn her over to Ross?

"Kaleigh?" his lips formed the word silently. Elayne flicked her eyes upwards at the stairs with a nod of her head.

In the space of a heartbeat, he pivoted squarely on his feet, bellowing, "*Dia Deònach bidh mi!*" He shoved Elayne behind him as the MacCollough warriors fell on Ross and his men in violent fury. *God willing I shall, indeed,* she reflected on their clan motto as the MacColloughs raged against those who escorted Ross into the hall. The clashing of swords rang through the keep. Elayne cowed back into a corner behind the tables as Hamish stepped in front to guard her from the horde.

Maimed and dead Ross men littered the hall in a field of gray and red. As the rest of the Highlanders worked their way out outside, Duncan held Donald Ross immobile, dragging the beleaguered man to where Elayne remained with Hamish.

"Ian and the others dispatched most of the men of the outer yard as we crept in the back. Hamish!" Duncan hollered at the young man, "next time warn a man if ye plan to leave a trap in the way! Christ's blood, I caught my leg fierce on that hanging rack!"

Duncan's attention refocused on Elayne. "Milady, while this one here led the invasion on our land, too few men accompanied him. My conviction is he has other plans." He shook the squat laird, making the man quiver all the more. "Where are the rest of your men?" Duncan hissed at him.

Donald remained silent, only offering a bloodied smile flecked with broken teeth. His eyeballs rolled in his head, and Elayne was convinced he had lost all reasoning. Duncan threw the man to heap on the ground, where MacCollough men dragged the demented, defeated Laird toward the dungeons.

"What do you mean, other plans?" Elayne questioned, coming around the table to meet him.

"If he attacks the castle, or those inside it," he regarded Elayne, "Laird MacCollough could align with other clans, or the King himself, in retribution. If the Laird himself is killed though . . ." Duncan left the words hanging as Elayne grasped the gravity of his implication.

"Ye think more of his men are going to my father's land? To what, ambush my husband?" Her nails dug into the palms of her hands as she clenched them, flush with both fear and anger.

"Aye, to kill the Laird most likely, and any who may stand in their path. Milady—" he was unable continue as Elayne repeated her wedding day stance and scrambled atop the trestle table.

"My husband's men!" She called out, straining her voice. Casting her sights at Duncan, who bowed imperceptibly, she continued. "*My* men! Our Laird is in danger from these crazed invaders! Cast the lot of those still breathing in our dungeons and prepare to ride to clan MacNally!"

Duncan clasped her arm to help her down from her platform as the MacCollough Highlanders, in stark contrast to her first days in the hall, scurried to follow her command.

"Milady, we will return with your husband —" he began again, but was shushed by a sharp wave of Elayne's hand. She still clenched her sword, surprised she did not drop it in the fray.

"We, Duncan." She hefted the sword to rest its solid weight on her shoulder. "'Tis no' just my husband, but my father, and when he dies, all of our lands and people. I will not let one madman alter that fact. If ye desire, Hamish can serve as my guard, and I will be armed, but I shall accompany ye." She sighed at the prospect. "We must hope we are no' too late. They have quite the gain on us."

While his ire rose at her commanding tone, her words struck a chord. He bowed again and made to move away in preparation. Elayne reached out and tugged on his hauberk.

"I will collect the women from upstairs and appraise them of our departure." Here she paused, her eye crinkling in a grim smile. "And thank ye, Duncan, for coming to our aid. I ken that assisting me must have left a foul taste with ye."

"Ooch, aye, it did!" He tried to stop the smile that pulled at his whiskers as he walked away. "But the Laird would have had my head otherwise!" he hollered over his shoulder as he ducked out the doors to the yard.

Chapter 26: The Valley of Shadow of Death

They retrieved the women from the safety of the chambers above and informed them of what transpired, nearly sending Senga into an apoplexy. Her wrinkled hand grabbed at her chest as she pleaded with Elayne to stay in the manse.

"Nay, Senga. With both my da and my husband at risk, I can no' stay here and watch. Have ye every known me to stand by and observe?"

Elayne flung a heavy plaid around her shoulders, anticipating a cold ride. With the wind stirring up as the afternoon passed, she was certain the journey to her father's would be raw indeed.

Senga grasped the edges of the wrap, holding Elayne back.

"Please, milady. Let the men, the warriors, take care of this! Ye should remain behind to oversee the keep!"

"Nay, I have a chatelaine for that." Elayne's gaze flicked to Bonnie's, hoping the lass took her suggestion. Bonnie, the clever young woman she was, did. She stepped up next to Senga.

"Aye, Lady Elayne. We will set the castle to rights, clean the hall, and make sure everyone remaining here is fed."

Elayne nodded, then clasped Senga's hand in her own.

"My willful nature has no led me astray yet." Senga squinted at Elayne in disagreement, and Elayne huffed. "Aye, not *completely* astray. And anytime it seemed to, it eventually directed me to the right path. And here I am, wed, with a keep of my own, so who's to claim differently?"

Elayne placed a quick kiss on Senga's delicate, withered cheek. "I will have Hamish for protection," again her eyes glanced toward Bonnie, "and I shall return by the morn, I am certain."

Elayne leaned in close to Bonnie. "Say your farewells," she told the lass, and Bonnie did not waver. She flitted to Hamish like a small bird, and he enveloped her in his warm embrace, speaking soft words for her ears alone. Bonnie kissed him for a long moment, then thrust herself away and, blinking back tears, disappeared into the kitchens. She said her goodbyes.

Elayne gestured dramatically toward the doors of the hall, open to the yard where the MacCollough men awaited. "Shall we?"

"Aye, milady." Hamish took her by her elbow and escorted Elayne to her horse standing in the muddy, battle-worn yard. She mounted, and with Duncan leading the way, the assemblage rode for MacNally land at a fierce clip.

***

They did not let the horses falter or slow their pace, for Ross' men had the advantage. MacNally's men would defend their lands and homes from these meager Ross warriors; however, the greater concern was that the traitors came upon Declan and Torin while the two traveled the road. Two men, great warriors that they were, were little challenge against any large number of Ross warriors. And at the tail end of those worries was apprehension at encountering the Ross clansmen themselves as they journeyed to Elayne's father.

The wind whipped at Elayne's hair and chilled her to the bone as she rode as hard as the rest of the MacColloughs. She tried to remain hopeful that her husband arrived safely at *Akedene* and the Ross men lost their opportunity to extract a madman's vengeance against a chieftain Laird loyal to the King himself. Her prayers, however, did little to settle her mind from worry.

Several of the Highlanders rode ahead, assessing the clearing, searching for men from Clan Ross. The only sound was the mucky hum of hooves on the soggy ground. Soon they arrived at the manse of Clan MacNally, some of MacNally's clansmen greeting them with curiosity as they approached the bailey.

Elayne and her kinsmen were also surprised. They had expected conflict and Ross warriors, yet here they were, openly welcomed to the keep. Duncan and Hamish exchanged a cautious glance before dismounting and handing the reins over to MacNally clansmen. The normality of the outer yard struck a hard contrast to the chaos they left back home. Elayne dismounted, threw her shoulders back, and ascended the steps into her father's home.

She paused at the domestic scene of her father and her husband amid a large meal, the warmth of the fire and the familiarity of the people hitting her full force. House servants bustled about, the lively din of castle chatter filling the hall. Her father spied her first and half rose out of his seat to welcome her in his booming voice.

Hamish and Duncan joined her just inside the doorway. Elayne's arrival at her father's home with wind-blown hair and a coterie of Highlanders gave Declan pause for concern. He rushed to her, clasping her icy hands in his.

"What has happened, 'Layne?" Declan turned to Duncan. "Is naught amiss?"

"Ye are fine here?" Elayne interrupted. "Ye are, dining?" Her furrowed brow caused him greater distress than her questions.

"What is it, Duncan?" Declan's stern tone demanded a response.

"We were attacked, Laird," Duncan's words came out in a rush. "Ross' men, after ye left with Torin."

Declan cursed under his breath, his hand subconsciously reaching to his side for a sword that presently rested near the hearth.

"But no' many, Laird," Hamish supplied. "Ross arrived with some warriors. He would have liked to have brought Lady Elayne low, and the clan, but we heard them in the woods and prepared, surrounding the men. But not enough men. I — We — believe they have a larger target in mind." Hamish and Duncan both regarded Declan pointedly.

"Where is the old man now?" James MacNally joined them, asking about Donald Ross.

"The dungeons, father," Elayne replied.

"And did he enlighten ye as to what his plan is? What set him upon this path of destruction?" Declan asked.

Hamish responded. "We think he is, uh, not quite right in the head?" he suggested. "The old Laird finds the MacCollough singularly responsible for the success of the Bruce. He wants to destroy our clan, our allies, and find ye, Declan. He thinks ye ken the Bruce's location. His aim was to obtain that information from ye, then kill ye most likely."

Elayne shivered at how casually Hamish spoke over a plan that involved the death of herself and her husband. Her pride extended to her husband's clan, which apparently deserved the Beast clan name, if not for civility then for readiness in battle. She tossed her hair back to clear her mind of these dismaying thoughts. Elayne drew herself up to her full height and shared what she knew with her husband.

"The clansmen at *BlackBraes* have the remaining Ross men contained, but Ross suggested that another party of his were on their way here. 'Tis why we rode like devils to reach *Akedene*. But, nothing appears amiss here . . ." Her voice trailed off as she scanned the hall once more.

Declan peered over Elayne's shoulder, surveying the ajar hall door, as though he was searching for Ross' men right in the yard. Then he, too, cast his sights around the full hall, pulling Elayne into a brief embrace.

James MacNally acted without hesitation. He clasped Duncan's arm, then Hamish's, pounding them each on the back. "Naught will concern us this eve. *Akedene* is soundly defended. Come, invite in your kinsmen. My daughter and her clansmen will stay the night with us, and we will leave at daybreak." James cast a knowing look to Declan, who gave a slight nod in return.

"What will ye do with the Ross?"

Declan scratched at his beard, considering. "I will have to write to the Bruce, for certain," he explained after a pause, all but admitting he did have knowledge of the absent King's whereabouts. "Most likely, he will want the Laird and his men sent to either the Buchanan's or Campbells to be dealt with by the Bruce later. For now, I will permit the cretin to reside in the comforts of my dungeons until I receive a message from the King."

Declan then attended Elayne and seated his wife next to him near the hearth. What had been an ordinary meal became a festive evening, complete with MacNally warriors patrolling their land throughout the night, searching the frigid mist for any gray-clad figures hiding in the wood.

***

After spending a sleepless night at her father's, Elayne dragged herself to the inner bailey to join her husband and father. MacCollough's men brought the horses. Several of MacNally's clansmen had already mounted, armed to the hilt, Claymores and rough-hewn shields glinting in the dusky light of early morn.

Mounting her mare and wrapping her plaid more snugly around her, Elayne braced herself for the uncertainty of the ride back to *BlackBraes*. The sobering mood of the morning weighed on everyone, the Highlanders eyeing their surroundings as they prepped their horses, keeping their ears open for any sound foreign in the glen.

Declan and James MacNally rode near the front of the entourage, with Elayne ringed by men for her safety. She and her husband shared harsh words the evening before over her riding to her father's under such a threat. Declan called it a "crazed woman's fancy," and Elayne raised her renowned eyebrow, declaring that she hardly considered her husband's security "crazed" or a "fancy." To settle the disagreement, she agreed to ride home with him, surrounded by clansmen, and here she was, trotting far behind Declan in a silent circle of MacNally and MacCollough warriors.

How her horse stumbled mystified her, as did her resulting tumble off the mare. An accomplished rider, she did not fall from her horse. Blath's left leg had somehow slipped, and the neighing of the horse broke the eerie silence. Elayne landed in an awkward heap next to her horse where she became bogged down in the chilled mud. The commotion drew the attention of Declan and James who slowed their horses at the lead.

Torin realized he had the bad luck to be directly in front of Elayne's horse and reined his steed around toward Elayne. He noted the blood on the mare's leg as he raised his hand at Declan. What seneschal would he be if he allowed his Laird's wife to sit in the muck? Declan tipped his head to catch sight of Elayne amid the throng of Highlanders. She assured him she was uninjured with a wave of her mud-coated hand, and Declan and James returned to their place, leading the group farther up the road. Several men held back with Torin to assist Elayne as the rest moved forward.

Brushing at the damp sludge on her gown, she felt the burning heat of her blushing cheeks. To fall off her horse, and now Torin was impelled to aid her? She was humiliated at being an impediment. Embarrassed and covered in mud, she fit the image Declan had of her "crazed woman's fancy." A grimace pulled at her lips all the more as Torin dismounted next to her.

"Are ye well, milady?" Elayne could not be certain, but Torin's tone sounded mocking. She glared at him.

"I ken I put ye out, Torin. No need to school me for it. I dinna ken what happened. The mare?"

Torin's agitated sigh rankled Elayne more than she already was. "The mare trotted up toward Hamish. I will dump you on your mare's back once we catch up."

Aye, Elayne thought to herself, *definitely a mocking tone. Would the man never find accord with her?* She resigned herself that at least he offered to help her, though it was surely to appease Declan. It was a start. Biting her tongue stopped her from voicing the abrasive words that would not improve her relations with Torin. Instead she accepted his proffered hand as an offer to help her mount his steed. She turned to place her hands atop the enormous horse when she heard a hard grunt. Torin's hand fell away from her. Swiveling back, she discovered Torin on his back, clutching at his bloodied arm, a short-nicked arrow embedded deep in his left shoulder. She screeched and reached down to assist him, when he threw her to the ground and grabbed his shield with his right arm, stopping another arrow before it could reach its mark.

The horses and men reacted without delay, circling Torin and Elayne, shields up and swords drawn. A moment of heightened anticipation passed as Declan stormed back, barreling down on the circle of men.

"Elayne!" he yelled. "Torin!"

"We are here," came Elayne's muffled response from behind the horses. "Torin is injured, but no' gravely."

Her answer appeased Declan. He and the other warriors spun their heads around, searching the grasses of the glen for any invaders. They kept the horses moving — no need to make the archer's job easy as fixed targets. Another arrow flew past their shields, striking into the mud, the horses stomping in agitation. Hamish pointed to a gathering of trees off to the east.

"Tis the only real covering in the glen, Laird."

Declan nodded in accord, marveling at the accuracy and distance of the arrow. No mere crofter or lowly warrior, but a trained man, a knight from England or Wales, perhaps? He lifted his shield up farther, trying to avoid the chance of another well-aimed arrow. The wind picked up, blowing and masking any sounds from the trees. Or from themselves.

"His aim is hellishly accurate, Hamish. And we are at the disadvantage. Why do they not invade?"

James nudged his mount forward. "Mayhap they await elsewhere? As Ross himself is in your dungeons, I can no' think of what their plan is."

Declan and James evaluated their current position, trying to think like a madman. What could Ross have told his warriors to do? Surely not shoot the Lady of the clan and depart. *Did they know of their Laird's current whereabouts?* Hamish caught sight of Elayne's mare, limping as she trotted to them.

"I ken how she fell. Look at the mare's foreleg."

A wet drip of blood stained the white hair just above the hoof. 'Twas not enough to hobble the horse, but enough to cause the animal to falter. Hamish nabbed the horse's reins.

"If the Ross man can shoot as accurately as that, we can no remain here. In the open we are easy game," said Duncan. Declan surveyed the glen and the surrounding trees once more.

"We have no' choice, men. We are much closer to *BlackBraes*, and Torin needs his wounds bandaged soon. That is most likely part of their plan, to lure us into a trap, but 'tis what we must do," Declan declared.

James nodded in agreement, though in his heart he despised the idea of putting his daughter at further risk, if the arrow was indeed meant for her. A sudden, knowing look came over his face.

"'Tis like a net, their plan, I think. 'Tis what I would do if I had a foolhardy vendetta, and if I needed to keep ye alive. Otherwise, the bowman would have sent a rapid fire upon us. I ken what we can do."

Duncan and Declan leaned in close as James MacNally shared his idea of how they could defeat Ross and his clansmen in their mad plan.

He then pushed his horse into the center of the Highlanders where his daughter knelt, holding the bloody Torin.

"Weel, they did a job on ye, lad," James' voice boomed. He scrutinized his daughter. "Can ye ride, lass? Can ye mount Torin's steed?" Elayne pressed her pale lips together, nodding.

"Aye," James replied, his gaze dark and direct. "Then hand the wounded Torin over to me. Ye shall ride his mount, stay to the center, and we are for *BlackBraes*, ye ken?"

Elayne nodded again, scrambling up the stirrup of Torin's horse, and adjusted her twisted skirts to seat herself for a rough ride home. James handed her a small axe — "just in case" he admonished and turned his attention the bloody Torin. Duncan and James all but threw Torin onto the back of James' steed. "Ooch, ye weigh more than the horse!" Duncan commented as he smacked Torin's backside. After his indignant screech, Torin grumbled on how turnabout and fair play. They began their cautious ride home.

***

As Duncan and James wrangled Torin onto a horse, Declan rode to a few of the men at the rear, speaking to their bent heads. Those men slowly broke off, easing their horses from the pathway into the glen. The remainder of the group formed another loose circle, encapsulating Torin, Declan, and Elayne this time. Their arms were at the ready, horses kicking up chunks of mud at a steady pace toward *BlackBraes* and the tree line ahead.

Duncan tried not to slow their gallop as the woods closed in, but apprehension and a desire to listen for any strange movement outside their view got the better of him. His thick arm clenched his shield, keeping it high against any possible onslaught of arrows. His blood buzzed in his head as they neared the wood.

They had slowed to a steady trot when Hamish's high-pitched whistle pierced the air. Keeping the horses at a slow saunter, the Highlanders slid off their still moving steeds, blending into the surrounding flora as a sudden flash of gray and black plaid attacked from both sides of the road.

MacCollough and MacNally's men were prepared. Though outnumbered, they had were well-fed and well-rested from warm hospitality the eve before, unlike Ross' men who had the misfortune to sleep on the damp, cold ground and eat naught but dried haddock and stale oatcakes for the past day. Their tired, ragtag appearance belied the impact of their attack.

Ross' men also fought under the auspices of a madman, not with any heart, a realization not lost on Declan.

When the men rushed from the trees and brush, Declan leapt from the side of his horse, his Claymore ready in hand. While he did not fear the men he could challenge hand-to-hand, knowing a bowman lurked in the wood necessitated further precautions. Few arrows pierced the air, so Declan assumed the shooter had left or was now engaged in the combat on the road. However, he was not one to risk his life on a wrong assumption. Shifting his shield to guard his heart-side, he lunged toward a pair of men heaving their way past the circle of horses. A steed to Declan's left cried out in a panicked whinny. One of Ross' clansmen hacked at the horse to get by, and Declan focused his fury at him.

The gray-and-black-clad warrior burst past the wounded animal, and Declan brought his Claymore downward in a solid strike to the warrior's shoulder, separating much of his neck from where it met his body. The man grunted once and collapsed to his side, the mud burying half his bloodied face. Declan stepped over the dead body, singularly focused on the next Ross clansman.

The horses had scattered, leaving room for a small contingent of MacCollough men to ride up behind Ross' men from the north, taking them by surprise. James' suggestion had been that, in a party of twenty men kicking up muck on the road, four or five men fewer would not be missed, especially if the attackers directed their attention at Declan and Elayne. And James was correct — a madman has a singular target, and Donald Ross had ordered the attack on the focus of his twisted vengeance: Declan.

Elayne watched in shocked stillness atop Torin's steed, the axe her father provided her clutched tightly to her chest. Few Ross warriors ventured close enough for her worry on employing the small weapon. For those who did, Torin, angered over the arrow in his shoulder and at being attacked unawares, used his right arm and the claymore he held in retribution. He slashed at any man in gray who came too close to himself and Elayne, producing a small pile of death and destruction beneath James' warhorse.

As the numbers of Ross' clansmen decreased, so did the spirit of their fight. Declan took the opportunity to inform them of their Laird's entombment, hoping Ross' men might pull back. Declan's ragged voice carried through the wet leaves of the wood.

"Ye are defeated already, men! Your Laird presently resides in my dungeons, wallowing in the misfortune of his own lunacy! Your design against Clan MacCollough is at an end!"

One slender man in a stained gray tartan paused, his expression registering Declan's words. In response, the warrior mustered his clansmen, retreating with them back into the cover of the woods. *The only one with sense,* Declan thought to himself as he gave chase to a lingering Ross clansman, running the man off the road to join the others.

Declan held up his hand, halting his men at the tree line. 'Twas not worth their lives or the lives of his wife and her father to pursue the Ross clan any further. Donald Ross himself was ensconced in his own dungeons and could be dealt at a later time, after some counsel from Robert the Bruce. The fate of the Ross clan could wait, along with its chieftain.

Declan dropped his arms to his side, finally feeling the weight of his weapons, when he heard the mucking sound of someone stepping on the mud next to him. Reeling, he nearly raised his sword on his own wife. Elayne did not pause. She nudged his weapon to the side with her fingertips and pressed herself against his muddy, blood-stained body, wrapping her arms around him and pulling him as close to her as their clothing allowed. She held him thus until his breathing returned to normal and the rush of the battle quitted his body.

He calmed himself in his wife's embrace before speaking.

"Are ye unhurt?" he breathed.

"Aye."

"And Torin?"

"His wound needs attention, but he is otherwise fit. Able to use this other arm enough to fend off invaders as they approached."

Elayne's grubby tartan brushed against him as she moved aside, permitting Declan a unobstructed view of Torin, who complained stridently atop James' steed. While the man put on the pretense of handling his injury with ease, his pale face revealed otherwise.

Urgency roused within him. He wanted to bring his old friend home to tend his wounds; he wanted to check the state of his manse after Ross' men dared invade it, but mostly he wanted time alone with his wife. The fury of battle may have exited his body, but the thrill of the fight lingered, and he wondered if his cockstand was noticeable under his kilt. He rallied his men for home.

"We must depart! Donald Ross and his men await their fate in our dungeons, and Torin's wound must be attended."

He grasped Elayne's arm, escorting her to Torin's horse. His breath on her ear when he spoke to her warmed her very being. "And I need to have my shaft in my wife. Without delay."

Embracing her close, he lips pressed upon hers, searching for her tongue, lathing with as much intensity as he dared in front of his men, most of whom had no compunctions of cheering him on as he assailed his wife's tender lips. Then, just as quickly, he thrust her away and boosted her up onto Torin's steed, his hands slipping under her skirts for a lingering moment.

They left what remained of the deceased Clan Ross on the road for their clansmen to collect later. Declan mounted his warhorse, and they departed for *BlackBraes*, tattered and bloodied, but all alive and accounted for, a definite win for Clan MacCollough.

Chapter 27: Homecoming

Declan did not hesitate once they arrived at *BlackBraes*. His manhood raging, he had one singular intention. He left Torin in the capable hands of Senga and Bonnie, then turned his attentions to his wife. Clasping her hand in an iron grip, he led Elayne up the stairs, almost dragging her as he climbed. The door to their chamber shuttered its hinges as he kicked it in, sweeping Elayne into his arms and lifting her over the threshold of their chamber. He dropped her on to the bed, stepped back long enough to hurl his shift off over his head, and pull off his tartan, his erection full and wanting.

Her eyes widened, and her mind reeled at his ferocity. After all, they had been through this past day, how could he be so ready for her? As she reached up to touch his heaving chest, he lifted her off the bed to tear at her soiled kirtle as she stood statuesque. Elayne tugged off her skirt, exposing her bare flesh for his needy eyes. His intense golden gaze roamed over her, devouring her. Then, though a raging fire had burned behind his gaze and in his loins, his whole visage softened as he clasped her face between his hands.

"Never put yourself as risk like that again, my love. I felt as though my heart would tear from my chest," Declan whispered, catching her bottom lip with his teeth.

She opened her mouth to accept his tongue that delicately touched hers. His hands lingered on her, then trailed down to cup her breasts. Her skin prickled at his touch, both light and fierce, and her nipple hardened under the attention of his thumb. She exhaled softly.

Elayne reached around his hips to clasp the solid, round globes of his buttocks, and Declan moaned into her mouth. She could feel his attempt to keep his need for her in check, a sensation of him both pressing forward and pulling back. To release him from his self-constraint, Elayne ran her nails over his hips and enveloped his raging cock in her hand. This time he groaned deeply, his entire body clenching in wanton yearning. With a hand on his cock, she clasped her other hand across the back of his neck, guiding him to the bed.

Declan's raging need for her overrode any rational thought. Bypassing the bed, he pressed her against the wall, hot and demanding, his desire for her unsurpassed. His manhood could not find her opening soon enough, but he took a moment to ready her, moving his lips from her mouth, kissing her throat. His tongue skimmed along her collarbone, and she shivered in response, raising her leg to wrap it around his hip. She worked her grip up and down his throbbing shaft. Nearly exploding in her hand, he clenched her fingers in his own, lifting both of her hands above her head to capture them in one of his, imprisoning her against him.

He slid a finger into her silky opening. She was wet and waiting for his cock. She raised her eyes to meet his gaze.

"Now, my love," she breathed, and he roared into her, thrusting hard and deep into her welcoming velvet sheath. He held himself deep inside her, his arms shaking with exertion. Elayne did not let him wait. She shifted her hips, stroking him with her nether lips. His cock stroked against her mound and sent ripples of excitement buzzing through her. Elayne's body undulated in ecstasy with Declan's thrusts. He dipped his face to hers, abrading her cheek with his beard, kissing her ear and hair as he rocked in her. The cold of the stone wall battled the pounding heat of her husband, and her woman's sheath pulsed and trembled, building her to orgasm.

Declan at first wanted to reign in his throbbing desire, but Elayne's thrusting hips and the heat of her sheath inflamed his manhood, and his need built, pulling from his arms and chest, as though his whole being would come inside her. Unable to control himself, he groaned and gyrated harder. Elayne's entire body lit on fire at his movements, his cock rubbing and pulsing, and she dropped her head against the rough stone at her back, crying out his name as her waves of pleasure shuddered from her mound, exploding through from her toes to her fingertips.

Declan was at his moment, calling out to her, his cock flexing and spilling his seed, filling her. His seed mixed with her own wetness and their combined sweat, dripping down their legs as they tried not to fall over from exertion. Elayne's hair stuck to her face and neck as she regained her breath, her breasts lifting and falling in cadence to Declan's breathing. He released her hands, supporting himself on his elbows on either side of Elayne. His chest, glistening from his efforts, pressed damply against Elayne as they took their time recovering.

"I apologize if I took ye too fast," Declan's breath tickled the hair covering her ear.

"Nay need to apologize, as I was more than ready for ye," she whispered back.

"Aye, good then," he breathed, lifting himself from Elayne, releasing her from her position against the wall, seating himself on the bed. In the absence of his heated skin against hers, the chill in the air settled on her, dimpling her skin.

She moved to reach past him for her gown, when he grasped her hips, sitting her on his lap. He ran his fingertips over her body, up around her breasts, over her shoulders, down her arms, and this time her skin pimpled from his delicate touch. He caught her stormy gaze with his hazel one.

"I could have lost ye, Elayne. Ye are my family, now. I need ye, aye, but I want ye as well. I want ye as my wife. I ken why ye needed to come with my men to your father's — ye are no' a woman to sit at home sewing." Elayne glanced to the heavens at this comment, but secretly overjoyed that he understood her. "Please dinna throw caution to the wind so much next time. I want ye here with me for the rest of my days."

Elayne let a soft smile tug at her mouth as she held his face in her hands, her thumbs rubbing at the golden stubble on his cheeks.

"Are ye saying ye love me, my Laird?" she asked him.

"Aye, that I do, Lady 'Layne." He nuzzled one of her hands. "And ye, 'Layne. Do ye love me?"

It was the first time he had asked. She could no longer deny his feelings or the emotions she kept inside under lock and key.

"Aye, my Laird. I do love ye. Though many would think ye crazy to want the love of a Harpy."

Declan shrugged and kissed her breast, then looked up at her shining eyes. "Many would think ye are crazy to love the chieftain of the Beast clan. So I think we are well met." Elayne lowered her head, her lips brushing against his. "Then we shall be crazy together," she told him, kissing him long and hard.

***

Elayne and Declan did not leave their chamber until midday, enjoying each other in the warmth and safety of their bed. With the servants of the keep bustling below, the house functioned without them, and they had no desire to welcome the reality of the day. As for Ross and his men, they could rot in the dungeons until the second coming for all Declan cared. Any message to the Bruce could take its time as well.

Only when they heard an announcement of riders from the east did either of them leave their chamber. Fear struck Elayne's core and Declan's face hardened; his golden eyes turned to hooded slits, caution overriding every other emotion. Leaping from the bed, he donned his shift, plaid, and leather boots, hooking his sword to his belt as he raced from their chamber.

Elayne followed, tugging her gown over her head in the hallway, the stone of the stairs cold against her bare feet. When she reached the doorway leading to the yard, she halted at the top of the steps, taking in the presence of a man and two women on horseback inside the gate.

Declan, Hamish, and Duncan formed a line of defense at the base of the stone steps, hands on their sword hilts, waves of cautious expectation wafting off them like heat from a flame. Declan bounced on his toes, the strain of the past fortnight adding to his guard. Pity filled Elayne's heart at her husband's apprehensive stance, at how easily he transformed from a position of ease to one of resistance. Her attention focused on Declan, she did not notice the riders had dismounted and approached the keep.

The man of the group held back as an older woman wearing rich walnut robes strolled directly toward Declan, her gaze steady upon him. Her ashy blonde hair caught in the wind, lifting into a golden halo around her shoulders. The woman drew herself close to Declan, near enough to touch him as she lifted a worn hand to his face, pressing her palm against the scruff of his cheek. He jerked himself back.

"What are ye doing, madame?"

The woman's lips split into a huge smile, lighting up her face, and her visage struck a chord with Elayne. A sudden and uncanny sense of déjà vu fell over her; the woman was both a stranger and familiar to her.

"Oh Declan, how tall and strong ye've become. How I've missed ye." Her last words were soft but carried on the icy wind. Elayne stumbled back, her hand gripping her woolen gown against her chest in recognition of the woman.

"Missed me?" Declan responded, his brows furrowed, but his commanding stance stock still.

The woman continued to touch his face, searching his eyes with hers.

"'Tis been a long time, my sweet. I dinna expect ye t'remember your mother."

Now it was Declan's turn to pull back in shock, his countenance pale at the woman's announcement. Hamish placed his hand on Declan's back to catch his chieftain who appeared ready to faint. To Elayne, the resemblance was astoundingly clear. For all that Declan was a powerful man, his golden gaze and hair were mirrored in the woman who stood before him.

Declan glowered at Elayne, his eyes angry slits. She silently shook her head. Once she promised to stop searching for his mother, she burned the remainder of the letters and the two missives she received in response to her inquiry. Her disbelief of the blonde's arrival must have exhibited on her face, for Declan's stance softened, and he returned his attention to the woman who called herself his mother.

Declan, however, did not share in his mother's joy. His furious stare focused on her, and his ire carried in the words he spoke.

"My mother left when I was a lad. I dinna have a mother." He spit the last words at the woman. She did not react, her smile only widening and her whole face shining with elation.

"Aye, ye have such a right to be angry, my lad."

She reached her hand out to touch him again, but paused her hand when Declan flinched back. Duncan and Hamish remained unmoved, flanking their Laird, supporting him in whatever move he made.

"What did he tell ye? Egad, Nels always worked his for his own gain." The delicate blonde woman spat on the ground, casting the evil eye, and Elayne's grin tugged at her lips. She liked the woman already.

"Did he say I left ye, my only son? That I left ye with that beast of a man?" The blonde paused, placing her hand on her throat to calm herself. "My apologies, my son. I do no' mean to speak ill of the dead. I have been with the Welsh for these last years, working as a chatelaine for a Welsh lord. I had not learned that the old *bauchle* died until I received a letter from the Mother Superior of the ColdStream nunnery.

Evidently her convent received a message from a Lady Elayne MacNally MacCollough?"

At this, the blonde, who must be the estranged Davina Mary MacKenzie, tipped her head to the side, peeking past Declan to rest her softened expression on Elayne. The happiness in the woman's heart shone through her gaze. Elayne said nothing, bowing her head in concession.

Davina turned back to Declan. "So I am here to see my son, explain to him why I left, and hope he can find it in his heart to forgive me."

"Why?" he croaked, choking on emotion. "Why are ye . . .? Why did ye . . .?"

This time when the blonde reached for Declan, he did not shy away. She placed her hand on his chest, patting it like one would a small puppy.

"Why am I back? And why did I leave?" she asked. Declan nodded. "I left, contrary to whatever your da may have told ye, because 'twas the only choice I had. He threatened me, ye see. Well, nay, not quite. He threatened ye."

Davina bit her lip, forming her words carefully. "Ye see, he could no' get to me. I lost a bairn before ye. Your father could be violent, ye ken? Not always, but at times. When I had ye, I was over the clouds with happiness, your da notwithstanding. But the anger that imprisoned his heart grew darker and more volatile, and he oft turned that anger on me. I was leaving him, with ye. I had a bag packed and an ally ready with horses.

"Your father accosted me in the hall as I held ye tight to my bosom. I feared he may take his violence out on me one last time as I was leaving. Nay, he did something far darker. Nels removed his dirk and held it to the back of your neck. He had a knife on my bairn! He said I could leave, but he would see his son dead 'afore letting the lad leave with me. I did no' ken what would happen if I stayed, but I did ken that if I tried to escape with ye, he would kill ye, my boy, and not me. That horror struck a knife deeper in my chest than that foul man ever could. I left ye, there, in that dark hall, your da's scarred hand on your shoulder.

"A few of the clansmen promised to watch over ye. I had to have faith that Nels wanted ye for his own, and ye could grow up hale and strong. As I rode off, I could hear ye crying for me, and that sound has haunted my dreams all of my life."

Declan blinked over and over, trying to halt the tears that threatened to spill over. Davina's words washed over him, granting him validation he lacked all his life. His mother had not abandoned him to a monster of a father; rather she was forced to leave under the threat of his own death. She sacrificed her motherhood to save his life, and the weight he carried since childhood took flight. He breathed in, contentment blanketing him in a way he had not before known.

"And ye are here?" he asked, stepping forward. Elayne's own heart soared at the simple movement.

"Aye. The message from the Mother Superior read that a Lady MacCollough was searching for her husband's estranged mother. I ken at once it was ye, daughter-by-law," she peeked at Elayne again as she spoke. "And ye, my son. I left at once, with Eghan here," Davina's cloaked arm flapped to the man reigning the horses, "and with Caitrin."

The hooded woman named Caitrin stepped forward to stand by Davina's side. Davina grasped her hand, leaning into her and speaking low so only the hooded woman could hear. The woman lifted her head and pulled back her hood.

Elayne gasped and caught herself on the stone wall to prevent herself from falling over. She clapped her hand over her mouth to stifle a cry, her heart ready to beat out of her chest. The hooded woman was a lass, with wild blonde hair and golden hazel eyes, just like Davina. Just like Declan.

Declan froze, his blood rushing to his head, and he stumbled back. Hamish and Duncan steadied him, both trying to understand what the presence of this young girl portended.

Pulling the girl by her hand, Davina presented Caitrin to Declan. The girl grasped the sides of her tartan skirt and curtsied in a graceful movement.

"Your sister, Declan. Caitrin Marie MacCollough."

For a series of heartbeats, no sound entered the yard, no movement disturbed the frosty air. No even a rogue leaf dared scuttled across the earth. For a man who had little to call family for most of his life, Declan found himself once again a son, and now a brother. Davina reached for Declan's hand, placing it on Caitrin's and held his other hand in hers. Her face radiated with clarity — as she had both her children in her arms again, a moment she never dared to hope for.

"You see, Declan, I had to leave. Your father was not a man at peace with a wife, or with children. I was fortunate with you, a strong, robust lad. He could find a use for you. He even seemed to have some care for ye. But what if the child I carried then was not a strong lad, but a weak lad? Or worse," she regarded Caitrin, "a lass?"

She shook her head with surety. "I could no' stay with the man and risk the second child. I was no' sure he would even let the child grow in my womb. I had to make a choice. I had faith ye would live, grow strong, and become Laird one day. And I had to keep faith that ye would one day meet your sister and find forgiveness for me."

Davina's eyes blurred with tears as she looked upon her children, her aching need to have both her children with her emanating from her like incandescent heat.

Elayne regained enough of her senses and strode up behind Declan, shoving him in the direction of his mother. "Get ye into your mother's arms!" She hissed into his ear. "Most do not get the chance as ye have presently!"

She prodded him again, making him stumble off the stair, out of Hamish and Duncan's reach, and into the embrace of his penitent, long-lost mother.

Davina did not hesitate but embraced him as he fell into her. Declan kept his arms rigid by his sides at first, and Elayne feared he would not find forgiveness for his mother's choice so long ago. Then Declan's whole body deflated, softening into his mother's arms. He hugged her back, his strong arms completely enveloping her.

Caitrin, who Elayne guessed from the tears the young woman shed since her introduction, was the emotional type and leaned to the two of them. She wrapped her arms as best she could around both her mother and her brother.

In that moment, Elayne wanted burst in happiness and love. Over the last few months, where she had been rejected, she was now accepted. Where she was once despised, she was loved. Where loneliness tread, companionship reigned. Where a clan was failing, it was now respected. And where a family was lost, a mother and sister were now found. Elayne had achieved her heart's desire by losing all she thought was hers.

Under the dappling light, they were a family — mother, son, daughter, sister, and brother. As the frigid winds blew through the land, Elayne's tartan whipped against her. The taut green and black plaid still pulled flat against her belly. Elayne laid her hand against the wooly fabric, excited over the secret she had only recently confirmed. Soon the plaid would cover a rounded belly, and the family that neither she nor Declan enjoyed as children would soon be realized.

Peace infused her entire being as she held her stomach and watched the heart-rending scene unfold before her, the stillness of the moment broken only by Davina and Caitrin's sobs and the lonely caw of a loon in the distance.

Excerpt from The Exile of the Glen

T he brilinn struggled over the rough, freezing waters of the Minch well into the night. While Alistair did not know how long the ride would be, he knew they would most likely arrive sometime the next day. He needed to prepare himself for these unanticipated changes to this trip.

The strange men wandered away, leaving Alistair to wallow in his own blistering cold misery. He shifted slightly, moving his head away from the alcove to catch a view of the dark sky. A few dim stars struggled to peek out from the clouds. A pale moon also strained to provide its muted light onto the water, lighting their path over the water. The winds favored them, blowing continually throughout the evening, cutting through the fabric of Alistair's tartan.

A flapping sound attracted his attention, and he found a scrap of tarp billowing near one barrel. Tugging on it, it slipped free, and he wrapped it around himself to fend off the cold air of the night. He huddled under the tarp as the feeling began to return to his fingers and toes.

Alistair felt small under the wide, dark sky, smaller even than when he was under the rage-filled scrutiny of his Uncle. His thoughts drifted to the past few weeks and how his life had changed so abruptly, so miserably. Just a few months ago, he was certain of his future, potential leader and husband, active in his clan, beloved by his family. Now here he was, freezing on a small vessel on the even colder Minch, his future uncertain, any hope for leadership or a wife gone. No clan, an embarrassment to his family.

He did not want to image his father's reaction when he learned Alistair's fate. His mother would never forgive her brother, no matter how justified MacNally was to demand his exile. Tears formed in the corner of his eyes and he had to blink them back lest they find their way down his cheeks. Most likely to freeze as they fell. *The plan seemed sound. How did it all go so wrong? What happened to me to take it all that far?* His stomach churned worryingly, and he had to swallow several times to stop the vomit from rising. Whether he was sick from the cold voyage on the sea or from the depth of his regret, he did not know.

Regret is a painful awareness of a misguided reality. And under the shadowy skies on the small boat on the Minch, Alistair could do nothing but let regret overwhelm him. A small part of him harbored hatred and anger over the loss of his position, his family, his life as he knew it, but the farther out to sea he traveled, the less space those emotions occupied. Instead, the weight of regret pushed it to the side. He had learned a hard lesson at the hands of Elayne and Laird MacNally, and he hoped that, in the future, he would not act in such a rash, crazed manner has he had in the past fortnight.

He formed the idea into a prayer, asking God for clarity and guidance, and sent his prayer up to the mysterious stars above him. Perchance this trip to the Isles could be an opportunity for a new life, a rebirth, to become the man he knew he could be, not the broken, disturbed man he left behind in Scotland.

A Note on History —

I endeavor to keep my narratives as closely aligned to actual history as possible. But it IS fiction, at the end of the day, and that is where creative licensing comes into play.

Both *To Dance in the Glen* and *The Lady of the Glen*, while mostly historically accurate, do contain some intentional errors or anachronisms – elements I inserted to contribute to the story.

The largest inaccurate aspect would have to be the use of the tartan or plaid. The Scottish clan tartans as we know them today did not really exist before the 16th century (the 1500s). My timeline is close, and plaids were in usage, but not specific colors or patterns to identify different clans as we see today.

I also took liberties with clans themselves – generic in their locales – as the clans in my books are invented. These people did not exist – or if they did, any similarities were coincidental!

However, infusing actual characters from history, like Robert the Bruce or John Comyn, or real places, like Methven, create a fictionalized realism that I adore. My favorite writers often do this, so I am only standing on the shoulders of giants (*nod to those greats who came before).

A Thank You–

In addition to my friends and family, who are always my most staunch supporters, I need to bow my head to a few others who stepped up to help me make *The Lady of the Glen* the best it could be.

My English colleague and friend from high school, Julie Peterson, helped edit the book and provided some amazing feedback. Thank you for helping me see the forest for the trees.

I also need to thank Jamie Brydone-Jack, a beta reader who took a chance on a Goodreads connection. Her feedback helped me get out of my own head and see more to my story that I could sitting behind my laptop. Thank you, Jamie, for helping me with those Scottish nuances!

I would also like to thank the indie writing community, particularly the romance writing community, for advice, support, feedback, and general cheerleading. Every author needs a cheering section!

Finally, I of course need to thank my beloved children, who just want to see mommy happy in whatever she does, and my Michael, my own Happy Every After.

And if you haven't read *To Dance in the Glen,* be sure to go to your favorite online retailer and get your copy today!

About the Author

Michelle Deerwester-Dalrymple is a professor of writing and an author. She started reading when she was 3 years old, writing when she was 4, and published her first poem at age 16. She has written articles and essays on a variety of topics, including several texts on writing for middle and high school students. She is also working on a novel inspired by actual events. She lives in California with her family of seven.

You can visit her blog page, follow her socials, and sign up for her newsletter at: https://linktr.ee/mddalrympleauthor

Also by the Author:

Glen Highland Romance
To Dance in the Glen – Book 1
The Lady of the Glen – Book 2
The Exile of the Glen – Book 3
The Jewel of the Glen – Book 4
The Seduction of the Glen – Book 5
The Warrior of the Glen – Book 6
The Echo in the Glen – Book 7 coming soon

Celtic Highland Maidens:
The Maiden of the Storm – Book 1
The Maiden of the Grove – book 2

Men in Uniform
Night Shift – Book 1
Day Shift – Book 2
Overtime – Book 3
Holiday Pay – Book 4
School Resource Officer – Book 5

Printed in Great Britain
by Amazon